WITHOUT DISRUPTION

CARRIE FRENCH

Carrie French

wishing you
true 'harmony'

First Edition

Paperback: 979-8-9851390-3-7

Ebook: 979-8-9851390-2-0

Audiobook: 979-8-9851390-1-3

www.carriefrenchauthor.com

WITHOUT DISRUPTION

CARRIE FRENCH

PROLOGUE

IN PROCESS

I looked down at my naked body and saw the mangled threads of discolored flesh — all that remained of my scorched arm. Swallowing back the rising bile in my throat, I stood up and began to spin my attention around the room. My search for a door kept my attention away from the injury.

I was nearly sick again from the thought of it.

"During process, you will feel no pain." Vie's voice echoed and filled the small, square room, which was sealed with glossy white metal on every surface.

I didn't feel any pain. I also didn't physically feel anything at all. My breath didn't blow across the tiny hairs inside my nostrils. The bottom of my feet didn't make sensory contact with the floor. Was I dead?

I rotated again with dizzy unease. I couldn't make sense of what I was really looking for. An exit? A distraction?

"You have reached the end of this lifecycle, but you will start again."

The voice sliced through me and dragged a helpless chill down my spine. It explained a condensed version of everything I already knew and laid out the web-like pattern of a soul's lifecycle. The speech droned on, fading numbly into the background of my awareness.

I no longer knew if I believed any of it, but I hoped it was true. I prayed to Vie, the system, or whatever this really was. This couldn't be the end for me.

"Harrison, you did not find harmony in this cycle. In harmony with time and for the sake of all humanity, you must move forward without disruption."

This exact same phrase had played out thirteen times over the course of my life, but never like this… For the first time, Vie's timbre was ice cold, and it wasn't posed as a question.

"The system is designed to carry memories forward through your final transfer. In order to preserve and save this evidence for future reflection, you may dictate a record of your experiences. When you are finished, speak the phrase, 'Process my soul into the next cycle.'"

I stood in dazed silence until the stillness was broken by another message. With uncaring persistence, she echoed the script word for word.

How long do I have left? How long can I survive in here?

Vie repeated the message three more times, but I didn't know how to respond.

My first instinct was to work out a plan and force my will toward a solution, but I was emotionally drained, enervated, and completely exhausted. There was nothing left to do.

As instructed, I recounted the story of my life — first hesitantly, then settling into a rhythm of remembrance.

"I had a pretty normal childhood… and, um, yeah… some experiences stand out… but everything worth remembering really set into motion on the day of my seventeenth birthday. That was the first time I had harmony in my grasp and mindlessly threw it away…"

PART 1

EXPLORATION

1

I checked the clock. Only a few minutes left.

"Harrison and Harold, my first-born twins. You were always the steady pillars that balanced this family. Happy seventeenth birthday to my darling boys. You've grown up so fast." My mother's voice soared above the incessant murmur of conversation that spilled out around us. It warbled and shook, but the strength of her honeyed tone shone through.

During her speech, I admired the spacious community center, which looked as I had always known it: alight with shared activity and boisterous energy. As H-sibs, this was our local gathering spot to eat, play, study, and help each other throughout the day. Dozens of children ran across the upper-level balcony, darting around felt game tables, disorganized bookshelves, and clusters of couches that had been pushed together and piled high with fluffy pillows.

The majority of us, numbering well over 200, were sitting, chatting, and sipping on tea at long, butcher block tables that filled the center atrium and cafeteria. We naturally clustered into small groups, but there was a sense of fluidity to every conversation as H-sib members easily shifted back and forth between parties.

Our table was crammed with empty teacups, water glasses, and chipped plates. Many friends dragged chairs over from other tables or craned their necks to listen as our loosely organized birthday celebration devolved into a goodbye party.

Harold and I set our teacups onto mismatched saucers and, dusting birthday cake crumbs off our laps, stood up in unison.

Mother wrapped her arms tightly around us, burying our faces into her bony shoulders. "Wherever your paths take you, know that your birth names will always be written in love, and I'll never forget you. I love you so much. We all do."

"Mooom," Harold whined as a blush crept across his face. His left cheek crinkled with a prominent line, pushed up and back by his wide smile. When he let loose and grinned with total abandon, it was always slightly crooked. He hugged her tighter, if only to find more cover from the line of eyes that looked up at him. Quietly, he said, "I'm building a family right here, just like you. We've already talked about this. I was born into balance, so I don't have to go looking for it."

"Even if you did…" she started to protest.

"I don't," he said with a reassuring smile.

"*But* if you ever choose to transfer into a different alpha-class and set off on your own path like your brother, I hope you know—"

"I won't." He cut her off again with a quiet reply that signaled the end of the conversation.

I found my brother's hand in the mess of tangled limbs and squeezed it tightly. I knew how hard it was for him to stand up in front of everyone, even during an important moment like this.

Although our features were mirrored, our personalities

were not. I was emotional and impulsive, a dreamer who wanted to make an impact on the world. He, on the other hand, was happy to walk calmly down any path that opened up before him. Regardless of our differences, he was my number one supporter and closest confidant.

Before releasing us from her strangling embrace, my mother turned her face toward me and whispered, "You'll always be my baby. You'll always be Harrison to me." She took a small, hesitant breath that echoed in the hollow of my own chest. "My sweet boy… Please don't think you're cutting our time together short. It's ending right on schedule, and this was just the opening chapter of a hundred happy years. You're growing into yourself as an incredible young man, and I'm so proud of you. I know in my heart that your happiness is guaranteed — it's just not here with me. I'll always love you."

"I love you too, Mom. Always!" I gave a huge smile. "Take care of everyone, okay? Your support and love mean the world to me, especially as I've been getting ready to leave. I'll always be grateful to you." Addressing the wider room, I added, "You were the best family an H-sib could have hoped for."

Three bright, resonant chimes played out over the speakers, interrupting our heartfelt goodbyes and thanks. An exuberant cheer ran through the hall as everyone stood up from their crowded tables en masse, squeaking well-worn, mismatched chairs across the hardwood floor.

Seventeen o'clock.

This routine happened every day, at the exact same hour, without fail. The chimes rang out immediately after late afternoon tea, and crowds barreled into the street — either to gather at home for dinner or to join a loved one's procession to the V tower.

I had been expecting the chimes while I counted down

the minutes, but they still caught me by surprise. With shaking hands, I flicked my finger through the air to pull up a private screen. The familiar dashboard sprang to life with vibrant color and a hazy wash of light that almost obscured the real world. My gaze swept past a scrolling newsfeed in the bottom-left corner and my contentment score summary in the top left.

I had spent endless hours navigating through this view screen in recent months. Harold and I had lain back-to-back on our cramped bottom bunk, our eyes glazed in concentration as we read through the alphaclass guidelines over and over again. He never even considered transferring, but he still took the time to review the options with me.

Now, on my seventeenth birthday, the grayed-out transfer tab was accessible and fully lit with a cerulean border.

I stalled for a second to stare and felt the persistent hum of my family's eager energy shadowed by excited whispers. I couldn't keep them waiting.

I tapped my thumb and forefinger together and called open the transfer application for the first time. The top of the screen was split with my current contentment score at the left and a detailed graph on the right. A tiny blue arrow pointed at the center of a flat line, showing where I was today at 17 contentment points — perfectly on target, but Vie's prediction showed a dip down to 16 in the near future. It was only a guess by the system, and I could still make changes to prevent it, but now that the choice to transfer was unlocked, I felt increasingly certain that transferring *was* the change I had to make.

I waved my hand to scroll through the alphaclass list, sorted in alphabetical order:

A-aut

B-stud

C-spen
D-view
E-sit
F-nat
G-paw
I-con

Wait, it skipped H-sib?

I wouldn't ever be able to transfer back to an alphaclass I had already been in, but it was shocking to see that the list of available options had already shrunk by one. My scrolling hand twitched, and I accidentally selected J-dev.

As my transfer application proceeded to the next screen, Vie read the J-dev alphaclass summary in my ear.

J-devs achieve 17 points of contentment through meaningful public service, specialized religious study, and complete devotion to Vie. In exchange for the guarantee of harmony, J-devs must give up 3 points of contentment by living exclusively for the system and not for the self.

I awkwardly flexed my hand and waved the screen back to the selection list.

Harold, always so in tune with my emotions, noticed that I was flustered and placed a hand on my shoulder. He whispered, "This is a big moment for you. Take your time. We're not in any rush."

My shoulders rose, carrying his warm hand, and I blew out a deep breath. I kept scanning through the alphaclass list as I scrolled all the way down to reach my target at the bottom: N-star.

Warmth spread across my cheeks as Vie read the summary I had memorized.

N-stars achieve 17 points of contentment through fame, prestigious notoriety, and public recognition with dedicated fanbases. In exchange for the guarantee of harmony, N-stars must give up 3 points of contentment by following groupthink procedures with a uniform lifestyle of shared decisions.

After the stress of my initial decision was over, I flew through the rest of the application's questions. I requested a mixed-gender house and asked to continue living in the same region, if possible. I selected my new name, confirmed everything, and submitted the form.

Please proceed to V tower 1675 for transfer. Vie's soothing voice echoed in my ear. I dropped the private screen, and my glassy eyes regained focus. Renewed cheers rose from the table as I flashed a V sign with my fingers and lit up with a smile.

As we all moved toward the rotating outer doors, small children were ushered forward in groups. Babies clung to their mothers' chests, sleeping peacefully through the echoing noise. Couples walked hand in hand all around us, ranging in age from sixteen to ninety-six.

I had experienced this daily seventeen o'clock procession so many times that it had entirely lost its meaning to me. Now, it really mattered. Today was my day, my moment.

Most people filed out of the community center to return home for dinner and evening activities, but part of the crowd was clustered around me. They pushed me forward as we headed in a different direction, marching along the busy, central street toward our local V tower, which rose, shimmering, above the modest valley town's skyline.

Another large group trailed behind us, celebrating the hundredth birthday and death day of a woman who had organized weekly gift exchanges for at least as long as I had been alive. Our reasons for visiting the V tower were different, but equally exciting: I was transferring to start a new chapter of my life, and she was processing the end of hers, right on time.

The atmosphere of both groups was electric and optimistic, but the pace of our youthful steps soon eclipsed her feeble walk, and we pressed on ahead.

As school friends and cousins waved goodbye, my smile stretched wider than I ever thought possible. Quick hugs and pats from neighbors made me feel so loved and uplifted. Even as they hurried away, back to their own lives and routines, I felt the warmth they left behind. I knew in my heart that they truly wanted me to settle into balance with 17 contentment points. It was my turn to set out and build a stable, happy life — whatever that looked like for me.

My brother clung to my side in the throng of bodies. Leaning in, Harold admitted in a small voice, "We've never spent a single day apart… It's hard for me to accept that you're never coming back."

"I know. I wish you wanted to come with me, but I'd never ask you to do that."

"And trust me, I'd never ask you to stay!" he replied quickly. "I'm in balance here and you deserve a stable, balanced life as much as anyone else. But still… I'll miss you."

"I'll miss you too."

An autocab passed by on the open road and chirped a harsh warning when Harold stepped too close to the edge of the sidewalk. The noise shocked him out of his melancholy.

"Most likely to crash an autocab?" Harold asked with a smirk.

I snorted and remembered how we used to rank the alphaclasses in 'most likely' lists to pass the time. "They're called auto for a reason. They literally drive themselves, so I don't even think that's possible!"

"Exactly. That makes the list even more interesting!" he insisted.

"I'm tempted to put L-rush at the top because I can only imagine how wild things get by the end of the night with blackout party crowds and an endless supply of stimulants, but…" I trailed off, thinking hard. "I'm gonna have to say I-con. Yep. I-cons all the way!"

Harold laughed incredulously and ran a hand through his dark, voluminous curls.

"No, seriously!" I argued. "If anyone's going to crash an autocab, it's an I-con. You know how rigid they are with their schedules. Consistency, consistency, consistency. That's their 17. If any of them were ever running late, Vie forbid, there's no way they would let the autocab cruise along at its normal speed. They'd hack it and crash it!"

Harold and I grasped hands — wrist against wrist, like when we were little boys. Harold's other hand was clasped around his wife Huna's waist so that he could delicately pull her forward at our pace.

Huna's tiny feet tripped excitedly alongside him, and she beamed at me across Harold's towering body.

"Where are you going first? Where do you feel led to? When can I see you next? What should I call you?" She blurted out her string of questions in fast succession, breathless and eager.

I stood up taller and prouder. In doing so, I felt Harold's grasp loosen in my own. This brief separation swept a chill through me, the first of an entire lifetime.

"I know my balance path seems exciting, but really — you're the lucky ones! You both get to be monos forever," I replied, with as much breezy generosity as I could muster.

A soft, personal look was exchanged between them, and my brother's eyes crinkled in the corners with a soft smile. His connection with her, and everyone else in the community, was so genuine, deep, and effortless. Seeing yet another sign of how perfectly content he was, I felt even more resolute in my decision to go. It just wasn't the same for me here.

"Uh — wait, I forgot, what did you ask?"

"Where you're going, obviously!" she exclaimed brightly, giggling into Harold's chest.

Huna was the youngest of fifteen children. She had watched so many H-sibs, both biological and communal, wander away, but she never got sick of the routine. Every day, she was one of the first people to congratulate transfers and deathdayers as soon as the chimes sounded — whether they were part of her close circle or seated on the opposite side of the community hall. She always said that her balance was clearly spelled out with three straight lines — a perfect, capital H. Still, she was enthralled by the possibility of change.

I leaned in across my brother and playfully raised an eyebrow in his direction. He arched his back away from us to create a symbolic bubble of personal space for Huna and me.

"My next name is Nicolas," I whispered in her ear with an uncontrollable smile. "But I'll be Harrison until the transfer, and it'll always be listed at the top of my ID. I'll carry my first name with pride."

Huna's eyes grew wider and brighter in surprise. "Woaaaaah." She exhaled under her breath. Whispering back across our imaginary circle of secrecy, she said, "I knew it! You've always craved attention. How fitting! I can't wait to see you on screen as an N-star."

The crowd was thinning out as community members stepped into rotating entrances, resigned to the quiet comfort of home. As H-sibs, our doors were never closed to visitors — metaphorically or literally.

I looked around and saw the procession from a new angle. I had walked this route hundreds of times, but I was always at the back of the group. Whenever an H-sib signaled that they were ready to transfer, we all cheered them on and patted them on the back. We focused the entirety of our love and energy on them until the moment they walked through the V tower's glass doors.

I had the same number of friends, family, neighbors, and community members around me as any other day, but now I was in front. Helga, my mother, caressed my back. Huna and Harold were at my side. The buzz and clamor of footsteps were overwhelming.

Two N-stars walked toward us on the sidewalk, clad in full-length magenta robes. The heavy silk fabric was cinched up in an ornate, circular pattern across the hip, and both of their skirts were hemmed to precision, floating a hair above the smooth cement.

We stepped into the road to clear the walkway and let them pass. Halting our conversations, we bowed our heads low and I strained to catch a glimpse of them under my heavy lashes. They rolled their eyes at our reverence, and one of them reached out her hand to me. In a trance, I raised my hand to return the gesture, bowing even more deeply and never taking my eyes off the mesmerizing swirls of fabric draped at her hip.

She wrenched her hand away in feigned disgust at the exact same moment her companion burst out laughing. "Niha! You're not honestly stopping for the adoration of an H-sib, are you? They're basic breeders..."

Quick to retake her rightful place on top of the joke, she reached down and grabbed a shriveled, dry leaf off the pavement. "Pretend this is the trash you deserve," she said through hiccupping laughter as she flung the leaf up into the air. It loped down on the breeze and landed on top of my head. The thick stem rested in my curls until Huna reached up to pull it out.

We all gaped at their singular beauty and confident poise as they continued down the path. When they were a long distance away, the voices of our group slowly returned, first in whispers of shock and talk of chance meetings. Everyone placed friendly bets about where I would transfer, as if I couldn't hear them. Finally, it was back to the raucous, energetic din.

Despite our social rank and all of the jeers, taunts, push-offs, and trash-throwing that came with it, we found balance with each other. Our 17 points of contentment came from the uplifting support of family, communal generosity, and enhanced fertility. Growing up as an H-sib, I was never lonely. How could you *not* feel wholeheartedly loved when you were part of such a huge, interconnected family? Together, we were everything, and we were enough — that's what I was always told.

I convinced myself it *could* be enough until I was old enough to decide it wasn't. As soon as the chimes rang out, the self-soothing illusion transformed into a sign of childish delusion.

We finally reached the steps of V tower 1675. The three-story building was a pinnacle of light that reflected the pink-orange glow of the late autumn sunset. Every mirrored window was awash in transient color.

Its heavy glass doors looked imposing — not only because of their weight, which I assumed was substantial, but mostly because of its anchored design that was so unlike our rotating entrances at home. My face grew hot, and my breath quickened. I faced the door and took in the gravity of my decision. This was only the *first* challenge of an entire lifetime. I would never be able to reverse the wind that would blow back from the door's sweeping gesture.

But then again, I knew I had already opened the door in my own mind. I couldn't go back. The wind was already whistling through, seeping under the threshold of every interaction and decision that I made. I had to leave.

My instincts kicked in, and I stepped back in time to

watch a C-spen part our crowd with a flick of his wrist and glide up the tower steps. His disdainful glare hit me harder than ever before.

Just like everyone else, he thought we were embarrassing or downright disgusting because we were H-sibs. For our guaranteed harmony, we had to put up with the social pressure of being universally hated and ostracized. For the most part, it brought the H-sib community closer, but it still stung.

We all leaned on each other and healed emotional wounds with the salve of familial love. If anyone hesitated to put back on a joyful attitude, they would be cradled in the warmest, tightest hug with at least half a dozen arms wrapped around them. I could lean on their relief and support right now, but the second I walked through that door, I would be alone for the first time in my life.

With one easy movement, the C-spen grasped the thick, vertical handle, which intersected the glass in a long, clean line from top to bottom, and wrenched it open. A thousand tiny jewels were suspended from his collar, and they hung serenely among a curtain of silk threads. I heard the faintest tinkling sound when he took his first step through the door, sending the jewels swinging.

Harold thumped my back, Huna grabbed both of my hands, and my mother folded me into a fierce embrace. Hsiu, my school tablemate, brushed her ankle against mine, like she had done every time we sat down together to study. Hollis, my baseball coach, whistled a loud, shrill chirp. All of my younger siblings crowded in at the edges. Was that Holly, my girlfriend, rubbing my shoulder in slow circles? *Ex-girlfriend*, I supposed.

My mind went blank while I spent all of my energy absorbing theirs: every touch, embrace, whisper, and whistle. A familiar chant started up, though I couldn't tell who started it.

"Your balance is there. Your family is here! Your balance is there. Your family is here! *Your balance is there. Your family is here!*"

I had cheered this phrase so many times and watched countless H-sibs stumble up these steps in delirious delight, but now my mouth was closed in a tight-lipped smile and my throat felt dry, as if all the water in my body had rushed up behind my eyes without permission.

My breath caught in my throat as I bravely took two steps up the mirrored stairs and approached the entrance. I replayed the C-spen's movements over and over in my mind, silencing the tumultuous shouts that echoed behind me.

My balance is there. My family is here. I steeled my shaking hand to grip the foreign handle — something I had never done before. I wrenched it back with excessive force, slamming the glass door into its safety-stop magnetic field. The metal and glass elements vibrated from the sudden stop and rang out with a sonorous pitch. I caught myself on the top stair and held my position — wide-eyed and frozen, facing into the shadowed lobby.

Over the years, I had seen so many other H-sibs stumble down the stairs in fits of embarrassed laughter, but I had never quite understood why. I always thought that as an H-sib, I would have to try *harder* to mold myself into the next alphaclass. It never occurred to me how easy this could be. If the free-swinging door was any indication of how my balance path would go, I thought I had reason to be optimistic.

No glance back, no regret. I took my first step inside, and my rubber sole squeaked against the polished steel floor.

Squish. Squeak. Squish.

The sounds echoed unevenly around the cavernous lobby, and I chuckled. They were the same pair of shoes, so how could they possibly create such distinctly different sounds? It suddenly struck me how funny Harold would think it was; he'd probably tell me it was a metaphor for us as polar opposite twins.

I started to go back. This would be one last thing to laugh with him about before I made my transfer.

A woman's slender fingers wrapped around my forearm and pulled me back to face her, away from the door. She tapped the glossy white band that encircled my right wrist. A small light screen popped up, which was only visible to us.

"Harrison?"

"Yes?" I was breathless with the anticipation of this magical moment and the surprise of her touch. I bowed my head and averted my eyes. It was sheer habit. *I'll have to retrain that,* I thought.

"Don't even consider it. You know better," she scolded while dragging me over to the nearest white podium with a floating intake monitor. "We can never move backward." She tutted and tsked in perfect time with her crisp, heeled steps.

"Yes, I know," I insisted. "Thank you for the generous reminder." That ever so slightly released the crinkled line between her eyes. "I just..." I started, craning my neck toward the door. It had already swung shut and stood still. Then I paused and shifted my weight squarely back onto both feet. "Sorry, yes, I'm ready."

Was that a genuine smile tugging at the corner of her lips? From an I-con, no less? I couldn't help the puzzled expression that rose up and rearranged my features. I bowed even more deeply, and she laughed. Actually laughed!

"You'll only be an H-sib for a few more minutes, but don't worry — the transition is easier than you'd think." She glanced at the empty stand next to her and farther over to another intake manager who was initiating transfer for the C-spen. Then she leaned across the glossy white surface of the stand and said discreetly, "I was born with the name

Helen, so I learned the chant backward too. Trust me. Your family was there. Your balance is here." She rolled her eyes and swiped through the light monitor that floated brightly between us.

I took the deepest breath I could and tried to relax. My shoulders rose tensely, stretching the tight muscles around my ribs, and I released the breath with audible relief.

"Oh, and one more thing," she whispered. "Don't call it balance. It sounds so ridiculous. Everyone calls it *harmony*. Vie, H-sibs can't do anything right… Figures."

We stood in awkward silence while she worked. The instinct to bow overpowered my deep desire to take a better look around the room. Instead, I studied the white rubber toe caps on my favorite pair of sneakers.

Finally, I worked up the courage to ask, "What do you like most about being an I-con?"

She continued swiping through the air, performing a slew of digital check-in tasks, and I bit my lip in embarrassment. I assumed she would simply ignore my out-of-bounds question, but eventually she granted me a reply. "I enjoy that my life has precision and clear expectations. Every day is the same, or as similar as I can make it, and I take a lot of comfort in that. My routines bring me peace, like a seamless meditation practice that lasts for years."

"You have to work," I mused. "Doesn't that take away from your 17 points?"

"Oh, knock off the stupid H-sib act, you know the guidelines as well as everyone else — no one *has* to work. The system is self-sustaining. But yes, most I-cons do choose to pursue casual work. Personally, I like to fill my day with structured activities, and working at the V tower helps me stay focused. It's all about finding *balance*, as you like to call it. Maybe you'll transfer and become an I-con later in life." She chuckled softly. "Then you'll see what I mean."

It was my turn to laugh under my breath. "I was always a wild child. I can't stick to much of anything for very long, so life as an I-con wouldn't be a good fit… For my twin brother, that sounds perfect. If he wasn't such a mononomer and set on life as an H-sib, I definitely think he'd become an I-con next."

Her eyes refocused as she tapped out of the private screen. Softening, she said, "I'm so sorry you and your brother have to separate." Nodding, she returned to her work. "It's for the best. Besides, life as an H-sib is an absolute and utter waste. There's no way anyone finds harmony by popping out a dozen kids, babysitting all day, and planning an endless parade of birthday parties. Breeding isn't living. If life as an I-con has taught me anything, it's the importance of setting a schedule and knowing that there's always a precise, perfect time to transfer. At least you had the decency to do that. You're moving on, right on time."

I stared at my sneakers again and nervously picked under my fingernails.

"Well, Harrison," she said brightly, breaking the silence. "I double-checked your most recent scores and passed on your information for transfer. Vie is ready for you. Remember, when we all give up 3, 17 is guaranteed. Goodbye and good luck… Nicolas."

I moved behind the row of white intake desks and ended up walking right alongside the C-spen.

Technically, it's wide enough for two, but I really shouldn't… I cut myself off mid-thought. It would have been unthinkable for Harrison, an H-sib, to walk next to a C-spen, in his luxury clothes and perfume, but Nicolas had chosen his place and he deserved it.

Warm purple lights ran along the length of the corridor, sending one beam up each wall and another horizontally across the hard steel floor. For one step, we broke the beam together.

Then, like linked minds, I stole ahead, and he moved back. The next beam illuminated my foot alone, and I no longer registered the embarrassing squeak and squish of an H-sibs's shoes.

2

My wristlet vibrated and a subtle chime rang inside my ear as I approached the fourth transfer room on the right. I tipped my head to the side, peering closely to find a handle. Then the door rotated on its hinges, seamlessly and automatically.

I gazed down the long room and took my first step inside. The door closed behind me with a quiet whoosh of air. A bank of lights turned on, bathing the glossy, all-white interior in an angelic glow.

I reasserted my most confident posture, even though I was alone. My shoulder blades clasped together and pushed down, lifting my chest. I stood there for a few moments, assessing how strange the posture felt in my bones and noting the muscles that already tired under the expectations of their new roles.

Vie's warm, familiar voice sounded quietly over the room's speakers. "Welcome to transfer. Today you will step out of one life of discontentment and enter another life of opportunity. Leaving everything behind, you can only carry forward a record of your previous name. The decision you make today will affect the course of your life forever, and it requires careful consideration. If you would like to rescind your application and return to the lobby, this is your last opportunity to do so."

I bounced nervously on my heels, but didn't dare take a step back toward the door. *I'm ready.*

"If you choose to proceed and claim your new name, you may never return to the alphaclass you have left behind. Repeat transfers are forbidden in order to guarantee harmony and stability for all. Do you agree to these terms?"

"I agree."

Numerous light screens sparked to life and floated in a seamless circle around me, sealing me in.

"Harrison," she intoned. "You did not find harmony as an H-sib and your scores indicate that you are prepared to seek it as an N-star." Her voice sounded minutely different when she read out the alphaclass names – sharper and more metallic, as if the sounds were both tentative and forced. "In harmony with time and for the sake of all humanity, do you agree to move forward without disruption?"

"I agree," I replied as a genuine smile split my lips.

"Remove all of your belongings and place them on top of the pedestal for disposal."

The floating display seamlessly transitioned to show an illustrated view of everything I had in my possession. I eagerly ripped the soft, cream-colored cable-knit sweater over my head, but one of the yarn loops caught on the back of my stud earring.

"Fuck..." I muttered, trying to work the sweater over my shoulders while unclasping the metal clip from my ear. *Calm down. Be cool. You have time. You're fine.*

Untangled and released, I folded my sweater neatly on

top of the pedestal in front of me. Then I poked my bronze stud earring through the sweater's stretched-out collar and admired how the metallic letter H glittered against the fuzz. I had worn this little stud every day for eleven years, and it was the one thing I hesitated to part with. My linen button-down came off next. I stepped on the heel of each tennis shoe and kicked them off in turn. Then I yanked off my favorite pair of maroon socks, which had been lovingly embroidered with a thousand tiny Hs by one of my younger brothers.

One by one, the on-screen illustrations faded as I placed my items on the pedestal lid.

My wool trousers had a skinny fit that still dared to look baggy on my narrow frame. Even at the age of seventeen, I was growing up faster than I could put on weight. I undid the buttons and they dropped to the floor, weighed down by polished rocks, handwritten notes, and vintage, dog-eared N-star cards in my pockets. I took out each item and laid them around the rim of the glossy pedestal. Not to linger over them, I assured myself, just to make sure nothing was missed.

Only one image shone on the display. I took a deep breath, slipped my cotton underwear down to my ankles, and tossed them, unfolded, over the otherwise neat pile.

There was a whistle of air as the chute opened and sent my items back home. I was already moving on, two steps ahead.

Glancing down at the white circle around my wrist, I noticed that the outside was engraved with a new name next to the inlaid button — Nicolas. I slipped my thumb inside the metal band and made space to look at the side that faced my skin. Some of my tension faded and I felt unexpected relief when I saw my birth name etched there, unchanged. I padded barefoot into the next chamber, where a new bank of lights rose up to greet me.

Vie's ethereal voice sounded softly behind me as I passed through a succession of half-partitioned rooms. I stepped into a steaming glass shower to rinse off. My loose curls, which had grown unchecked past my ears, were trimmed short by an autostyler and finished with shiny oil. A retina infopod screened all of the recent N-star news and basic alphaclass guidelines in front of my eyes in a series of fast, blue-tinged light flashes.

The final bank of lights illuminated an identical pedestal to the one I had left behind. This time, it was already loaded up with a neat pile of clothing. I jogged the last three steps and picked up a set of heavy magenta robes. Running my fingertips across the gorgeous, never-worn fabric, I saw an infinite string of Ns woven into the fine fibers.

The fit was flawless. These robes were identical to the ones I had seen the N-stars wearing on the street earlier in the day. I expected as much, but I was still overwhelmed by how perfectly tailored they were. They were hemmed to my exact height, and I looked perfectly proportioned for the first time in my life.

Vie's voice broke through my self-absorbed daydream. "Nicolas, it is time to recalibrate your scores."

Without hesitating, I waved to accept the command and pressed the inlaid button on my wristlet with the tip of my thumb. The band hummed in its usual way, but I felt different. For the first time in years, I was excited to hear what the score would say.

Vie's voice spoke in my ear, repeating the familiar phrase with a new name. *17 out of 20 contentment points. Congratulations, Nicolas.*

My score hadn't changed, but it finally *felt* right. The promise of true, stable harmony and balanced contentment was laid out before me — no more, no less.

The external speaker system invited me to exit the room

and I prepared to grab the door handle, but it swung open automatically. I exhaled a breath of relief and stepped out to join a group of N-stars clustered in the hallway.

3

It was dizzying. *Everything* was dizzying. I was on the verge of passing out, but I didn't want to miss a single second of my new life.

I was still a full stride away from the group when a boy stepped in my direction and reached out to me. Before I knew what he was doing, he touched the button on my wristlet and pinged up my ID screen, just between us. His glazed, distracted eyes scanned through all of my personal information, including my birthday, Vie alerts, and names: Harrison, Nicolas. His confident, unexpected touch sent a spark of electricity through me, and I flushed.

The boy seemed so familiar… intimately familiar. It was unsettling how precisely I recognized and knew the soft features of his face: the curve of his rosy, upturned lips, the flat line of his mahogany brows, his gentle, sloping nose… We were strangers, and yet I had a bizarre sense of déjà vu. Hazy memories glitched through a lifetime of close encounters that had never happened. *How do I distinctly know a guy I've never even met?*

"Nicolas!" he bellowed with surprising warmth. "We love

the name Nicolas, don't we? It's a fan favorite!" He gently squeezed my wrist and continued to hold onto it, even though he no longer needed touch to access my information. "You're so lucky you got to transfer today. It's card day!"

"Every day is card day," a girl replied with equal force, laughing and rolling her eyes.

The boy leaned conspiratorially in her direction and whispered loudly, "Well, maybe he didn't know that yet! We love a little fun. Don't spoil it!"

"Come on, even new transfers know that. Just imagine if we ever went an entire day without giving the other alpha-classes an update. Their scores would drop straight to 12s!" she shouted.

"Why are you all talking so loudly?" I couldn't help but ask.

"It's just for today. We all decided. We want to make sure we're heard loud and clear!" he yelled, leaning back on his heels and cupping his hands around his mouth like a megaphone.

Overwhelmed, I let the sound wash over me as I studied my companions. I noticed that everyone's hair shined with the same oily glaze as my own and that the girls' hair was beautifully styled in neat, close buns.

"I'm Niam," the boy said, then he pointed around the circle and introduced all three girls in turn. "And this is the rest of our group — Nyla, Neela, and Nieve."

The girls broke into giggling conversation and jabbered so loudly that it echoed down the steel-floored hallway. Niam flung his arm over my shoulder and pulled me against him. He was at least four inches shorter than me, so he had to stand on his toes to reach. His long, draping silk sleeve tickled the back of my neck as it brushed by, and my skin pricked with goosebumps.

"Little Nicky seems pleased," Niam, the handsome, dark-haired boy teased.

I was unaware I had been smiling, and my cheeks stretched even wider.

"It's Nicolas, actually." I flashed a smile down at him.

"Well, Nicky... Nicolas, we're ready to head out." He shifted his weight back down onto the balls of his feet and boldly took my hand in his. He held out the other hand to Nyla on his right and we stepped forward in unison. "Let's give the people what they want!"

As it turned out, there were no people. Our tram was empty. The cloudless sunset that had escorted me into the V tower had been fully overtaken by a dark sky and a narrow crescent moon. Nieve spun demurely around one of the standing posts in the center of the tram car and hummed a quiet song. Her pale, rose-tinged skin seemed to reflect the tram's overhead lights with a ghostly glow. Nyla lay gracefully across a row of seats and chewed on her full lips, deep in thought. Shortly thereafter, Niam upended her, slid into a seat, and laid her head back down in his lap. Mirroring their playful confidence as best I could, I lay on the opposite bench and shook my head in amazement. Trailing fingers down my forearm, I twirled the lush silk of my sleeve into little roses.

Fifteen minutes later, I watched the city center roll away for the very first time, and I gazed across the spacious countryside. I could breathe again. There was no tightness in my chest. Bubbly, full-voiced conversation rolled around me in cheerful circles while my thoughts floated away.

"We don't sleep on trams," Nieve whispered in my ear, coaxing me awake. "But we'll give you a pass because it's transfer day." She kissed me playfully on the nose. "This is our stop, Little Nicky. Forward! Always forward!"

I was swept up in it all. Somehow, I kept up.

A short walk from the station brought us to a tall,

imposing wall that extended in an endless curve. It was stacked up with gray bricks and each one was intricately carved with a repeating N pattern. We stopped at a shimmering energy fence that filled a six-foot opening.

My companions breezily passed through the flickering, translucent light waves and ushered me forward with unbridled laughter.

"We get exclusive access," Neela giggled.

Niam talked over her, encouraging me. "Oh, hurry up — you're an insider now!"

As I tentatively reached out and broke through the field with one fingertip, my wristlet skimmed against the heavy silk sleeve of my robe. I remembered my new name, etched with all the privilege it deserved, and stepped forward. The temperature rose slightly as I passed through, much like stepping from a shadowed overhang into the full face of the sun.

"We're exhausted," one of the girls whined next to me as we walked in a line through beautifully tended gardens. A wide concrete pathway led up to the minimalistic white house, which was one of many identical abodes in the complex.

Niam grasped the front door handle with two hands and pulled it open in a grand, showy gesture. Doing so, he winked in my direction. Niam was the only one that had touched my ID screen, so only he knew that I used to be an H-sib and grew up with revolving doors. The joke felt warm and intimate, just between us.

I followed my guides through the maze of rooms until we arrived on an expansive sleeping porch. My eyes slowly adjusted to the dark, and Niam patted an empty bed next to his own. It was positioned next to a huge picture window that spanned the entire wall. The glass had a seamless curve that stretched up to a tall, domed ceiling. Niam slipped off his shoes and crawled into the crisp white sheets, tossing back a heavy quilt. I took off my own identical shoes and placed them on the floor next to his.

"We're really glad you're here," Niam whispered through the dark.

"Thanks. That means a lot."

My body molded so perfectly into the soft foam of my mattress. It felt heavenly. Rolling onto my side, I noticed something hidden in my pocket. As quietly as possible, I reached down and removed a screen card from the folds of silk. The metal was cold and smooth in my hands, but I immediately knew what I was holding.

It looked so unlike the vintage paper N-star cards I had removed from my pockets earlier in the day, but there was no mistaking it. I pulled the covers over my head and tapped the back with my forefinger. It blinked to life. My name! My photo! There was even a looping video clip from when I first walked down the V tower steps with my companions! I was officially a celebrity — someone worth remembering, and this was the proof. I curled my body up tight and held the N-star card in front of me. Tomorrow, adoring fans and collectors would beg me for this exact screen card and an autograph. Studying it in disbelief, I was lulled to sleep.

4

Days and weeks passed in a blur as I fell into the contented cycle of my new life. Every morning, we woke in unison, stirred gently out of sleep by the subtle tingle of energy that emanated from our wrists. I would tap the wristlet to update my scores and hear Vie speak in my inner ear: *17 out of 20 contentment points. Congratulations, Nicolas.*

Inside our private bathpods, Vie always had the day's fashion neatly laid out. The grooming tools never struggled to work my curls into the decided style, and I enjoyed seeing myself try out so many new looks. Niam and I always stepped out of our bathpods at the same time and spoke softly on our way back down to the living room.

"How are we feeling today?" he asked one morning with a sweet smile.

"We're doing well, I think… We think? We're still getting used to this new way of speaking."

"It's a little awkward when you're not used to it. Honestly, I… yes, I." He tapped his chest playfully. "I don't think it really matters all that much. It's just a silly social norm to keep everyone linked together. More of an expectation than a rule. When we speak as a group, we act as a group, I guess."

"That makes sense." I nodded.

"Hopefully this isn't too personal, but why did you choose to become an N-star? Trust me, your gorgeous face was made for the screen, and I've secretly been stashing your N-star cards away for my private collection..." He laughed nervously. "Hey, I'm kidding! Well, about the cards, not about how cute you are. I really am curious to know."

"I don't know... a lot of reasons."

"Care to be a little more specific? If you don't want to talk about it, you don't have to," he said, brushing the back of my hand with his. "But if you do want to share, I'm here to listen."

I bumped his hand in return and said, "It *was* a lot of reasons. It seemed like the polar opposite of life as an H-sib, for one thing. I've always been drawn in by the popular crowd and I care what other people think, even though my family tried to tease it out of me as a kid. Plus, I have a twin brother, so we were always called 'the twins' like we were a single unit. I wanted to build a life for myself and attract attention on my own, if that makes sense."

We were approaching the living room and heard the girls' chatter cascade over the top of the partial wall, cheery and bright. Our soft-soled shoes barely sounded on the gleaming white tiled floor. We slowed and Niam thrust his head back questioningly toward the bathpods. I turned around, relieved the conversation didn't have to end so soon.

"I was an only child, but I think I get it," he said. "You want to be independent. That's normal."

"What about you?" I asked.

"What do you mean?"

"I'm assuming you weren't born an N-star, so why did you choose it?"

"No, I wasn't born into the celebrity life, but I should have been! You've seen me on set. Unless I'm completely delusional — and tell me if I am — I know I'm absolutely crushing it for the fans. I adore the attention, I won't lie." He playfully wiggled his brows and his eyes lit up with faux charisma.

I shoved his shoulder playfully to get him to cut the act. "Yeah, yeah, yeah! I've already seen you charm the cameras. Were you always that way? Were you born for this?"

"Hard to know. I couldn't exactly practice my on-set persona until I came here, could I?"

We reached the bathpods at the end of the long hall and sulkily spun on our heels, forced to return to our real destination and wrap up the private conversation.

"It's weird… I knew *life* would be different without Harold, but even *I* feel different. Maybe I was only reckless and spontaneous because I knew he was always watching out for me. Looking back, I don't recognize the fast-paced kid I used to be. I'm not quite sure who I am without him. And now that I'm alone…" I glanced up and blinked away tears. "Sorry, I don't know why I'm laying this all on you."

"Hey, you're not alone. You've got me," Niam said, wrapping his arm around my waist for a few drawn-out seconds before slowly pulling away. "So, um, did you grow up around here?" His pale cheeks burned pink, and he took a boyish double skip to realign our steps as we walked leisurely down the quiet hallway.

I tugged awkwardly at the hem of my soft lavender shirt. "Yeah… I grew up in the city center. Right down the road from the V tower in 1675 where we first met."

"Did you ask to get placed in the same region, or was it random chance that Vie matched you here?" He shifted a fraction closer to me and stretched out his arm, dragging knuckles and fingertips across the white wall.

"No, I asked to stay close... if I could."

"Huh." Niam's shoulders rose in a tentative shrug.

"What?"

He blurted out, "You seem like an adventurous guy, even if you're feeling a little guarded while you recalibrate. I don't know why, but I have this gut feeling that you're an explorer at heart." Niam squinted one eye and slowed to a halt, studying me. "Somehow, I see you jet-setting to every corner of the world, walking through pre-Vie museums with baffling levels of concentration, and never getting bored with the immensity of your options. How far off am I?"

"K-trav was my second choice, actually," I said. "Have we really never met before?"

"Trust me, if we'd met, I'd remember." His striking smile caught me off guard, and it was hard to believe it was meant for me.

THE N-STAR COMPLEX glimmered with clean, utilitarian precision; it was so unlike my childhood apartment and bustling community center. I was used to seeing sentimental keepsakes and trinkets on every windowsill, and piles of hand-woven blankets and knit shawls that wrapped you in love, not only warmth. The layers of patchwork rugs, hand-stitched drapery, and gifted furniture had always made those spaces feel like home.

The distinct H-sib style was a constant source of teasing from other alphaclasses, but it was also one thing they never seemed to understand: we didn't live that way out of necessity or lacking; it was always a purposeful choice. Before we brought a new item home, it would be passed around through at least three different owners. Then, it would return to us, scuffed with the bustling energy of running children, knocked around in the heated distraction of love-making, and radiating the warm energy that could only be bestowed by friends.

We, we, we. Snap out of it! I chided myself internally. *They, they, they. I'm not an H-sib anymore.*

As N-stars, we either ate breakfast in the front garden or in the studio. Occasionally, we took the tram back into the city to celebrate a special event or attend the opening of a new restaurant. Breakfast was served a lot later than I was used to, but it was also the largest meal of the day. I was never disappointed by the vast spread of food that graced our table, and it tasted a lot better than the cafeteria-style dishes I'd eaten most mornings in the community center.

Throughout the day, Vie sounded subtle cue chimes in my ear and I watched my wristlet rotate, gently tugging me in the right direction. Her guidance made it easy to follow the flow of activity and remain in lockstep with the rest of the group.

There were automated cameras all around the complex, so I knew we were being scanned throughout the day, but those tapes were only published for low-tier broadcasts, like H-sibs, D-views, and L-rushes. At the sound of Vie's bell chime, we would simply wave at the mounted cameras as they flashed and continue on our way. The studio, on the other hand, was something special. That was reserved for our real fans. On studio mornings, we took our time and stretched the breakfast event into a full-fledged talk show with exclusive footage and guest cameos.

We occasionally worked jobs, but only when it suited us and offered something new to the filming schedule, like tending gardens, answering voice calls, and teaching video lessons for fans. Once, we even worked as volunteer tram conductors, but the surprise show resulted in transit delays across the city! During our free time, we walked the grounds and explored the expansive complex, meeting new friends and expanding our social circle.

When I made the decision to transfer, I didn't only want to experience something new — I craved a radically different lifestyle. For the first time in my life, I felt cared for and adored both inside and outside of my home. I didn't have to worry about walking in the wrong place, looking at someone the wrong way, or generally being wrong. Everything was *right* and perfectly timed with the other N-stars. All of the negativity I had faced from the outside world as an H-sib evaporated the second I took on my new name. It was unbelievably empowering to truly feel like an icon.

I was also amazed at how familiar everything felt to me here. I had grown up watching N-stars stroll through identical hallways, lounge in identical gardens, and cuddle on identical beds, but I had never seen it from this angle – I had never had the opportunity to live it.

We got along with everyone, and the atmosphere in our house was always pleasant. Nieve, Niam, and I formed the closest bond right away, so the three of us led the pack together, arm in arm. Nieve was bubbly, brash, and incredibly witty. Niam's personality was magnetic. He not only knew that he possessed charm; he knew how to use it.

Sometimes Nieve would wander off with the other girls and leave the two of us alone together. We all decided how the group was going to split up, if at all, so Niam and I couldn't *ask* for time alone, but those quiet moments of private conversation and laughter were special to me. I had a feeling they meant something to him too.

On the last day of February, the entire N-star complex filed out to attend a special awards show. The mass gathering was located in 3112, which was only fifteen minutes away by plane. Our autocab ride out to the airport took twice as long, but that was mostly due to the overwhelming rush of N-star traffic.

I was the only one who had never flown in a plane before, and I was secretly terrified. We bounded up the stairs and into the spacious interior with jovial energy, but I had a hard time maintaining my smile.

There were nine plush white couches along each side of the plane with plenty of space to seat three.

Niam seemed to sense my anxiety in choosing a seat, and he whispered in my ear, "Pick that couch in the middle of the plane, on top of the wings. We'll have the smoothest ride there." Nyla and Neela split off to the left and settled in alongside one of our middle-aged neighbors.

Niam's hand lingered on the small of my back as he guided me forward. His supportive touches continued to surprise me in a good way: he squeezed my hand during takeoff; his fingers trailed aimlessly across my knee; he reached his arm around my shoulder to point at something out the window. My heart fluttered with every brush of skin, but hesitation quickly pulled it back into rhythm. Everything was still unspoken.

Unlike our day-to-day events that were scheduled around breakfast, this was a special overnight trip for prime-time evening programming. Neela squealed gleefully, remarking that every screen around the world would be displaying our faces. Nyla chattered endlessly about how excited her fans would be for the opportunity to see her in a real evening dress for once.

"Want to watch a music video?" Niam asked, tossing his arm over the back of the couch and leaning into me. "It's one of my favorites."

"Share on your screen?" I asked.

"Yeah, tap in and I'll show it to you."

I wrapped my hand around his warm wrist and touched the button, pulling up a shared screen between us. As he opened the entertainment portal and swiped through his content library, I felt the tendons in his arm flex under my touch.

"Wait, slow down!" I said. "I want to see what you've got saved in here."

"Hey, I offered to show you an incredible new song. I wasn't exactly planning on giving you a tour of my mind." Still, he slowed his motions. "Maisie here is an amazing illustrator, so I have several of her pieces saved."

"For the record, I would like to take the full tour of your mind sometime. Let me know how to get tickets," I interjected.

He ignored me, but his voice sparkled with laughter. "Morgan creates trippy videos with shifting perspectives and gorgeous color editing, so if I ever look glassy-eyed and distracted, I'm probably watching that. Um, what else... Marcus is a talented piano player. You *need* to check him out."

"You've got a lot of M-self content on here! Do you not watch the system's stock entertainment? There's not much to choose from unless you're a D-view, obviously, but I still think the selection is pretty decent."

"No, not really. I'm a people person at heart. I prefer content created by *real* artists, and I like to think I'm helping them on their harmony path too. Wouldn't it be depressing to spend your entire life creating art and then find out that no one even cared to watch it?"

"Coming from the N-star who's obsessed with fan attention? Makes sense. Maybe M-selfs find contentment in making it, not just sharing it?" I suggested, tipping my head to rest on top of his for a moment.

He laughed and continued scrolling through. "Fair enough. This woman... Miriam. She's an all-around *artist.* That's what I wanted to show you."

We watched with quiet, shallow breaths as a woman danced in silence, alone under a solitary spotlight. Alternately, she twisted on the stage floor and leaped into the air. Then she flexed her hands in a slow, even pattern that matched a simple bassline. She sang in a husky, urgent tone that propelled the song forward, even while the fluid accompaniment behind her remained cool and meditative. Her lyrics were a string of random, open vowels and misplaced consonants. The nonsense words created a special kind of language, and I felt deeply in tune with her story. I crossed my ankles, flexed my feet, and my pulse pounded harder as the music swelled. Eventually, the singer pulled away from the constrained instrumentals and ran off the empty stage, singing with wide vibrato while she spun in giddy circles. The song faded out and the screen transitioned into a pure white square.

"Wow, that was... incredible." I released the button on Niam's wrist and didn't pull away.

"I know, right? I discovered it the other day and thought of you."

I bit my bottom lip, trying to contain a smile. "Thanks. Really, that means a lot. It was beautiful. What do you think she's saying in the lyrics?"

"I don't think it matters. M-self censorship or not, she clearly knows how to tell a story. At least, I heard one."

"Me too."

While we prepared to land, Niam firmly clasped his hands over mine. I felt more thrill than terror as we watched the ground rise up to meet our plane on the landing strip. I breathed out a huge sigh of relief and squeezed his hands in thanks.

"Little Nicky landed safely! We love to see that, don't we, girls?" he said brightly.

It only took a few words to pop our private little bubble and link back up with the group.

"Absolutely! Nicolas, you looked like you were going to pass out! We were worried about you," Nieve added.

"We're a lot better now that we're back on the ground," I said.

Would you like to update your scores?

We all waved in the affirmative, answering the voice that chimed in our ears.

17 out of 20 contentment points. Congratulations, Nicolas.

Then we disembarked the plane and walked over to the line of autocabs at the edge of the runway, arm in arm.

AN IDENTICAL N-STAR complex had been built for this annual prime-time event. Niam explained that it was always kept in pristine condition, exactly like the complex back home. The bright white interiors glimmered under the dazzling coastal sun, and a salty breeze blew through the house when I threw open the garden doors.

The awards show was scheduled to start at twenty o'clock, right before sunset, which meant we were free to spend our day playing on the beach.

Inside our individual bathpods, Vie had laid out teal blue swimming suits printed with white Ns, crisp white towels with matching teal stripes, and silver sandals. I changed, stood, and stared at myself in the mirror. My ribs poked out, my belly button looked weird, and my elbows looked even more awkward. The swimming suit fit me perfectly, like everything else Vie had ever laid out for me. I hadn't felt this clunky in months; self-conscious thoughts suddenly dominated my psyche. I couldn't help but think of how beautiful all of my companions were and how out of place I was going to look walking at their side. I already stood inches above the rest of them. Now I had to walk around shirtless too? Briefly, I considered asking to stay behind.

The button on my wristlet spun toward the door, but I couldn't take a step. I heard the faint tinkling of an in-ear chime a few steps in front of me. The band's energy physically tugged at me, escalating. Still, I was frozen, stationary, stuck.

Niam and the girls pounded on the door of my bathpod with exuberant, lighthearted screams. That was enough to jolt me back to life. I leaped into motion and pushed the door open with a broad smile.

THE BEACH WAS FILLED with N-stars in matching teal swimming suits. White towels and silver sandals littered the sand. All four of my companions had attended this event and visited the ocean before, so I was the odd man out, which felt even more embarrassing in swimwear.

The crashing waves were crystal clear; blue water shined almost as brightly as my swimming bottoms. Nieve and Niam ran straight into the water, mirroring each other stride for stride. Neela, Nyla, and I were slightly more reserved as we splashed into the surf, but we were still only seconds behind.

After an hour of swimming and snorkeling, Nieve and I decided we needed a short break, so we sat on the cool sand under the shade of an umbrella.

Nieve's platinum blonde hair had fallen out of today's ponytail, and the saltwater transformed it into crimped, tangled curls as it dried. Her missing hair tie was long gone, floating somewhere in the ocean. There was no use taming her hair, so she chose to let it whip around loosely in the wind.

I grabbed handfuls of sand in my fists and let it pour out in a slow, even stream. I was so happy to be here, watching everyone play and celebrate. It was a magnificent day and the view around me was as much proof of harmony as I would ever need. Dressed in the same garments, following the same schedule, and broadcasting to the same crowds, we were all equally admired. Our status as the most popular and iconic alphaclass was cemented and guaranteed, just like the promise of 17.

Looking out toward the water, I admired how well the bust of Nyla's suit was cut to fit her form. The high-waisted bottoms finished exactly at the sloping curve of her natural waist. Niam's swimming bottoms fit him just as well, and I had to actively stop myself from staring.

"We really like him," Nieve said, cocking an eyebrow in Niam's direction, where my gaze had been fixed a lot longer than planned. "Is there something going on with you two?"

I looked at her conspiratorially.

"Oh come on, we can talk about anything. And I'm smack in the middle of everything! We need to know how we should split up, that's all."

"Well, we're not supposed to ask for time away from the group, so…" I started.

"We're not prying, we're curious," she said. "Now spill."

I grabbed another handful of sand and squinted across the beach. Niam had his arms wrapped around Neela's waist as he spun her in circles. He dipped her all the way back so that her ponytail touched the water. Then he paused to brush a loose strand of hair back from her face. For a second, I thought they might kiss. But reality split away from my imagination, and I had never felt so relieved to be wrong.

"Can we just say I?" I asked.

She laughed and smiled. "We can."

"I really like him, Nieve. I feel this magnetic attraction and I can't stop staring. He's so handsome. And funny too! He always knows how to make me laugh and there's never a dull or boring moment with him. His energy is infectious and he carries himself with so much confidence. I've never been interested in guys before, but there's something different about him." I leaned in closer and dug my fingers deeper into the sand. "This is going to sound bizarre, but when Niam and I first met at the V tower, I felt a weird sense of déjà vu. I was flooded with unreal memories I can't quite pinpoint… It's hard to explain, like we've already been through this in another lifetime – him and me. Maybe this is what it's like to find your soul mate. Love at first sight, I guess? Vie, that's weird to say out loud!"

"I don't believe in love at first sight, but he *is* really good looking. I'll give you that," she agreed, shielding her eyes with her hand.

"I think he's giving me signs that he likes me too."

"He definitely is! The nicknames? All the handholding? I swear, he's inventing opportunities to get his hands on you."

"I know, right? And when he does touch me, it's electric. There's a spark between us that makes me want to get even closer to him."

"Okay, then why don't you?"

"I don't know. My mom always criticized me for being impulsive and rushing into things, but with him, I feel like I'm second-guessing everything. A few weeks ago, I was telling him—"

"What is there to second-guess?" she interrupted.

"The group dynamic. It's difficult… We can't choose to run off and be alone whenever we'd like. I'm an N-star now, so I can't *decide* to go rogue and make a move on my own. How would I even go about that?"

"What do you mean?"

"I don't know how we'd start dating in the group house… Assuming he even *wants* to take things to the next level."

"Just do what Nyla and Neela are doing. They're a couple and it's not weird. If things get more serious between them, we'll get new roommates, but it's fine for now — 17 is guaranteed when we all give up 3. That doesn't mean you can't have a relationship or start a family. It's just a little harder to make things work within the group. Underscoring is just as disruptive as overscoring, so we've all got to find a stable middle ground."

"They're together?" I said, shocked. My attention flew back over to where Neela played with Niam on the beach.

"Ha! Yeah! Why do you think they always head off alone when we decide to split?"

"I didn't even think about it. Huh. Good for them. Does Niam know?"

"Yeah, of course! Honestly, I'm surprised you didn't know." She looked perplexed. "We saw it coming."

I tried to backtrack and bluff my way out of the mistake by pretending that I was just as aligned with the group dynamic as everyone else. "Obviously we all saw it coming. I meant it happened a little sooner than we expected."

Our three companions called us back over to the water, and Nieve's attention dropped away from me.

As we were getting up from the sand, I said, "One thing, though. I'm worried I'm reading too much into this. He's so touchy and upbeat with everyone. That's part of what makes him such an amazing N-star. What if he's playing a role? He had his hands all over Neela in the water. Is he just being charming? Should I be jealous?"

"No doubt he's a charmer and he wants to be liked! I

wouldn't read too much into it. I think he might be insecure, if I'm being honest. He knows how to draw a crowd and rake in the compliments, but that's partly because he seems to need and want the validation. I guess that's true for all of us. Otherwise, we wouldn't be here. We're all charming people who crave attention."

"You really think I'm charming?" I shouted as we splashed into the water.

"Of course we do!"

THE AWARDS SHOW was set up under an expansive line of tents on the beach, and everyone from our complex filed down exactly five minutes before showtime.

We all had our hair braided into neat, tight lines, and the special event demanded a bold red lip from everyone. Most of the girls stepped onto the sand in full-length, layered tulle skirts with strapless bodices. The dark blue fabric was speckled with tiny white stars that looked like the night sky. I could have chosen to wear the dress tonight, but I preferred a matching suit instead. It was one of the first decisions that had been posed to me, and me alone, in months, and it felt like a big step, even if it was a one-time, annual exception.

Automated cameras hovered everywhere and the flash of lights was unreal. Light screens were set up in front of the ocean playing live reaction videos from our fans, and it was clear the world really was watching.

Our banquet table was laden with silver-rimmed dishes and a towering bouquet of bone-white tulips. I trailed my fingers over the navy linen napkin that draped across my plate. Our names were stitched in sprawling white script and I noticed that Niam's seat was across from me. My view would be fully obscured by the massive floral arrangement.

Glancing up, I saw Niam's sparkling, dark green eyes set on mine, even as he talked animatedly with a large group of people near the outer edge of the tent. He gave me the faintest wink, and that was all the motivation I needed. With a swift yet casual motion, I whipped Niam's and Nyla's personalized napkins off their plates, as if they were carried away by the wind. Resettling them in their rightful places – according to me, I smiled with smug satisfaction.

Niam was already on his way back to the table. "Nicky, you're full of surprises." He beamed and settled into the seat next to mine.

"Aww, you boys look so handsome in your suits tonight," Nieve said a few minutes later. With a coy smile, she urged, "Scoot closer. I'll take a picture!"

We shuffled our chairs on the crumbling sand until our knees bumped together, igniting a buzz of warm energy between us. Even after the camera flashed and our composed, celebrity smiles transformed into genuine grins, neither of us shifted even an inch away.

We created a private corner of conversation, tucked together and shielded by tulips. I told him about how my mother was such a terrible cook that we had to eat every single meal in the community center; how I had crashed my first bike riding down a set of stairs in the school lobby because I was dared to and couldn't bear the humiliation of saying no; how Harold and I always shared our birthday gifts and convinced ourselves that it meant we got double of everything. It felt like a victory every time I made Niam laugh. Our banter was split between his hilarious stories about the overly talkative guy who lived in the house before me; how his childhood as an E-sit flew by so fast, he sometimes wondered if it even happened at all; how although he had no idea how to play, he had fallen in love with the sound of the violin because it was soaring and dynamic, but could also be delicate — just like me.

After dinner, the awards got underway. Because there were hundreds of attendees and every group was going to receive a prize, the winners were announced simultaneously with in-ear prompts.

The categories were read out and the vast crowd sat in total silence, shadowed by the sounds of crashing waves.

Squeals of joy and congratulation poured out all at once as every person heard about their prize.

"We won most charming!" the table behind me yelled.

"We won most influential!"

"We got most glamorous!"

I cheered with my companions and we toasted sparkling glass flutes of champagne as we shouted, "We won most elegant!"

We clinked glasses for the cameras, posed for exclusive fan photos, and gave speeches about how much the award meant to us. The noise in our tent was deafening as everyone recorded their acceptance speeches simultaneously, but Vie's microphone system managed to give everyone a voice.

It was nearly two o'clock in the morning when we stumbled back onto the sleeping porch. Our beachside complex was identical to the one at home, but it was built facing a different direction. The giant window wall next to my bed now captured a perfect picture of the full moon.

I was the last one out of the bathpods and I slowly shuffled across the dark room toward my bed.

"Hey," Niam whispered.

"Hey."

"See that incredible view of the moon?"

"Yeah, it's amazing." I heard Nieve's reassurances in the back of my mind and decided to take a chance. My heart thumped in my chest as I said, "It's bright next to the window. Do you mind if I sleep in your bed tonight?"

His moonlit face brightened as he flipped back the quilt and patted the empty space next to him. I slid under the covers and he pressed his body against mine.

His touch always felt intimate; this was different. I wrapped my leg around his and felt the thud of his heartbeat, which was racing in time with my own. We settled into the moment, listening to the sound of our breathing as we trailed light, exploring fingers across fabric and skin.

He turned my face toward his and we were suddenly so close our noses almost touched. "I'm incredibly proud of us for winning most elegant tonight, but you deserved to win most handsome." He grinned widely at the cheesiness of his own comment. It was obnoxiously cute and he knew it.

I tipped my face into his shoulder and stifled fits of laughter, trying not to disturb the girls. "You're too charming!" I whispered. "No one has ever been this charming in the history of the world! It's super weird!"

"You love it!" He pulled me tighter into the crook of his neck.

"I do." I couldn't stop smiling. Neither could he. His green eyes were mesmerizingly expressive, even in the low light. He studied my face just as intently as I searched his.

"What are you thinking about?" he asked softly while slipping his hand inside my shirt to brush against the skin of my lower back.

I flinched and flushed with surprise at the heat of his touch.

He quickly returned his hand to the outside of my shirt, as if it had never happened. "Sorry, sorry. Am I rushing things?"

"No, no, I like it," I whispered with a hint of embarrassment. "I've just never done this kind of thing before."

"What kind of thing? What exactly *are* we doing, Nicky?" he replied, with a playful arch of his brow.

I allowed my hand to wander under his shirt this time, and it was reassuring to feel the prickle of his skin in response. "I don't know. I really like you and I've been drawn to you since the first day we met, but I was nervous about putting myself out there. You make me want to slow down and be careful. I don't want to mess this up. Tonight, I want to make it clear where I stand and see where this goes."

My mind skipped forward in an uncontrollable loop, already lurching through scenes of us together in bed, inviting him into my bathpod for a shared shower, and tracing circles on his bare skin in the light of dusk.

"I'd like that too," he said. I couldn't tell how clearly the fantasy reel played out on my face, but I felt a physical response from him that signaled I wasn't alone.

"I've only ever dated girls," I blurted out, tipping my face into the pillow we shared. "Is that okay with you? This is new for me."

He smoothed my hair and waited for me to look at him again before saying, "Of course. I've only ever dated guys. Is that okay with you?"

"Of course."

"Then there's nothing to worry about. We'll take things slow and, like you said, see where it goes." One of his hands twirled through my curls while the other explored the curve of my shoulder. He shifted even closer until there wasn't an inch of space between our hips.

"I wish we were alone," I said.

He gasped in mock surprise, saying, "Alone? That's a forbidden word around here." His eyes flicked down to my lips and my heart fluttered in anticipation.

Then he lifted his chin and touched his lips to mine. Sparks shot off within me that balanced the softness of him. The kiss was gentle at first, but the surprise of it took my breath away. As he turned his face to kiss me more deeply, his stubbled jawline scraped against my own. Tracing my fingers along his chin, I yearned to feel him even more closely. His fingernails scraped over the skin of my back as he pulled every part of his body against mine. Eager anticipation turned into silent exploration as we shared a single breath.

5

A few weeks later, I heard the faint tinkling of in-ear cue chimes, but decided to continue lounging on the cushioned swing on the front porch. Then, all of a sudden, I saw my housemates wandering toward the outside gate in an even row, chatting softly among themselves. I grabbed my shoes from the hallway and sprinted after them, hopping ridiculously on one foot while I tried to attach the decorative button clasps and keep moving at the same time.

"We're going out?" I shouted.

"Yes, Nicky!" Niam called back over his shoulder. "Hurry up, we're leaving for a breakfast event in the city!"

With both shoes securely fastened, I ran to catch up with them. When I finally reached the group, I tossed my arm around Niam at the end of the line and waved to the girls.

Near the tram station, we passed three I-cons on the street. They each took a tiny step back, mesmerized by their luck of seeing N-stars in person. We smiled, waved, and passed by without breaking our formation. I was struck by the hilarious contrast of their simple work clothes against our matching haute-couture ensemble. When I looked back, I saw a little girl standing half-hidden behind her father's leg. She stared at me, awestruck.

Releasing my arm from Niam's, I walked over to her, knelt down, and held out my screen card as a gift. "My name's Nicolas." I winked. She took the card in her hands, unmoving and mouth gaping. Her parents murmured words I couldn't hear, but I picked up on the mixed tones of amazement and frustration, so I reassured them, "Don't worry — you won't miss your tram. I promise you'll be on time and can stick to your schedule! It always waits for N-stars."

I hopped up from where I perched on the pavement and ran back to rejoin the group.

Reaching inside my pocket, I felt the replacement screen card. I knew by now that Vie would always have another one waiting for me, like magic.

Stepping through the restaurant lobby, Niam and I nodded to our friends and wandered off toward a small table in a quiet corner. We slumped into the booth, which was covered in smooth velvet and trimmed with elegant, angular pleats. The light tan fabric was a few shades brighter than today's camel-colored wool suits. A large silver pearl glinted in everyone's hair, which was styled with a windswept, casual look. It was a large event today, and there were dozens of N-stars I didn't recognize from other complexes.

"Nicolas," Niam said.

"Yeah?" I pulled my gaze from the wider room and back to our table.

Niam studied my face with the softest hint of a smile. "We really like you," he said quietly.

"We really like you too!" I grinned back, shifting forward and resting my elbows on the glass tabletop.

He leaned forward too and glanced around quickly,

measuring our privacy. "I have to ask you something..." He paused. "This morning, you weren't ready to leave with us."

"That's not a question!" I teased.

"Nicolas, come on."

"What do you mean?" I let out a quiet laugh. "We were only about six steps apart... We met up right at the gate."

"Six steps behind is not in line," he said with serious, sculpted features.

"I guess? We... I didn't realize we were leaving."

"Exactly."

"Exactly what?"

We both paused. The restaurant was softly lit with flickering candles. Opaque glass lanterns hung from the navy ceiling. It was a breakfast event, like all the others, but this restaurant somehow managed to capture the dining atmosphere of early evening. Cradled in a narrow corner booth, the soft, diffuse candlelight was incredibly gentle and intimate.

His dark green eyes searched my own, and I admired their dramatic, jewel-tone clarity.

"We left and you weren't ready. All of us heard the in-ear chines that signaled it was time to go, so how did you not know? Didn't you feel your wristlet twist and tug on you when we all got up to leave? Or were you just ignoring it?"

"Niam," I said with seriousness, "we were all ready. We were all together. I was only six steps behind."

"We're worried about you," he whispered, leaning even closer and holding my hands in his. "No... fuck it, *I'm* worried about you. We all decide, we all know exactly what to do, and we all follow through. That's how this lifestyle works. But *you* weren't ready. And that little trick with the I-con – giving the little girl your screen card? No one else bothered to stop, but you did it anyway. Vie, Nicky!" He cursed under his breath. "I can't keep dragging you along with us. What if the group splits and I'm not there to help guide you when you're ignoring the guidelines?"

I was dumbstruck. My mind was blank. I couldn't even begin to process what he was saying, much less form any kind of response.

"I'm worried about you," he repeated.

"Don't be," I said. "My contentment scores are 17 — not under, not over — exactly like it's supposed to be. Vie confirmed it this morning."

He took a long, slow breath and then flopped his head down on top of folded arms.

I squeezed his shoulders reassuringly and smoothed my palm around his back in wide circles.

"Nicky…" he muttered, barely audible through the woolen mask of his sleeves, "I couldn't stop thinking about it during the tram ride and I wasn't sure when we'd get a chance to talk alone. I hope this isn't a bad sign… You know how I feel about you, right? Our relationship has felt like a whirlwind so far, but I want it to last. I need you to be content here so that we can stay together."

"Niam, we—"

A petite N-star walked up to our table and brought the conversation to an abrupt halt as she squeezed onto the seat next to me. The small booth was only big enough for two people, but she seemed accustomed to molding the world to fit her wishes. And so it did. Niam popped his head upright again with an unruffled smile.

He forced out a loud laugh. "My favorite Nicky and Little Nicky finally have the chance to meet!"

She turned to me expectantly and cocked a tapered brow. "How do we decide who is who?"

"Check your screen card, maybe it's on the newest update?" I teased.

She took a screen card from her pocket and pretended to study the cold metal with feigned interest.

"Come on, you know you're our favorite," Niam said to her, interrupting the charade and blowing her a kiss.

Fuck, he's so charming! I thought. *He knows exactly how to make everyone feel special and adored... Am I delusional to believe he really feels something more just for me?*

"Oh, we're in such a bizarre mood today! Vieeee…" Nicky drew the pitch of *veeeee* off into a breathless tenor.

"We're quite pleasant, actually," I said with a smile.

She gazed back at the kitchen doors as they were ceremoniously thrown open. "It looks we're getting served any second. Do we mind sharing a table?"

Niam and I said, "Actually, we do," and, "Of course we don't," in perfect unison and total discord.

Our resulting, uncomfortable laughter transformed into something loud, stupid, and infectious; it spread around the restaurant with unplanned ease and suddenly everyone was red-faced with giggles. No one even knew what the joke was or where it had started.

A sea of plates levitated on autoserver trays and floated across the crowd, landing on tabletops with a delicate clink. The meal was impeccable and conversation across the room was light. I was certain that today's broadcast would be especially entertaining for fans. A few people pressed cupped hands against the restaurant's windows, trying to peek inside. The tone of the event grew even more lively as time went on.

Nicky's charm was spot-on, and our conversation flowed seamlessly. There was no question… she had the it-factor and everything you'd expect to see in an N-star. I pointed out the crowd of fans peeking in through the window and watched her face light up with genuine pleasure. Seeing them absolutely made her day. Niam's too.

It was a glamorous, entertaining event, but I couldn't focus. Throughout our idle conversation, a thought was lodged and unshakably moored in the back of my mind: I hadn't wanted Nicky to squeeze onto the narrow bench next to me. I really, really hadn't. But there she was. So I guess *we* did.

6

I sat cross-legged on my bed and stared out the expansive picture window. A thin layer of snow speckled every surface, but the dry, fresh flakes weren't even close to blanketing anything. It was a fluke storm that wouldn't stick around for long — probably no more than a few hours. It was early April and the spring season was fully underway when a bizarre cold front blew this pitiful snowstorm down from the north.

As children, we would all rush into the street at the faintest murmur of snow. We took turns — one keeping watch for passersby while the rest of us had our heads tipped upward to study the heavy cover of clouds.

I wiggled the toes of my left foot, which was crossed under me, and felt the needle pricks of sleep. I turned to lie face up across the foot of my bed, bending my knees off the side so that my feet dangled a few inches off the floor. From this position, I could look straight up at the sky without obstruction. The huge pane of curved glass had caught my attention the first night I arrived, and I was still mesmerized by it.

Harsh sunlight streamed in all directions, unbearably bright.

My thoughts wandered away and I was dozing in boredom when the foam mattress dipped next to me.

"Already read them?" a voice asked.

"Yep," I said softly.

"Well, that was quick." He whistled.

"Already read yours?"

"I got distracted."

"Well, that was quick," I repeated, matching his tone and cadence.

I turned my face to the side and found Niam lying beside me. The sheets stirred as he swung his feet back and forth off the side of the bed in time with my own. His dark green eyes were so familiar to me now — how they turned down slightly and widened at the outside corner. They were framed by commanding, dark eyebrows that sat horizontally when his face was at rest.

"What are we looking at?" he whispered, turning his head up toward the sky.

"Just everything," I said quietly. "Watch the clouds… There's a fast current up there. We can see snowflakes before they fall. We can see the sun shift toward the horizon. You know, everything."

He sighed. "We love that."

"We do."

We passed lingering moments in silence. The sound of Nieve's recorded fan mail passed through the window, light and bubbly. Nyla's voice buzzed softly through the thin walls. No sound carried in from Neela, so she must have been farther away in the garden.

This was the only individual time allotted in our schedules, and I looked forward to my brief escape every Sunday. Each of us split off to a different part of the house or city, depending on what we were doing that day, for an hour of solitude dedicated to answering fan mail.

When I had first arrived, my stomach was in knots and I was nervous to open my private screen. After all, I was a new N-star, and I didn't know how long it took for transfers to build a following. To my surprise, my private inbox was immediately overflowing with messages from fans. They said how much they loved my transfer day robes and how they fit me even more perfectly than any other N-star. Fans laughed along with a feed clip from the breakfast event when Niam and I started giggling and it took over the room. They also sent sketches and virtual collages of me lounging during breakfast in the studio. I responded to as many messages as possible within the sixty-minute slot, always saying how much we appreciated their support, how we did it all for our fans, and what a privilege it was to open our mail every Sunday.

The first few weeks, I meant it. Then months passed when I wasn't sure. Finally, I stopped opening them entirely.

Niam slipped his hand into my own and squeezed it sweetly, starting an unspoken conversation.

"I think I have to move forward," I said. My eyes were locked on the snow-dusted glass above us.

"I know... What's your score?"

"It's 16... not terrible, but obviously not enough. I know that if I stay here any longer, it'll hurt everyone, and I can't do that to you." I paused, working through my thoughts before daring to speak again. "I'm honestly so disappointed. I know that transferring is normal, and it's all part of the process. Most people are trinomers, and that's the point of having all these lifestyles to choose from. It takes time. It's a process. I get it! Everyone has their perfect place, and I believe that. I was just so excited to come here, and I thought this would be *it*. And we haven't had enough time to define what's going on between us yet. I know how strongly I feel about you, even if we haven't officially had 'the talk' or whatever... When we first met, I saw an entire lifetime of experiences and memories between us. I've never had déjà vu for a *person* before, but that's what it felt like. I just can't bear to leave you until I'm sure I absolutely have to. I guess that's why I've been hanging around here for so long, even after my scores first slipped."

He unlaced our hands, grabbed my forefinger, and pressed it onto his wristlet, revealing a private screen between us on the bed. "I'm a trinomer, you know," he said.

"No, I... I didn't know. You saw my ID the first day we met, but I haven't seen yours yet," I said, focused in study. "Hey! You're three years older than me? I knew you must be older because — you know, my birthday transfer was a dead giveaway..."

"That's your only takeaway?"

"The trinomer thing doesn't matter to me. Wherever you've been is part of your journey and now that you've settled into harmony, it was all worth it. That's how it goes."

Niam interjected, "How can you be so sweet and supportive with me but so hard on yourself?"

"You were born an E-sit, you tried A-aut, and now you're here as an N-star. That's it. That's perfect!"

"It was until I met you." Niam relaced our fingers, releasing his wristlet button. The screen disappeared and revealed a clear view of his sunlit face. The corner of his lips tipped up in a shy smile, but his eyes were set on mine. He was serious.

"Niam, don't talk like that. You're in harmony here — I can see it, your fans can see it, everyone can see it! You're clearly built for this lifestyle. It's part of your charm! And that's partly how I can tell that it's not a good fit. For you and the girls, everything flows. It just *does*, and I don't even know how to explain it. I see how flawlessly you're all fitting in, and I'm… not."

"I know," he said.

"That's why I have to leave. I'm out of balance." I corrected myself quickly. "I'm not 'in harmony.'"

Niam's smile stretched wide. "Ah… Harry is poking through. Not a good sign."

"Come on, don't tease me!" I said, playfully trying to extricate my hand from his grasp.

"We don't have much time, Nicky," he said, back to seriousness.

"Yeah, I know." I popped my own screen up to check the time. Only five minutes left in the hour.

"I agree, this isn't the right alphaclass for you. I think it was a knee-jerk reaction to the way society treated you as an H-sib, but it's not what you truly want. Maybe you thought you were in harmony at first, but trust me, I've been through this before. When I was an A-aut, there was one day when I felt… I don't know… *lacking*. I mulled my scores over and realized that things weren't adding up. The best, most fulfilling parts of that lifestyle weren't enough for me, and I was settling for more than the 3 points that bring us into harmony. I realized that my guaranteed 17 wouldn't show up there, so I had to leave." He steeled his resolve and continued, "We both know exactly what day that was for you. Six steps behind, right?"

"Six *fucking* steps behind."

"I know."

"You're all so in sync with the scene. You know exactly where the cameras are rolling, the connection with your fans is unbelievable, and you never seem annoyed by the group plan. But don't you ever want to say fuck it and skip a studio session? Or choose your own dinner? Or go for a walk alone?"

"No, I don't." After a moment of thought, he continued, "That's just a little sacrifice to me. So what if I can't pick my own clothes? It doesn't bother me at all. Sometimes I feel exhausted when I have to wake up early with the group and I'd prefer to sleep in… but that's just 3 measly points! We all settle for 3 to guarantee 17. Maxing out 20 points sounds perfect in theory, but we all know it's unsustainable. That's unrealistic."

"I know," I said, a little defensively.

"Right now, with you, I'm genuinely tempted to say fuck it and skip this whole thing."

I laughed despite myself. "Fuck it, huh?"

"Fuck it." He smiled. "I've never met anyone like you. This is new and I don't want to overstep, but I think we've got a real connection and I want it to last. Maybe two other alpha-classes could make it work, but if I continue living as an N-star, I'd never be able to see you again. With these strict groupthink guidelines, I wouldn't be able to head off into the city alone to meet you for a dinner date… This can't be the end of us. If you're going, I'm going too." He tipped his head forward and kissed me with sincerity. It wasn't our most passionate embrace, but it signaled something important — a shift in expectations, a bold assertion. "I'm confident I'll be able to settle into harmony again, but I'll never have another chance to meet you. I wasn't flooded with a lifetime's worth of déjà vu when we met, but I still felt instantly connected to you. It's *corny*, but I honestly believe we belong together."

"But Niam – honey, you can't give this up for me. You can't give up *your whole life*," I whispered, shaking my head morosely. "Your screen cards will be wiped for forever, even your most devoted fans will forget about you, you'll have to change your name… And if you go with me, you can't ever come back. This is a life-altering decision that I *can't* ask you to make. If things don't work out between us, I never want you to blame me for stealing you away from the place where you were truly happy. You have to–"

His sudden kiss stopped my words, overwriting desperate emotion. "I think Vie's got a lot of things figured out, but what if *you're* my 17? What if it doesn't even matter where I am or what alphaclass I'm in? This is so stupid! All I know is, I can't lose you! You came into my life and changed everything so fast, and I–"

I kissed him back with more force. This time, it was my job to pause his rambling thoughts. I swept myself up and hovered over him as his hands gripped my biceps. "I think I love you. I've never been in love before and you're my first boyfr—"

He interrupted me, grinning. "*You think* you love me?"

"I take it back! You say it first!"

"Happily! Harrison Nicolas, I am deeply and completely in love with you."

"Did you really *think* about it?" I swept back a lock of his fine black hair and tucked it behind his ear, placing a soft kiss on his temple.

"Yeah, I did," he murmured. "I've thought about it a lot. You, us… where we're going — the whole thing. And I'm not kidding. I love you and I'm ready to transfer whenever you are. Life as an N-star has been fun, and I think it's a good fit, but it's nothing compared to the way you make me feel. Like Vie says, we have to move forward. I'll happily give up the chance to go back in order to get a future with the man I love."

"I love you too." Soft heat spread through me as I gazed down at his smiling face and felt the electric energy of attraction ring between us. "But you won't ever be able to come back, even if you change your mind down the road."

"I know."

"You think I'm worth that risk? We're really committing

right here, right now to build a new life together?" I asked, genuinely cautious and concerned.

He wrapped his arms around my waist and leaned up to whisper in my ear, "Where are we off to next, partner?"

THE NEXT DAY, Niam and I said goodbye to our friends, passed through the warm energy fence, and left the complex for the last time. I ran my finger along the N-stamped bricks, my other hand wrapped in his — warm and steady.

Even though he was by my side and united with me in this decision, it was still the first independent action I had taken in months. I had almost forgotten how liberating it was to walk in silence down the street and set your own pace.

We wore our last set of matching N-star clothes with pride, including a fitted, brass-colored top with puckered shoulder plumes and a prominent black zipper. My black silk trousers were beautifully tailored, as always, and I could feel the off-kilter weight of one screen card pulling down my right pocket.

As I had expected, yesterday's dusting of snow was already gone, replaced by a surprisingly warm breeze with blue skies. It was like it had never happened at all.

I handed out screen cards while we rode the tram into the city for the last time. As I pulled them out one by one, my pocket magically replaced the card in an endless cycle. The crowd was star-struck. I even dared to quietly offer a screen card to an H-sib who stood huddled against a wind draft at the back door. As I did, a twinge of painful energy pulsed out from my wrist, like I had crossed an invisible barrier meant to make me grimace and recoil. Still, I refused to pull back right away. A tiny bronze H pendant hung around his neck, and it brought back memories of the stud I had poked through the collar of my sweater during transfer — the one physical item that was hardest to let go.

Niam rolled his eyes and leaned close to whisper in my ear, "Harry, I can't take you anywhere." He kissed me on the cheek and a camera flashed in front of us, capturing the moment. A G-paw beamed up at us, juggling her camera and the tangled leashes of more than half a dozen dogs. We smiled politely and agreed to take a posed photo with her to go along with the candid one.

"Keep an eye out for our response on Sunday," I reminded the crowd as we exited the tram at the city center station. "We always write back to our favorite fans!" We waved goodbye and continued walking in contented silence, knowing that we would never reply. They would be quick to forget.

Niam pulled open the V tower's heavy glass door for me. With an eager laugh, he led us inside toward a pair of pure white podiums on the right side of the lobby.

7

During my first transfer, it was liberating to wrench off the heavy second-hand sweater and empty my pockets. Sure, I had felt a pang of nostalgia and the frightening twinge of loss, but I was also being tugged forward with dreams of what was to come. It was a specific mix of emotions and something altogether impossible to replicate. The first time you leave home and set out on your own is a singular experience.

I no longer had my close-knit H-sib family or lockstep N-star community to lean on, but Niam was right… with him, I would never be alone. As a K-trav – a global explorer – I would soon discover how loneliness and isolation balanced with independence and autonomy.

My second transfer was speedy, and I was giddy with both enthusiasm and expectation. If I hadn't been so eager to reconnect with Niam on the other side of the door, I might have lingered.

How many N-star cards would I have been able to stack up on the white pedestal? Would the floating screen around me have dimmed and regained its illumination every time a new card appeared in my pocket? Or would Vie's illustration have remained constantly lit, unamused by the trick?

At the time, it never even crossed my mind to try. I hurried across the narrow room and passed through automated hygiene stations that molded me into a new version of myself.

Niam was already waiting for me on the other side. He looked unusually small, standing alone in the dim light of the hallway without a cluster of N-stars around him. With his hands stuffed into the pockets of a utilitarian, navy-blue jumpsuit, he looked uncomfortable and out of place. The heavy fabric pooled around his wrists and ankles, and the top seams of his sleeves hung limply over the edges of his strong shoulders.

He turned to greet me, and I threw myself into his arms.

"17?" I asked enthusiastically.

"17."

Just like me, his gold-flecked hair serum had been rinsed off during transfer, but a lingering trace glinted above his ear. It warmed my heart to see him carrying a tiny token of his former N-star self. It had passed imperceptibly under Vie's careful scrub, and I secretly hoped he would never lose it.

"Well… Harry, Nicky, partner? What should I call you?"

"Let's do IDs at the same time. Simultaneous reveal?"

"Trust me, you're going to love mine," Niam said with a wink.

I pinched my lips together and feigned thoughtful estimation, but I couldn't hold the pose for long. My emotions overwrote the teasing gesture, and I flashed a wide smile.

My black rubber ankle boots faced his white sneakers head-on. We counted down from three and tapped each other's wristlets.

His private screen popped up and laughter burst out of

me, unfettered. "Khiam?" I gently punched him in the chest, pushing him off balance. "Honestly? Niam… Khiam?"

"Hey! There's something really familiar and beautiful about the way that name rolls off the tongue."

"Are you even trying?" I chuckled, offering my hand to steady him and pull us back together.

"Well, Kasey. It's so nice to meet you. You know, you look a lot like my old friend Nicolas. Nicky, we used to call him. It's uncanny!"

"Yes, you can call me Kasey!" I said. "I want to do this transfer right. A new name is a new opportunity. You know the drill. In harmony with time and for…"

His voice joined my own: "…the sake of all humanity, I agree to move forward without disruption."

He continued, "I know, I know! But I couldn't resist picking a sound-alike name. You fell in looove with a guy named Niam, and I wanted to make sure you wouldn't forget him!"

"Khiam," I said with a straight face and soft voice, "you know I never will."

"TURN OR STRAIGHT?" Khiam asked when we neared the end of the first city block outside the V tower.

"Hmmm… let's do a turn," I replied.

"Left or right?"

"Right."

Khiam prompted me for directions at every juncture and insisted that I set our course, even though we had yet to decide on a destination. Off we went, zig-zagging aimlessly through the city as the night grew darker and darker.

Our loping, directionless path led us to a long bikeway

where we walked under the light of a full moon and sparse overhead lamps.

On our left, a small grove of maple, fir, and oak trees grew tall and unrestrained. The dense undergrowth was kept mostly under control. A few trees had been chopped down and fresh wood chips were scattered over the dark, muddy soil like traces of evidence at a crime scene.

The path also ran along the edge of a mixed alphaclass neighborhood. Most of the residents had drawn their curtains closed, but we were unknowingly invited to peek inside a handful of others. I observed the neatly organized furnishings of I-cons lined up with absurd precision. G-paws played fetch with a large group of dogs and E-sits lounged in low light farther down the road.

"It's really dark outside… and chilly," I whined.

Khiam shivered beside me. Without the warm spring sun overhead, it was easy to replay yesterday's falling snowflakes.

"We could run?" I ventured. "Get a little heat that way."

"I don't know if I can keep up with your long legs."

"We could turn around and go back to the city? I know there's a hotel near my childhood community center."

He kept moving forward. "Is that what you want?"

I thought for a moment. *What do I want? In this moment, right now, what would make me feel most content?* "I want to go to bed and I don't care where that is as long as there are lots of warm blankets!"

"And me too, right?"

"You do make a pretty good heater."

"That sounds so nice. See, this is why I put you in charge of the directions today!"

I laughed. "I have no idea where I'm going!"

"Yeah, but we're K-travs. We're *guaranteed* 17. We just have to lean in, give it a solid try, and discover hidden gems along the way."

"Okay, and what's that got to do with this?" I asked, with a sweeping gesture toward our surroundings. "Khiam, we're on a path to nowhere. In the dark. And it's freezing!"

He blew warm air into his hands and rubbed my shoulders vigorously, creating a pitiful amount of friction heat. It did make me smile, if only for the effort.

"Now at least you're not freezing," he said. As we passed under the warm glow of a lonely street lamp, he continued, "And at least it's not dark anymore."

"Only for about ten more steps!"

"Hey, that's something!" He winked. "I'll let you in on a little secret. We're not on a path to nowhere. Trust me."

I guffawed.

"No, really! It's not much farther," he insisted. Khiam took my hands and held them inside the wide kangaroo pouch pocket that ran across the middle of his new jumpsuit.

"If you say so." I sighed tenderly and we quickened our pace down the dark lane.

Our hotel that night was a tiny establishment with seven small rooms. It sat on a hill that overlooked a tidy field of farmland and another forest grove, much like the one we had passed on our walk. Two bikes rested against the front gate and a car was parked at the side of the building, covered with a black tarp.

Vie's automated system scanned our wrists and checked us in.

Our room was unbelievably cozy and welcoming. I carelessly kicked my boots across the room, flung myself headfirst onto the bed, and pressed one of the soft pillows over my head in an attempt to warm my frozen ears.

"Ugh!" I moaned, facedown on the white flannel sheet.

I heard Khiam unsnap the buttons on his jumpsuit and gently set his sneakers by the door. He slid into bed beside me, under the covers.

"What time is it?" I asked.

"Check it yourself!" He chuckled. "And scoot over. You're hogging the whole bed!"

I wriggled under the covers and flashed up my dashboard. "Twenty-two o'clock? Khiam! We walked for five hours! Whose terrible idea was that?"

"Well, I mean, technically you were the one who kept making all the wrong turns..." he whispered, eyes already closed.

"Because you refused to pick a hotel and make a plan!" I retorted.

"Hey! You finally got to make your own decisions for the first time in months. I wanted to maximize the opportunity."

I scooted closer to him, hugging my knees up to my chest. I still hadn't stripped off my bulky traveling clothes. "Okay, that's fair. I appreciate that. But before you go to sleep, I have to ask: how did you even know this place existed?"

His smile broadened in the dark. "Funny story. I was an A-aut for a while, you know that. Well, I watched some travel series as a kid and I always loved the idea of hotels. I grew up as an E-sit, so I was never able to travel, but it seemed magical, you know? Like how you can go anywhere in the world and Vie always has a bed waiting for you, just like home." He breathed out warm air that thawed my frosted cheeks. "When I had the choice to select an area of focus during A-aut transfer, I picked the hotel industry because I liked the idea of having a voice in the decision-making process. Where they got placed, how they were rated for alphaclass use, what design features got approved... that kind of stuff. This was one of my last projects. The stats for usage rates and local demand didn't quite add up, so Vie kept pestering me with tickets that I had to override, but here it is! That's the allure of living as an A-aut and having some authority, right? My voice mattered and I made something happen! It's amazing."

"A-auts can override Vie? You actually did that?"

He snorted a tiny puff of laughter. "Barely! Override sounds dramatic."

My skin felt warm again and sleep started to tug my eyelids down, so I finally got up and pulled off my outer clothes. I carelessly chucked the garments in the corner near where I thought one of my boots had landed.

"Why here?" I asked as I snuggled next to Khiam's bare skin inside our flannel cave.

He rested his head against my chest and murmured, "I don't know… I rode out here on a bike ride with my boyfriend at the time, a guy named Alexi. He was nice, but it wasn't anything serious. We rode all the way to the end of this path, climbed the hill, and that was it. Then we turned around. And I thought, wow… this would probably be such a good view to wake up to."

"I guess we'll see in the morning."

"Good night, Nicky," he whispered softly. "I love you."

"Kasey," I corrected. "I love you too."

His smile stretched against my cotton shirt. "Good night, Kasey."

THE EAST-FACING windows did put on a show. Khiam and I were gently stirred to wake as sunlight crested the horizon and crept into our room. I traced a finger down his pale bicep. He twisted his hands through my mess of curly hair.

I need another haircut, I thought.

"I like it like this," he murmured.

"I think I like the length on top, but I hate when it curls around my ears like a—"

"What?" he interrupted.

"My hair."

"What about it?" he asked, puzzled.

"You said you like it like this."

"Thiiis," he said, elongating the word as he waved his hand, palm up, at the scene of our messy hotel room. "Where did the hair thing come from?"

I laughed. "It's stupid."

"You're stupid," he said. Planting a kiss on top of my head, Khiam returned to twisting and teasing my curls.

I laughed gently and turned to breathe in the scent of him. It wasn't cute. We both needed a shower.

Beyond our picture window, sunrise cast a diffuse, warm glow over the fields and forest. The landscape was blanketed under fast-moving, wispy clouds, and the sun rose above a line of mountains on the horizon.

My bare feet sank into the lush, high-pile carpet as I walked over to the bathroom. I was glad to see that it was fully stocked with toiletries. I had never stayed in a hotel before, so I hadn't been sure what to expect.

"Have you checked your score yet?" Khiam called from the other room.

"No, I'm afraid to," I yelled back.

"Why?" A split second later, he was in the bathroom with me, leaning in through the doorframe.

"I might be too happy!" I kissed him on the cheek.

He took a step closer and ran his thumbs inside the waistband of my underwear, pushing them down and saying, "Good thing we're allowed a little time to recalibrate. Let's make the most of it."

We left the hotel around eleven o'clock. Vie's voice reminded us to check for forgotten items inside the room before we closed and locked the door.

Our walk back into the city was much more pleasant with sunshine at our backs. For the first time in months, my thoughts settled on Harold and Huna. They had always seemed so content together, permanently in balance. I wondered if our paths would ever cross again. It would be tricky to arrange a meeting with them because I couldn't talk to an H-sib openly in the streets, as a K-trav or any other alphaclass. Maybe I could slip through their door for a quick hug? That could work, as long as no other neighbors stopped by.

"You win. Today we can make a plan," Khiam said breezily as we reentered the city.

"We can still take turns, if you want. Keep practicing our newfound independence?" I offered.

"You're full of good ideas."

"I distinctly remember you saying I was stupid about four hours ago," I said dryly.

"I changed my mind!" He skipped boyishly ahead of me. "You go first."

"Shopping? We're not N-stars anymore, so no more private bathpods with our clothes laid out every day."

"I do miss that crisp, perfect fit," he replied dreamily. "And the status, I won't lie, it was great! Doesn't it hurt your feelings to walk down the sidewalk and have no one recognize you… or even notice you?"

"It's heaven!" I said, jogging across the empty street toward a small department store on the other side.

"Look!" Khiam gestured up at a nearby billboard. "There's

a new episode playing from the studio and everyone's watching it. Two days ago, they were practically drooling at *our* feet. Now no one cares where we go or what we're doing."

It was true. A handful of people stopped on the sidewalk to watch the scene play out on the board above them. Another couple sat enthralled at an outdoor dining table, leaving their food untouched.

"But it was always so annoying to be *on* for the cameras. And you acted differently when we were in the studio versus when we were alone. Even with the rest of the group or other N-stars, it always felt like..." Searching for the right word, I continued, "I don't know, it seemed like you were acting."

"I was! That's the point! That's why it was fun." He rolled his eyes and continued into the store.

I followed him inside. An M-self was searching through bolts of raw fabric at the design bench reserved for artists in the back of the store. Otherwise, we were alone. Khiam walked over to a shopping terminal by the entrance, and I thumbed through a rack of K-trav clothes.

"Acting feels unnatural. It just wasn't a good fit for me. Hey! Speaking of fit..." I hoisted up a snow jacket with a neon-orange collar and matching puff sleeves, stamped with the letter K.

"Oh, come on! Get over here," Khiam begged as I returned the garish jacket to the rack.

At the terminal, Vie suggested a variety of travel packs and accessories. Before we could make a decision, we had to figure out where we were going. Wandering around the city was fine for a day, or maybe even a week. We could ride bikes across the valley and climb the foothills if we wanted, but there was so much left in the world to discover. We needed to make a plan.

I turned up my palm and placed my fist on top, silently inviting him to play a familiar game.

"Vie. On. Three," we chanted while rhythmically tapping our fists on our palms. On the last word, I steepled my first two fingers into the shape of an upside-down letter V. He chose to hold his letter V flat down against his palm.

"Yes! I win," he cheered as he slid his fingers under mine and sent my letter tumbling. "Wait, we forgot to pick a question first! Do it again."

"Winner picks the question, so you set the terms?"

"Okay then… East or west?" he asked.

"East," I said.

"You know if you go far enough east, you end up going west?"

I scoffed and held out my hands in the ready position.

"Vie. On. Three." My fingers were face up, his were face down. This time, I slid my fingers under his and flipped them over to signify my victory.

"Okay, so we're going east…" I mused. "We might as well get directions out of the way first. North or south?"

"North," he said with a wide grin. "I want to see some real snow."

"Hey! The question was north or south, not snow or no snow."

A few people entered and wandered around the shop while we worked through at least thirty more rounds of the childish game, but no one minded. It was the first time I could be in public without attracting the attention of other alphaclasses – positive *or* negative.

With a clear destination in mind and renewed enthusiasm, we selected several items and confirmed our order at the terminal by scanning our wristlets. Vie produced two complete travel packs under the counter in just a few minutes.

On our way out of the store, we pulled up private screens and initiated travel requests for 2588. An autocab pulled up to the curb within minutes and whisked us away to start our next adventure.

"Your stomach is grumbling louder than your snores," Khiam said in disbelief as he gently shook me awake and lifted me off his shoulder. I had fallen asleep during the hour-long drive to the airport, and he was right – I was starving. Our room service breakfast had been bland, so I hadn't eaten much.

After scanning in at the terminal entrance, I heard Vie's soothing voice in my ear, repeating our departure time and gate number.

Khiam dropped his pack on the checkered tile floor and slumped into the booth of the airport's 24/7 diner. He patted the light birchwood bench next to him, and I bumped his hip with my own.

"You're so lucky you got to take a nap," Khiam groaned through a large bite of cheeseburger. "Your snoring is more obnoxious up close."

"You love it!" I said, but an embarrassed blush ran up my cheeks. As a kid, I had been teased mercilessly by H-sibs for my sleep talking, sleep walking, and snoring.

He read my face and noticed the reaction. "Hey, I'm just giving you a hard time! I think it's cute."

"Total change of topic: does your food taste weird?"

"Yeah," he said, stuffing a handful of fries into his mouth. "I expected that."

"Oh yeah," I muttered. Realization struck me and I felt stupid for bringing it up at all.

"K-travs don't get the full sensory experience. If you have

the *entire world* at your fingertips, you've got to give up something equally big for the sake of system-wide harmony. That's worth 3 points, I guess. Everyone's experience has to be even and equal."

I picked up my grilled cheese sandwich and took another flavorless bite. "Whatever it takes. Just give me balance."

"Harmony, Harry. It's called harmony!" he corrected with a wry smile.

I stuck out my tongue at him and lightly kicked his shin under the table.

8

Vie's voice coaxed me out of sleep. *The time in 2588 is 15:44. The weather is twenty-four degrees with light snow and winds out of the northeast. Dense cloud cover will break at 19:12 tonight to reveal the northern lights. Would you like to update your scores?*

"I can't believe we only transferred yesterday," I mumbled through a yawn, waving off her request.

Khiam was fast asleep, curled up on the plane's couch beside me. The message from Vie wasn't loud enough to wake him, but I knew that she would repeat it at a higher volume if he didn't reply. All of the other passengers stood to gather their belongings from the overhead bins. I gently squeezed Khiam's shoulder and pushed back a lock of sleek black hair that fell over his gorgeous horizontal brows.

Nearly everyone on the plane was a K-trav, but I did see a lone C-spen packing up her belongings in the VIP area at the back. I was mesmerized by the luxe velvet bedspread and ultra-soft throw blankets draped across it. Our couch was spacious and comfortable enough, but it sure wasn't on par with *that*. Luckily, you could fly anywhere in the world in under three hours, so we weren't crammed together on the couch for too long.

We exited the plane behind a small family — small compared to what I grew up with. The father pulled down five neoprene travel packs from the overhead bin, all proudly stamped with the letter K. The woman was helping a toddler put on her shoes and quipping at two older boys to please help their father. All three kids shared the same chestnut brown hair as their mother, soft and straight. While velcroing the little girl's straps in place, the mother turned around and caught me staring.

I jolted back to reality and coaxed Khiam with less grace than before. As he sputtered awake and rubbed sleep from his eyes, the family trundled past us down the aisle to disembark with their belongings.

The woman stopped in front of me. "First time?"

"This was my second time flying, actually."

Her face changed in a flash. "New transfers? I meant first time here in 2588. Do you mind?" she asked, gesturing for my wrist.

"Go ahead."

We tapped each other's bands to pull up private screens for introductions.

"Kasey, it's so nice to meet you. You're an H-sib by birth?"

"Yeah," I said sheepishly.

"Most people are. That's nothing to be ashamed of as long as you had the self-respect to get out and pick a better life for yourself, which you clearly did."

Her toddler pulled at the pocket of her jumpsuit and asked to be picked up, so the woman obliged.

I responded, "Thanks, Kara. I just turned seventeen last year, so this process is new to me."

"Oh, that's so sweet. Young, eager, chasing harmony! I'm sure you'll find it here. Kevin and I have always been content as K-travs. I've scored 17 every day of our adventure – isn't that right, honey? And it's only the beginning! Is this your traveling partner?"

"Yeah," I said, half-lifting Khiam off the couch to stand with me. "This is Khiam, my boyfriend. We came from 1675."

The woman bounced her daughter on her hip and turned back to face the other family members who were lingering impatiently at the front of the plane. "We love it over there, don't we, Kevin? 1675 is on the west coast, in the heart of the valley, right? That's such a nice jumping-off point. Close to the mountain snow and an autocab trip away from the coast. Heaven!

Do you guys have any particular plans mapped out while you're here?"

A couple at the back of the plane appeared ready to disembark, so I picked up our packs and signaled to Kara that we would follow them out the door. "We've just been making decisions as we go along."

"That's the best way to do it." Kara hoisted her daughter onto her hip as gravity started to get the best of her.

I gave Khiam a knowing nod and he returned it with a small smile. I could tell he was still tired. His large eyes always dipped down at the outer corners, but now they looked absolutely droopy.

I spoke up. "I think a hotel is at the top of our list. Khiam needs a nap."

Kevin, the husband, proceeded to tell us in great detail about their favorite hotel in the city: a remodeled pre-Vie cathedral with towering white columns and three domes on top.

"Obviously, the interior has been retrofitted, but they kept the outside architecture. Vie will try to reroute you to a basic hotel in the water district if you're a first-timer, but this one's so much better," he insisted. "We're planning to check in there as well, so you can follow us over if you'd like. Share an autocab?"

Trudging through the slushy snow, my ankle boots felt woefully insufficient. We didn't have to walk far from where the autocab dropped us off, but it was far enough. A chunk of snow broke off over the top of my boot and fell in next to my sock.

Khiam must have seen my look of frustration because he lightly jabbed an elbow into my side and cheered, "It's snowwww, Harry!"

"It's Kaseyyyy," I said. "And yeah, snow. Fun. You're the one who wanted to travel north, not me." I took in a deep breath. The cold, wet air felt familiar in my lungs, but I couldn't distinguish the scent.

A six-foot-wide path cut through the snow and revealed steps of ancient brick leading up to the hotel in front of us. When new flakes touched the walkway, they immediately melted into a pool of water and dried into a warm mist. The level of thoughtful preservation baffled me. Someone must have removed the bricks, installed warming panels, and returned everything back to the way it was. Where I grew up, it didn't seem like anything was left from the pre-Vie era. Maybe that was just because nothing in the area was worth saving?

Six huge, white columns supported the massive façade, and a dozen more wrapped around each side. I wondered in amazement what it would look like to peer out of the 360-degree windows that circled the tall, domed tower on top.

"What was it before?" I asked.

"The hotel, you mean?" Kara smiled at my awed innocence. "I'm not sure. Maybe a pre-Vie government building?

Or a church?" She said this last word with the twinge of a disgusted laugh. "Thank Vie they did something useful with the interior."

———

We spent three weeks exploring 2588 and the surrounding area with our companions. They were gracious enough to slow their pace and stop with us to look at hidden gems that weren't listed on Vie's guides for first-time visitors. Her organized systems and structure felt so familiar here, even though we had traveled halfway around the world: N-star gossip still flashed on every screen, J-devs huddled together on street corners to hand out missionary counseling pamphlets, D-views were visibly absorbed in private entertainment, and I could still spot a C-spen's luxury outfits from three blocks away.

Kevin taught us that most cities had been remodeled to align with A-aut building codes, but the decision-makers were always careful to leave some parts of each location untouched — or, at least, as much as possible. How would K-travs be able to enjoy harmony if every city was a cookie-cutter model of the rest?

Our amateur guides led us through expansive parks and across the edge of a marina, which sat empty except for a handful of flashy yachts emblazoned with the letter C in glittering gold.

The old market hall, as it was dubbed by our in-ear guide, was a mesmerizing departure from the style of the rest of the city. The red-and-white bricks had faded a bit, but they still created a striking peppermint stripe. In the middle, the entrance had been retrofitted with a modern, seamless expanse of glass.

"V and O?" I mused, studying the letter-like pattern of

yellow and orange bricks that spanned the side of the building. "Why O?"

Khiam poked me in the side and whispered, "This is pre-Vie, Nicky! Stop trying to make sense of it."

I quietly corrected my name without any trace of barb. I secretly loved that he had his own nicknames for me. It made me even more convinced that he loved me for where I was in my journey, not only in spite of it.

Every day was a new experience. We had free rein to explore historical and cultural sites that were preserved across the city.

In the morning, we warmed our hands around tiny cups of lackluster espresso. At lunch, Kara carried out a heaping plate of flavorless potato sausages for us to eat in the park. For an afternoon treat, we stood at a café counter to eat cold-smoked reindeer and cured salmon. The texture was delicate and intriguing, but the taste was hollow. Holding a salmon cracker close to my nose, I could only smell the lightest whiff of brine and salt. Still, it was unlike anything I had ever tried. Before we left the park, I ordered a small tin of salmon from the kiosk and tucked it away inside my pack.

THE FAMILY'S OLDEST BOY, Karter, turned twelve the day before our departure. He tended to be passive and uninterested in what we were doing as a group. Instead, Karter preferred to ping up a private screen to get updates about Neeyana, his favorite local N-star. He thought we couldn't tell what he was doing (so easily fooled by the self-centered lens of adolescence), but it was obvious. Casually scrolling his hand through the empty air was a dead giveaway. Staring at a close-up light screen also gave his eyes a glassy, detached look that was easy to spot. His parents scolded him halfheartedly and threatened to set limits on his screen time, but they never did.

It was so interesting to watch the family dynamic and compare it to how I was raised. All three children were born several years apart, and although we met up with other K-travs for meals and tours, the kids rarely spent time with others their age.

Karter may have been distant and introverted, but he also seemed perfectly content. He was a child, after all. At that age, you don't know enough about yourself or the world to make life-changing decisions about harmony. Don't trust a twelve-year old to run away from home and fully grasp the reality of what it means to *never* go back. This was his opportunity to enjoy the full experience of the alphaclass he was born into. In five years, he would earn the right to decide for himself — then he could stay or go.

In honor of his birthday, Karter was granted full control over our itinerary for a day. Kale and Kaava, his younger siblings, instantly set to whining and moaning: "It's so unfair! He's going to waste our day. We're going to have to go into the woods *again*, aren't we?"

As the autocab rolled to a stop at the trailhead, Karter wrenched open his door with wild enthusiasm and eagerly gestured for us to follow. Kara was still kneeling at the back seat to help little Kaava put on tall boots over thick wool socks.

"Mind if we wander ahead? It looks like our guide knows where he's going," Khiam called back to the others.

Kevin waved us on, leaning against the round glass front of the autocab. He, too, had a habit of calling up his private screen when he thought no one was watching. Maybe that was why Karter never received the punishment that was promised.

Khiam offered a hand to Karter, but the boy ignored it and set off jogging down the forest path ahead of us. Khiam grabbed mine with a shrug and we walked on. Our pace was quick but not too hurried.

Every few minutes, Karter would pop back into view, racing to tell us between puffing breaths about an especially exciting tree. "There's an awesome... pine tree coming up on... the left! And it has a *huge*... sea buckthorn... thicket wrapped... around its base! Maybe twenty paces... You can't miss it!" And he set off running again.

"Where do you think *he's* transferring when he turns seventeen?" I chuckled.

"That's the definition of an F-nat!" He shook his head, grinning. "I love it when it's that simple: when you meet people who know exactly what drives them and where they're supposed to be."

"That's what my twin brother, Harold, was like. If we were standing still, no one could ever tell us apart, but the second we started talking or doing anything at all, it was crystal clear. I was always restless and impulsive as a kid, but he glided through life — content with his place back home. Everyone loved him. *Everyone.* And that's saying something in an alphaclass that's built on the gushy, lovey-dovey concept of devoted families and tight-knit communities. I was well-liked, but he was loved. I was always in awe of that. He knew exactly where he was supposed to be."

"Did he even consider transferring with you?"

"No way! There was absolutely no chance he was going to transfer on our birthday, and I'm convinced he never will. He started dating his wife Huna at age thirteen and they fell in love... It was disgustingly adorable. They were the first couple in our class to get married after turning sixteen."

"Sounds like our whirlwind romance!" He blushed and tried to backtrack. "Minus the marriage part…"

I laughed and playfully lifted our clasped hands to check for wedding rings. "I think they fell in love even faster than we did, if that's possible. And they were always so steady. No questions or hesitations, ever. They just knew. It was beautiful to watch, and I'm so glad I was able to walk him down the aisle on his big day."

"Aww, that's so sweet. I'm sorry you had to leave him behind."

"Me too. It was hard, but I knew it was for the best. Huna's probably pregnant by now, and I bet they're settling into a perfect life together, totally content. Can you imagine getting to spend eighty-seven years with the love of your life?"

"And always in the same place?" Khiam whistled a long, sloping tone.

"I guess the hardest part would be coming up to your death day and having to walk the other person up to the V tower doors before it's your turn. Huna is a little younger than us, so she'd have to spend the last two months of her life alone."

"After eighty-seven years, two months is nothing. And as an H-sib, you're never alone. Isn't that one of the major perks?"

"I guess."

"Besides, their love story is perfect. Two monomers falling in love with clarity and confidence? That's how the system is supposed to work! Not like us multinomers messing around until we find harmony."

"Hey!" I bumped his hip. "If we're all guaranteed harmony, then we also get to enjoy the journey."

"You don't have to preach to me. I'd be happy to spend the rest of my life with you anywhere. The journey we're on together is part of what makes our story so special. You'll always be Nicky to me."

We stopped walking and he wrapped his arms around my waist. His head rested against my chest while I placed kiss after kiss on his sun-warmed forehead.

Karter yanked us out of the moment. "*Guys!* I think I saw a rabbit!" Then he bolted away just as suddenly.

Lifting his face to meet mine, Khiam whispered, "He's a sweet kid when he's in his element, but *for fuck's sake,* we're trying to have a romantic moment here!"

"Always the charmer," I replied as we strolled hand in hand down the forest path.

Karter interrupted us at least six more times, and we nodded with awe and amazement, assuring him that yes, we did see the moss-covered boulder; yes, we were impressed by that tall spruce; yes, we did notice the cave entrance. How cool!

The wet stone path turned to duckboards under our feet, and they creaked serenely with every step. Birdsong echoed through the expanse. We shifted into an amiable silence and listened to the world around us.

When we finally caught up to Karter, he was resting on a polished metal bench in a clearing. It looked so harsh and out of place in this lush, natural environment. The boy's eyes were no longer scanning the woods for natural treasures; they were locked on his invisible screen.

He heard our footsteps, released the button on his bracelet, and turned to face us. "My dad said you're leaving tomorrow?"

"Yep," I said. "It's been fun hanging out with you all, but I think we're ready to go somewhere new. Any suggestions of places we should visit?"

"3102, 4489, 0148, and 0015," he said without hesitation, counting them off on his fingers. "Well, just outside of 0015," he clarified. "The city itself is okay… Mom really enjoyed the music there and she said the M-selfs had 'tapped into the local culture,' but the Sawn rocks and limestone caves were way better. Have you ever seen a pipe organ?"

"No…" we droned. I was perplexed.

"It's a type of instrument. I saw one in a museum when we visited 2790. I don't understand how it works, but the Sawn rocks look a lot like that."

"What?" I asked.

"The *rock* looks like an *organ,*" he clarified as if he were trying to explain the concept to an unmoving granite face. "You have to go see it in person! It's cool. I think you'll like it."

"Okay then!" Khiam chimed in. "We'll start in 0015 and work our way through your list." Without skipping a beat, he touched his wristband to make a note with Vie.

9

Over the next two years, we traveled to virtually every corner of the world, and there was still so much more to do. The immensity of our options left me wonderstruck. We could go *anywhere,* so we did.

The more I saw of the world, the more I resented my mother for choosing to settle as an H-sib and raise me in our small, crowded community center. You could make relationships and find community anywhere — with Khiam by my side, I was certain of that, so how could H-sibs possibly think that family was enough? Every day, society shamed and taunted them for their embarrassing lifestyle. How was it worth *that* when you could have *this*?

My father transferred away when Harold and I were seven years old. At the time, it was hard to come to terms with the loss and loneliness that enveloped me.

I remember walking with him to the V tower as the seventeen o'clock bells chimed. The path to get there was always the same. Just like my birthday procession, the group chanted with increasing energy as we made our way up to the entrance. Father knelt down to face Harold and me head-on. His words are too muddled for me to recall after all this time, but I do remember the touch of his hand on the back of my neck. He forced me to look him straight in the face, and it was clear that he wouldn't allow my attention to wander. He looked so excited, but his dark brown eyes glistened with tears. I asked where he was going; he shook his head. I asked what name he would take next; he said he didn't want to confuse my memories. Before he stood to grasp the stoic glass door, he tucked a scratched bronze watch into Harold's pocket and poked a tiny letter H stud earring through the collar of my sweater. Then he was gone.

Every night, my mom worked to convince us that he had done the right thing. But if he wasn't at home with us, how could that possibly have been true? I relied on Vie's quiet reassurances to keep me calm at night when my thoughts started racing.

In harmony with time and for the sake of all humanity, we agree to move forward without disruption.

We can never go back, always forward.

Harmony is guaranteed for those who seek it.

When we all settle for 3, 17 is guaranteed.

The phrases repeated in my inner ear, lulling me to sleep and quieting my discontentment.

My father had left us to chase his own harmony, and that was the right thing to do. By staying, he wouldn't have only hurt himself; he would have sown unhappiness and discontentment in our home. After enough years of separation and repeated speeches from my mother, I finally reached a point where I believed it.

Now it grated on me. It was infuriating for a different reason. What about *her*? There was no way my mother was content, and yet she stayed! If she could have had the whole world within her grasp like I did now, it was unbelievable to think that she chose to stay for the right reasons.

I thought back to all of the tight embraces and teary-eyed moments. Was that love? Life-altering, keep-you-there, always-enough *love*? Or was it fear? Who cared if you couldn't go back when you could be *here*?

I waded deeper into the steaming pool and floated out of my thoughts. The natural hot spring was one of hundreds of destinations that had left me feeling truly awestruck. Khiam was floating at the pool's snow-white edge where the water rose right up to the top, putting every other infinity pool to shame. The air smelled empty and hollow in my nose, even though the mineral water likely carried a strong scent. Two years into life as K-trav, my dull sense of taste and smell seemed normal. I simply avoided the foods from my childhood that held strong memories because the experience wouldn't be the same, and I didn't want to draw my attention to it. Otherwise, it was merely a subtle, slightly annoying shift in how I experienced the world around me. What I ate didn't matter as much as everything else I could experience, learn, and see.

The water lapped against Khiam's back as I approached. I couldn't help but notice the obvious cut of his spine and sharp shoulder blades.

Would you like to update your scores?

He waved away Vie's in-ear message, but I didn't.

17 out of 20 contentment points. Congratulations, Kasey.

Khiam crossed his arms over the pool's stone edge and rested his chin there. I mimicked the position. There was a mountain range in the distance, which held a soft, hazy glow from the summer heat.

"It's magical," I whispered over the lapping water.

"It really is."

"Pure harmony."

A tense silence surrounded us, which had been mounting for weeks. I had fallen into a habit of saying those two words when we experienced something truly breathtaking… like this. *Pure harmony.* Khiam used to repeat it back to me and we'd tap our bands to retake our scores. I couldn't remember when that stopped happening, but it had. I had tried to bring it up with him before, but he always shrugged off my inquiries and pulled up his display to make another travel plan with Vie.

I turned my head, still resting on my arms, so that I could look squarely into his dark green eyes. He did the same.

After a few minutes of calm silence, I said, "This feels familiar. Remember that afternoon back home when you had to have this talk with me?"

He groaned and turned his face the other way. "I'm just having a bad day."

"You've been having a bad time, not just a bad day," I said, rubbing his back. "I hate to see you like this. We're here in this magical place, *together,* and I don't know what to do for you. I don't know how to help you get to 17 because clearly you're not there."

"I know, and that shouldn't be on you."

"What's your score?"

"Kasey. Don't worry about it," he said harshly. "We'll pick a new destination and leave tomorrow. Somewhere wet and tropical again? That will probably help."

My lips relaxed and I dropped the forced smile. "So I'm Kasey now?"

"You always correct me when I call you Nicky or Harry, so tell me what you want! I'm just trying to keep up!"

I raised my hands in surrender. "Woah… Come on!"

He ran his hands through his black hair, which was cropped short. His softly freckled skin was several shades lighter than my own, but it had adopted a warm olive glow after weeks spent lounging in the sun and exploring desert ruins.

Finally, he said, "Look, I'm sorry. I don't know what's up with me."

"It feels like you're holding back. Just tell me."

He took a deep breath and exhaled slowly. "I don't know."

The wind picked up, rustling the lush green leaves of an olive tree on the nearby shore. We had set our packs at its base before diving in to soak. Mine was bulky and nearly impossible to close. Every pocket was filled with tiny trinkets and treasures I'd collected at every destination. Khiam's was slim and tidy. He was on his fifth replacement pack in as many months. He said that his old one got soaked and ruined in a tropical storm, but I knew that he really just needed smaller clothes that would fit his shrinking frame.

"You can tell me," I repeated.

Again, a deep breath. A slow release. "I feel lost. It's cool to see all of these new spots, and the pre-Vie access is fascinating, but it feels like we're doing the same thing over and over again. Doesn't everything feel… I don't know… flat? I miss the flavor of food! My mouth doesn't even water anymore when I think about my favorite dishes or strong scents and flavors. A sour lemon, strong coffee, any of it! And I miss dumb stuff, like the smell of grass and how your after-shave used to smell. Back at the N-star complex, do you remember how we always walked back from the bathpods together? Spoiler… that wasn't a coincidence! I used to finish my shower at the same time as you so that I could breathe you in on the walk back. Nicky, you smelled like a goddamn bath bomb! You can't even imagine how much I miss that! I feel like I'm stuck in a constant cycle of half experiences. I'm dragged along with you to all of these cool places, and I understand the appeal, but I'm not really here. My life feels dull, no matter what we do. How do you not care that we're eating tasteless mush? How does it only cost 3 contentment points? I've lost so much weight, and some days I can barely force myself to eat two whole meals. How ridiculous is that? It's hard to explain because clearly you aren't feeling the same way. I didn't want to worry you, but my score has been dropping for a while and Vie's alerts are ramping up. I don't know what to do."

I furrowed my brow in concentration, taking in his flurry of words. They had tumbled out with uninterrupted force – a stark contrast to our silent tension over the last few weeks. I saw how much he had been holding back from me and how relieved he was that he'd allowed himself to start talking.

"Do you regret leaving?" I asked.

"It doesn't matter anyway... I can't go back."

"I know. But do you?"

"I don't know. Maybe. It doesn't matter."

"It does," I insisted.

"Yeah... I regret leaving." He tapped the top of my hand with his finger. "But I don't regret you."

We settled back into stillness. My head was racing through scenarios and sentence fragments that I couldn't seem to voice. My mind spun out on a highlight reel of our time together. We crested the peak above 5557 and it took our breath away — we stopped our conversation mid-sentence and it never seemed important enough to continue on the hike back down. He lay next to me in bed every night, whining adorably about his sore feet after exploring new city streets. When I spent hours sitting in pre-Vie art museums, he would come back every so often to check on me, but he never demanded that we leave before I was ready. He always suggested a simple game of Vie-on-Three to sort out the details when we weren't sure where we were going. Travel had knit our lives together with infinite secrets and private memories. We shared everything.

I felt closer to Khiam than I ever had with my own brother — my first friend and other half. I had walked away from Harold without a backward glance. Could I let Khiam do the same thing to me?

I was so incredibly happy in this life, maybe happier than I ever had been. Was that because of Khiam? Or because of the K-trav alphaclass?

This level of freedom was something I had never experienced before, and it felt life-changing. I could spend my entire life wandering this planet and at the end of my one hundred years, there would always be more to do… more people to meet, more culture to discover, more art to see. Every day before I took my scores, I had to steel myself to feel *less happy*. Sometimes I felt guilty about it. Maybe I was taking more than my fair share.

There were tense moments and misunderstandings between us, of course there were. But I wanted to be with *him*. I had dated a few people in the past, but it was never like this. Not even close. The instant connection we felt had forged into something unbelievable, and he knew it too. Passion, playfulness, mutual adoration, and so much laughter. He gave me everything and had given up everything to be with me. His actions cemented it every day. He had been willing to put my happiness above his own, long before we even knew how unbreakable our bond would become.

I interrupted the silence, saying, "I don't know what I'd do without you. I *can't* go through life without you."

"I don't know what to do," he croaked. "I just need the spark of my life back. This isn't living. This isn't enough."

How could I let him walk away from me? If I stayed behind, I would lose him. If I went with him, I would lose this life. Either way, I was a coward.

I gently lifted his finger and placed it on his wristlet to call up a private screen. "You already missed today's transfer window," I said, "but tell Vie you want to leave tomorrow. I'm coming with you."

10

The retina infopod flashed a thousand images in front of my eyes. My pulse quickened as I got a better sense of what we were doing. I had never seen or met an L-rush before, let alone considered transferring to become one. All I knew about them was from alphaclass training programs that I watched as a kid.

Awareness settled on me like a weight, and I gripped the sleek white armrests that curved around me. I absorbed the safety recommendations, alphaclass guidelines, and recent L-rush news that Vie imprinted across my eyes. It was too wild, too loud – a total shock to my system, and I couldn't tell if the icy electricity was pure panic or adrenaline.

Deep breaths, I reminded myself. *It doesn't matter where I am as long as I'm with him. We'll get through this together. Who knows, maybe this will be a quick phase and we can move forward to something else.* A pang of worry sliced through my chest. *But what if compromise transforms into regret? Did I give up too much?*

My thoughts lurched back through time, reversing a dozen paces through the long transfer room:

"Kasey," Vie had intoned. "You did not find harmony as a K-trav and your scores indicate…" She paused.

My throat felt tense and tight as I tried to swallow. For a moment, I wasn't sure if she would let me transfer at all. I had fought back genuine pangs of dread, imagining Khiam standing on the other side of the door, waiting for someone who would never pass through to meet him. How long would he be willing to wait? How long could he? Would he understand? How would he even know what had happened?

In the weight of Vie's silence, tears welled up in my eyes and I attempted to push through the light screens that shined around me. I felt gentle pushback and familiar heat, exactly like the barrier fence at our N-star compound, but this time I wasn't being let through. My emotions spilled over and I slammed down on the wristlet button, pleading in distress, "Let me move forward! Let me move forward! I want to go forward!"

The last word broke into a sob that caused me to unravel. Panic and fear crashed over me.

Vie's voice picked up again, as if she had never stopped. "…that you are prepared to seek it as an L-rush. In harmony with time and for the sake of all humanity, do you agree to move forward without disruption?"

"Yes," I mouthed, unable to control my voice.

Through hiccupping sobs, I worked to reclaim my composure. I unearthed every item in my pack and set each piece down on the pedestal: a handmade web from the J-dev campus at the base of 6020, a paper photo card of the tower in 7895, a scrap of fabric from when my swimming trunks snagged on the reef in 3111, a can of cured salmon from our first visit to 2588. In that moment, I vowed never to forget these memories.

The first time I transferred, I had assumed that my items

would be returned home. Now I wasn't sure. Where would they go?

Even though I could never go back and would likely never see those destinations again, I told myself that I was content. I had to be.

I'm lucky to live in a system that has granted me the opportunity to glimpse those landmarks even once, I reminded myself.

Thank Vie I had the ability to experience the vastness of the world in any measure. I had seen up close how perfectly preserved and balanced the world was. That was something worth believing and trusting in, right?

Khiam and I had gone round and round during our conversations the night before, but I was steadfast in my decision. "We're young," I told him. "We have our entire lives ahead of us and this is only one small moment. This is only the beginning."

He was broken up over it, but I saw how he secretly hoped that he wouldn't have to leave me behind. The more we fought, the more convinced I was that I had to fight for him.

Khiam was waiting for me on the other side of the transfer room door, but unlike last time, I only made it halfway across the threshold before a teary, snotty mess of a man enveloped me. He pinned me against the door frame and planted desperate kisses across my cheeks, neck, and mouth.

"I was so worried! I didn't think she'd let you through! Or I thought maybe you changed your mind." He spoke through frantic sobs and clung to me.

I held him back, wrapping my arms around his short frame and whispering soothing reassurances into his hair. He smelled overwhelmingly of cucumber and eucalyptus. The fragrance was unbearably strong, but I didn't dare pull away or release my hold.

Several minutes passed, or hours. Slowly, our nervous energy transformed into relief, but the transition was halting and stilted. Living without him didn't seem possible, so I must have made the right choice. Vie had made me stand face to face with that reality when she paused and considered turning me away.

He took a deep breath and said, "You smell like a goddamn bath bomb."

I tousled his hair with a full, therapeutic laugh and said, "Have you smelled yourself recently?"

"Not in a *really* long time."

"What should I call you now?"

"Just guess." He laughed heartily against my chest. "What about you?"

"I'm Lokai," I said. "Or Kasey… or Nicky… or Harry. Whatever you prefer."

"Liam and Lokai. I like the sound of that."

Following Vie's in-ear instructions, we found our way to a three-story apartment building. Our steps echoed on the metal stairs, which twisted upward in a narrow spiral to the top floor. In our hallway, dingy tan paint was peeling and missing in large chunks across the plastered wall. Long-term water damage fed discolored pockets of mold that grew out of dark ceiling corners. Liam looked back at me in violent disgust after stepping on a dark spot in the carpet runner that squished with sickening wetness. He immediately hopped off and shifted over to the tiled edge, preferring the puckered, stained wallpaper to whatever had soaked through the floor.

A thin, wood-paneled door stood ajar at apartment 3C. Liam, who bravely took the lead, pushed it open with one knuckle. A tattered navy couch and stained yellow armchair filled the small living room. There wasn't enough room for the large glass coffee table that sat in front, but there it was, squished and forced into place. The room's large light screen broadcasted a live feed with footage from a local N-star complex. Parts of the picture were discolored and glitched in a violent, hypnotic pattern. AI commentary droned on in falsely excited tones, talking about the latest celebrity gossip, rumors, and fan ratings. I waved my hand through the light screen and turned it off.

My un-dimmed, restored senses still felt raw, like the sparking end of a live wire. I pulled my arm up to cover my nose. The perfumed fragrance of my sea salt body wash was a thousand times more pleasant than the reeking stench of dampness, stagnant air, and piss.

A grimy kitchenette filled the shallow wall opposite the living room. There was also an empty dining nook and a small window that was taped over with a piece of damp cardboard. Even after turning on the overhead light, the common area carried an eerie, dismal darkness. To the left, through the living room, there was a long hallway lined with eight doors. A wet towel was draped over the top of the first door, revealing a small bathroom; all of the others were closed. We held our wristlets out in front of each door until we heard two unlock.

The first room was roughly the size of a closet. Liam waved through the light panel at the entrance, but nothing happened. Our view was only lit by the dim hallway track light that flickered behind us. The closet-sized bedroom also had a tiny closet. Cream-colored sliding doors were visibly jammed with a tangled mess of wire hangers, limp T-shirts, hoodies, and jeans. Otherwise, there was only a narrow mattress and an unlit light screen to complete the space.

The other room was substantially larger, and at least it

had a window. We dragged in the first mattress alongside the other, stretched a thin bedspread horizontally across them both, and fell into an exhausted heap.

"So this is it?" I asked.

"It's not that bad," Liam said with only a hint of his usual charisma.

"Uh huh," I replied flatly.

Would you like to update your scores? Vie's voice swam through my head. I ignored her.

He twisted his fingers through my own, and the emotional weight of the past two days was finally pushed aside by sleep.

WE JOSTLED awake to the sound of crashing metal. A door slammed shut with impossible force and radiated shockwaves through the walls. A woman's voice shrieked with devilish laughter over a man's muffled scream. "Goddamn it, Lou!" Chaos spread through the apartment as two people piled into the room next to ours.

"Should we go out there?" I whispered.

"Maybe they'll leave," Liam said. I was already crawling across my mattress toward the closed door.

"Vie, why didn't you tell me we have guests? Lawrence! Come here!" The woman screamed over stumbling steps. Our door flew open without warning and slammed against the wall, knocking the handle into a ragged hole that looked like it was used to that kind of harsh treatment.

Her close-set, angular eyes were rimmed with smudged black liner and heavy fake lashes. One of the eyelashes was starting to peel away, and it lifted up at the inner corner of her hooded lids. Every time she blinked, it bounced a millisecond behind. She tipped her head back to peer into the other room and call for Lawrence's company. Her wide hips and narrow waist were accentuated by a pair of tight-fitting flared jeans that pooled over her sneakers. The back hems were badly frayed from the friction of her steps.

She launched her petite frame onto the bed between us and ripped the blanket off Liam. "We've been waiting ages to fill these beds! I'm so glad Vie hooked us up with some new roommates! Things have been so *boring*." On the last word, her chin dropped like a rag doll and rolled in a full, sweeping gesture.

We were speechless. Mere seconds out of a deep sleep, we were unprepared for this encounter.

Lawrence, I assumed, rounded the corner and stood in the doorway. His mammoth frame was a shock in contrast to tiny Lou. His huge shoulders stretched as he pulled on a heavy leather jacket. When he reached his hands up around the trim of the doorway, his white T-shirt rode up to reveal carved, muscular lines across his rich black stomach. Liam was incredibly handsome, but Lawrence was something else.

"What are you guys doing here?" Lawrence asked in a gravelly, low tone. He tossed a wink at Lou, who was still squished between us on the mattress.

"We just transferred… I mean… we just moved in. We live here," I spluttered.

Liam said, "Look, if we're in the wrong place… we followed the—"

Lou cut him off with a laugh and slapped her palm onto his chest. "No, he means, why are you hanging out *here*? It's not even one o'clock! We only came back to grab a jacket, and we're heading back out."

"Oh… um…" I wasn't sure how to answer.

"Names?" Lawrence called gruffly.

"That's Liam," I said, pointing at his ghost-white face. "I'm Lokai."

"Liam and Lokai, nice to meet you. Let's not waste your transfer night sitting around here!" Lou chimed, pulling us up off the bed. "Grab a sweatshirt, it's chilly." She searched through the pile of wrinkled clothing and tossed two fleece hoodies at us. The fabric's tiny square print caught my eye and I studied it: sets of interlocking Ls. Of course they were; how was I surprised?

She tapped her wristlet to check the time, saying, "Do you think they've already left? I know they were talking about hitting up Leonora's next. I don't want to take an autocab for nothing. Let's walk and try our luck there."

Lawrence nodded his approval, and the pair jogged back down the hallway, stumbling giddily against each other and the walls. "You guys coming?"

THE CLUB WAS PULSING with energy. Liam had managed to charm a stranger into giving up his barstool for me and we huddled at the back edge of a growing crowd. Electronic music radiated through my bones. The bar kiosk dispensed two beers, and we sipped them in silence. Even if we'd had the energy to talk, we wouldn't have been able to hear each other.

Leonora's, as the place was nicknamed, had a high ceiling and upper balcony with suspiciously dark corners. I tipped my head to peer around Lawrence's hulking back and saw an endless line of strangers moving back and forth from the bar to the dance floor. Their constant shuffling reminded me of a sickening throng of black ants.

Two-thirds of the way into my pint, I felt the beer buzzing through me. Compared to the watered-down drinks we had sipped on airplanes and in faraway destinations over the past two years, it tasted amazing. And it seemed so much stronger! The warm honey sweetness and earthy hops hit me like a truck with every delightful sip. I clinked my glass against Liam's.

"Another round?" I yelled into his ear, lifting our now-empty glasses off the bar and heading toward an open kiosk at the other end. "And maybe some food? Burgers?"

"Please!" he mouthed back, with a vigorous nod of his head. His eyes looked slightly unfocused, as if he were distracted by a private screen. Apparently the beer was hitting him a little hard too. But it was our first night out, and that was worth celebrating.

Lou skipped up behind me at the kiosk and stuck her arm underneath my own to edit the order.

"Two shots of… eviction?" I read.

"You're right. That's silly!" she said with a wild smile. "You're so far behind us. Let's grab four."

Lou and I each carried two glasses back to Liam at the end of the bar. The tapered shot glasses were filled to the brim with a deep amber liquid.

"What is it?" I shouted at Lou.

"Eviction!" she called back.

"I haven't heard of it… what is it?"

"Just drink it! You'll love it!"

Liam and I shared a knowing glance. We both dared the other to back down and secretly hoped he would. Neither did, so we tipped back the shots together.

Heat ripped through my throat and filled my chest like I was drowning in fire. We coughed and sputtered. Lou laughed along with the huge crowd that had turned around to watch us. After a few seconds, the pain turned into a sensational, warm numbness. My body felt looser, but my mind was sharper with superficial clarity. The chaos around me started to make sense as everything locked into a new rhythm. Liam pulled my hand up to his chest so that I could feel his heartbeat pounding. He laughed along with the group of faces that encircled us.

"Another?" he shouted, already picking up his second shot from the bar.

Time passed in a blur. Every time I started to settle into myself and feel stable again, some stranger handed me another shot and I sank back into the fire. I recalled traces of events in flashes, unable to grasp anything substantial: running my fingers through long, honey-brown hair; flinging myself on top of Lawrence's broad shoulders; unzipping my too-large jeans to urinate in the middle of the street; jumping headfirst off a bridge and being yanked back by something I couldn't see.

11

I blinked open my crusty eyes and forced them to focus, pulling me out of a stupor. Lou snuggled against my back, and my arm was flopped over a man's chest. The man wasn't Liam. Not even close. He must have been well into his sixties, with thin blonde hair that was mostly gray. I gazed down at his narrow face and sharp jaw, which was covered in unkempt gray stubble.

Rubbing my throbbing head, I sat up and the room swayed sickeningly. I steadied myself for a moment before standing up and moving into the hallway. This wasn't our room, but at least I had made it back to the right apartment.

I peered through our bedroom door; the combined, narrow mattresses were empty, so I proceeded back down the hallway toward the living room and kitchen.

"Hey. Lokai, right?" A young woman was sitting on the tattered couch, stroking Liam's face as he lay curled across her lap. She looked so familiar to me, but I couldn't place her. She gently freed herself, releasing him face-first onto the cushion. Her aura was so refined and quiet, completely at odds with the scene around her. She walked over to the peeling linoleum counter, popped open a white pill bottle, and turned back to me with an upturned hand. I took the tiny pink pill, which was stamped with the letter L across each side.

"You'll love it," she said in hushed tones.

I didn't have the energy to laugh, but I managed to mumble back, "That's what Lou said about the drink."

The girl smiled warmly and filled a dingy glass with water. "Trust me."

I swallowed the pill and returned the glass to its position in the crowded sink. Pain seeped out of me, cascading down from my head to tingle in my toes and fingertips.

Her delicate hand caressed my forehead, and she said, "Good. Your color is coming back."

I motioned to her wristlet in question. She nodded, so I pinged up her ID screen for an introduction. "Thanks, Leiko. Nice to meet you."

Her smile was involuntary. "We've *definitely* already met."

"Oh, shit! Sorry if I did anything ridiculous, or uncomfortable, or… I don't know, awful. It was our transfer night, and Lou and Lawrence woke us up to drag us to that club and…" My nervous babbling faded into nothingness as she waved away my explanations.

"You're good. We all had a great time. 17 contentment points, right on target."

"You remember everything?"

"Mostly. You'll get into the flow of it pretty soon. It's a rush to watch new transfers make fools of themselves the first time. We won't make you go that hard again… Maybe." She finished with a coy lift of one brow. I noticed how striking her heavy-lidded, narrow eyes were.

I winced with a hesitant laugh.

"No really, you're fine. We had a great time and I hope you did too."

In the corner of my vision, I saw Liam stirring on the couch, moaning and shielding his eyes. I refilled the water glass, grabbed a pill from the bottle, and knelt at his feet.

"Hey, love," I said, leaning in to kiss him softly on the forehead. It was clammy. "Take this, you'll feel a lot better." He groaned as I carefully shifted him into a sitting position and put the glass in his hand.

When he finally had the energy to respond, he cursed hoarsely, "What the *fuck* did we do?" His charm was always the last thing to revive in the morning, so he was still several minutes away from intelligent conversation, especially after the night we'd had.

I apologized to Leiko on his behalf, but she didn't seem to mind. She took a seat on the atrocious yellow armchair and motioned for me to sit with Liam on the couch.

"How old are you guys?" she asked quietly.

"Liam's twenty-four. I'm twenty-one."

"I figured we were about the same age. You saw on my screen — I'm twenty-two. And where did you transfer from?"

"We were K-travs, so we've been all over. Vie gave us a few location options for transfer. I didn't realize L-rushes don't live everywhere."

"Well, yeah… can you imagine how boring the club scene would be in a small town?"

"It makes sense, all part of a balanced system. We were traveling in 9032 and decided to fly back here to 0015. This was actually one of the first places we ever visited. A little over two years ago now." I smiled at the memory. "Have you visited the limestone caves near here? Or the Sawn rocks? They're incredible."

"No… I haven't, but I don't care much for rocks anyway."

"That's fair, but these ones… They're unlike anything

you've ever seen. And they're so perfectly preserved. It's incredible!"

"Nicky, you're boring her," Liam mumbled, working his way out of the stupor.

"Nicky, huh?" She lifted her dark, prominent brows in surprise.

"It's a nickname from when we met. I go by Lokai now," I said, flashing the engraving on my wristlet up to her, as if I needed evidence to support my claim.

"Have I seen you on screen, Mister N-star?"

"It depends where you've been. Unless you were near 1675 a few years ago, probably not. I think the fan bases are localized."

I saw her pull up a private screen, probably searching the world map.

"I grew up in a small city like that," she said warmly.

"And did you like it? Before you set off to find your balance?"

She caught the reference and tipped her head, studying me with interest. "Before my balance… ha! I guess I did! Oddly enough, my birth name was Harmony. You saw that on my screen." She chewed her lip and glanced away shyly.

I attempted to spin the conversation toward a new topic. "This is weird, but I have this bizarre memory of jumping off a bridge. Would you happen to know anything about that?"

She laughed and started to reply, but was interrupted when a man walked through the front door. I recognized his face, though I couldn't replay the scene that fit with it. He wore a dark gray T-shirt, and its stretched-out collar hung limply around his thick, pale neck. I had never seen a more muscular man in my life. Not only did he seem to recognize that fact, but he owned it.

The man kicked off his dirty sneakers by the door.

Lory? L-rod? My mind tried to grasp for a name, but it was a tangled mess.

"Hey, Lokai. Liam. Do you guys remember me?" His eyes were almost black, and they sparkled with luminous intensity under heavy, expressive eyebrows. He sat on the arm of Leiko's chair and enveloped her, kissing her hard on the mouth and tousling her long, honey-brown hair with passionate strokes.

I looked away, trying to be polite, and studied the cardboard-covered window in the corner of the room.

When he finally released her, he continued our conversation as if the kiss hadn't happened. Leiko's breathless panting and flushed cheeks were the only lingering proof.

"Helloooo? I asked if you guys remember me. That was a bit of a bender! I wouldn't be surprised if I got swirled up in the mess."

"Umm…" I said, closing my eyes to focus as I attempted to grasp the slippery letters of his name.

"I'm L'roy," he said. "Don't worry about it! I know, it's a lot to take in."

"Like E? Elroy?" Liam asked.

"Like L. L'roy," he repeated. "You get the joke. My birth name was Elroy and I liked the sound of it. I didn't want to rebrand, but you know the rules of transfer: new name, new opportunity."

I smiled at Liam. "He basically did the same thing. Niam, Khiam, and Liam. He's a bit of a rebel."

"L'roy has a thing for rebels," Leiko chimed in.

"No, I have a thing for you," L'roy said, nuzzling passionately into her neck for show. She laughed and pushed him off.

"How long have you two been together?" I asked.

They burst out over each other, "Oh, we're not putting labels on it," and, "It's just fun. Casual."

Leiko continued, "From the mattress mashup I saw in your room, it looks like you two are an item?"

"Yeah. We've been together for almost three years."

"That's cute," Leiko said with genuine feeling. "I hope you two are content here. I know things seem absurd when you're not used to it. Some people transfer the very next day. They realize *really* quickly that it wasn't what they were expecting, and hey, that's fine. Wherever your harmony is, go chase it, you know? But I think you'll get along with us. Just don't let Lawrence drag you into his drama. If you ever hear a juicy rumor that stirs shit up, it probably came from him." She laughed wryly. "It's all part of the magic, though. Part of the rush!" To L'roy, she added, "Hey, why don't you go rally the troops? I think the bike event is starting soon. We should grab some breakfast and head over."

I heard L'roy slam three bedroom doors and leap onto a mattress, sending up anguished cries from Lou and the old man I had yet to officially meet.

I showered, reveling yet again in the profound, blissful fragrance of my toiletries. Liam slipped into the bathroom while I was rinsing off and poked his head into the shower.

"Can I join? Am I invited?"

"You're always invited, but I'm ready to get out. I don't know how much longer this hot water will last, so we'd better not."

I wrapped myself in the least damp towel I could find and went back into our room to change. Vie's weather report said it would be a beautiful day, so I tracked down a plain navy T-shirt and a pair of gym shorts from the closet. The elastic waistband was stretched out, but I was able to knot the drawstring tightly enough to fit my lanky frame.

L'roy called Liam over to his room to scrounge for some clothes. They were roughly the same height, although L'roy's rope-like muscles gave him the illusion of a bigger frame.

The unceasing N-star feed playing on the light screen was grating on me, and my fully sober attention was drawn to the disgusting state of my surroundings. I tracked down a dry sponge and a crusty bottle of soap from the cabinet under the sink. Then I set to work cleaning dishes and wiping down the tiny countertop while I waited for everyone to get dressed. An orange glob of *something* was firmly adhered to the linoleum, so I worked to scrape it off with a butter knife.

"Hey, stop doing that," Leiko called softly from behind me as she entered the room. She scrunched her dripping hair into a discolored towel. Her features were strong and well-balanced with a beauty that wasn't quintessentially *pretty*, but was breathtakingly confident.

I returned my attention to the task at hand, managing to lift one edge of the glob up off the counter. "Why?"

"It'll just go back to the way it was."

"Not if we keep up with cleaning a little bit every day. I don't mind," I said, working away at the glob's other side.

"No... I mean, this is Vie. This is the system."

"What?"

"I've cleaned that counter at least ten times. Trust me, it'll be there tomorrow," she said, carelessly knocking a green plastic cup off the drying rack and back into the sink.

"Are you serious?"

"Yep! Every other L-rush will give you shit, tell you lies, and lead you on for a laugh, but you can trust me to tell you the truth."

"How does that work?"

"I don't know. Go ask the J-devs. They're obsessed with Vie and everything she does. I *do* know that the tram was never late as an I-con and the apartment is never clean as an L-rush. That's how things are."

"Hmmm." I contemplated this and worked up the courage to say, "This is a little awkward, but do you know what happened last night?" I blushed. "When I woke up, Lou was all over me and I was sleeping next to some guy I've never met. I don't think I would have done anything... *you know...* but I don't remember *anything*. It's blank."

"First of all, your transfer night was almost a week ago. You've slept in a lot of places next to a lot of people since then."

I frantically pulled up my private screen to check the date. "Holy shit!"

"I wasn't exactly babysitting you the whole time, but no... I don't think you have anything to worry about. You handled yourself very well over all, especially for your first week out. If your boyfriend is a rebel, then you're quite the gentleman."

I mindlessly lifted the remaining dishes out of the drying rack to put them away in dusty cupboards.

She leaned back against the counter next to me. "Look, you can clean if it makes you feel better, but that shit will get annoying after a while."

"Doesn't it bother you to live like this?"

She shrugged, tossing her soaked towel into the middle of the floor where a dining table ought to be. "It's a place to crash. This isn't the warm, cozy 'home is where the heart is' kind of life we grew up in. Everything worth doing is happening out in the city, so I try to spend as little time here as possible."

"And this is only worth 3 points to balance the scales and settle into harmony?" I said with visible disgust as I surveyed the room.

"For some. Not for most. Like I said earlier, some people barely last a day. Just embrace the 17 positive points and you'll see if things balance out. If not, at least we're young. You've still got choices."

"Yeah... I guess," I said, working distractedly at the glob

again. It sprang free and hit the edge of the sink with a tiny thud.

"... and she started riding me, right there! He didn't even have time to move his hand! I think the image will be burned into Lincoln's brain forever!" We heard the end of L'roy's story as he and four others came out of the far bedroom: Liam, Lou, Lawrence, and the old man I'd found in my bed this morning.

"Trust me, I've seen a lot worse," the stranger replied, punching L'roy hard in the gut. When he got to the kitchen, he stretched out his hand to me. I reached to shake it, but he tapped my wristlet instead. "I like to know who I'm living with," he said while scanning my ID screen. Finally, he looked up with severe blue eyes and a gruff, hardset jaw. "Lokai. Nice to officially meet you. You're really good in bed!"

I didn't have time to react before Lou burst in, bumping her wide hip against the man's solid frame. He didn't budge. "This is Lincoln. He's kidding! Stupid sense of humor. He's a mononomer, if you can believe it. He was born here, grew up here—"

"And I'll die here," he interrupted. "This conversation is boring me to death. Let's get out of this hell hole. We're going to the bike event, right?"

Would you like to update your scores? Vie's voice played in my ear, right on time.

On our way out the door, Lou offered everyone an eviction shot to start the day. Liam clinked glasses with L'roy and casually tossed it back.

I sipped half of mine and discreetly poured the rest down the sink.

With only half a shot in my system, I was better able to enjoy and remember the day. The bike event took place at a dingy arcade that was packed and screaming with energy, even at fifteen o'clock. There weren't enough playpods for everyone to participate and compete at once, but an enormous light screen filled the angled ceiling, bathing the room in flashes of light and color. Worn couches and loose padding filled the middle of the floor as dozens of people lounged with a drink and craned their necks up to cheer on competitors.

Liam, L'roy, and Leiko managed to get playpods for the first event. The rest of us settled in to watch.

I squeezed between Lawrence and Lincoln on a wide recliner built for two, and Lou flung herself on top of me, despite my best efforts to move her over to Lawrence's lap, which was much bigger than my own. Even after showering, freshening up, and reapplying her makeup, I noticed that one of Lou's rogue eyelashes still didn't quite adhere end to end. She chattered about nothing in my ear with so much friendly enthusiasm that I was torn between annoyance and genuine gratitude for her warm welcome. This close up, it was clear that she was at least a decade, maybe two, older than me. Smudged black liner blended out into deep creases around her eyes, but in studying her face and demeanor, I realized that her wild look wasn't an attempt to cover anything up; it seemed like an honest representation of who she wanted to be.

Suddenly, the starting bell rang out and the riders were off in their first match. I felt overstimulated watching them on the overhead screen. How challenging would it be to drive one of those things? On screen, electric bikes careened over rust-colored crates and around lava rock bends on a rugged desert track. Liam's avatar lagged toward the start — his engine had stalled. Even under the teal helmet and matching racing jersey, I recognized him. He pumped the bike continuously and tried to get moving. The rider in a yellow helmet was already spinning around the final corner, miles ahead of the pack.

Dang... he's about to lap Liam. No, he's about to hit *him.* Suddenly the screen was too close and Liam's impending collision felt too real. *This is a simulation, right?* I started to panic and pushed Lou off my lap, getting to my feet.

Lincoln's hand gripped my arm and pulled me back down. "You're blocking the view," he said gruffly. "Don't be such a fucking H-sib."

I watched in constrained horror as the bikes crashed together, sending the limp body of Liam's avatar tumbling off the edge of the raceway. The other driver sped on ahead while Liam's teal helmet dissolved and his player number blacked out on the scoreboard.

"It's just a game, sweetie," Lou said in my ear, massaging the back of my neck. "He's fine."

Leiko and L'roy stepped out of their playpods together, and he started into a passionate retelling of the match from his perspective.

My gaze was fixed on Liam's door, which remained firmly shut. *It's just a game, obviously. It's just a game.* But I had never seen anything like this, and although 'playpod' sounded harmless, everything looked shockingly real on the massive screen. If I had been watching a feed of N-stars attending a gala, I would have believed it just as much. How could I guarantee this was any different?

The door flew open. Liam's eyes burst out of their sockets and he ran his hands through his hair in manic exasperation.

"Can you believe it? That asshole! I had just gotten my ignition clicked back into drive! I could have at least beat the maroon fuckwad! Did you see him spin out on that tiny jump at the end? *Pathetic*!"

I had never seen him so angry, but it wasn't aggression, it was passion. Competitiveness? It twisted a knot in my stomach.

Lou, Lawrence, Lincoln, and I slipped into empty playpods and took our turns next, blatantly cutting the line that had formed around the edge of the room.

The small white dome of my playpod was immaculate. It had Vie's clean, modern aesthetic, which reminded me of the V tower transfer rooms, the inside of every hotel, and the bathpods at our N-star complex.

After the door sealed behind me, I breathed in the clean nothingness of its filtered air system. I climbed onto the glass seat and watched as the wall transformed into a light screen that placed me at the starting line of a desert racetrack. The immersive view made it easy to see where I was supposed to position my hands on the bike, even though there was nothing in the room to physically touch. Looking forward at the screen, it all made sense. My player avatar mirrored every motion, vibrations hummed through the empty air under my fingers, and the virtual machine supported my weight when I leaned forward, as if I were floating.

The only bikes I remembered riding were simple pedal ones, but I had an odd feeling that I had done this before too. Somehow, I knew exactly how the game mechanics were supposed to work. I flicked my wrist and revved the throttle to check my theory. The on-screen bike roared to life.

I racked my brain for the time and place; nothing came to mind. It was like a story I knew I'd been told, but could only remember in hazy fragments. *Maybe it was on the retina infopod during transfer?* I thought.

A quiet alarm sounded as someone slipped inside. Liam snuck up to me and kissed me deeply. I waved away the pod's warning, melting into his touch, and the door resealed.

"I missed you," I said when our lips parted.

"I missed you too. This has been such a fast-paced week. I feel like I haven't even seen you."

"Yeah," I said. "How much of it do you remember? Waking up in the bed without you this morning was super weird."

His pale cheeks reddened. "I really don't remember anything. Just flashes… Did we go bungee jumping?"

"No way! I think we did! It was probably a playpod. Lou said we came here a couple days ago. That's incredible! I remember a hint of that too."

"Cliff diving, bike racing, clubbing, concerts… I haven't felt this alive in years! And Vie's finally not fucking with me! I can eat and smell like a normal person again without feeling claustrophobic." Before I could answer, his lips crushed against mine. His tongue darted into my mouth with manic intensity, and his hands flew down to yank on the knotted drawstring that held up my shorts. "I can *taste* you again."

He was ecstatic, but I was on edge. "Did you take something? After Lou's shot this morn—"

A booming canon cut me off and flashing numbers started counting down from ten on the screen.

"Shit! Okay," Liam said, gripping his hands over my own on the bike's invisible handles. "Don't fuck this up like I did. Before the first jump, you can't rush the gear change!"

12

I nursed my drink throughout the day — just enough to dull my disgust and inhibition. Leiko saw me tip a half-drunk shot onto the bar's sticky floor, but she didn't say anything. She only studied me, biting her thumbnail between sips of beer. Liam and L'roy kept pace like it was a competition, bouncing off each other's incessant energy while they dragged the rest of the group along behind them.

For three weeks, we stumbled through empty streets, concert venues, and at least three bars every night. One evening, our routine was altered, and we settled in at a gambling parlor. Small, square tables filled the room, and all of the walls were draped with mismatched, stained velvet curtains.

How many drinks could have possibly spilled over the years to cover every single fucking surface? I wondered bitterly.

Scratched screen cards were shuffled and passed around the table. I had the strangest sensation of knowing how to play the game. As I tipped the cards up against my chest, I saw that they were hacked to display a number on top of old, barely visible N-star stats. Leiko quickly summarized the rules, and a tabletop kiosk requested everyone's bets.

Still, I was confused about one thing. "Wait… the system doesn't use money. That's a pre-Vie thing. What are we supposed to bet with?"

"We have our own economy. It's a secret," Leiko answered. "Nothing is physical, but we all keep track."

Lincoln snorted. "Leiko better than most! She doesn't give anyone extra time to pay their debts."

Her dark eyebrows lifted. "True. If it's owed, I want it paid. Lokai, it's not a big deal. Bet what you're willing to lose, nothing more, and you'll be fine."

"We don't have anything," I said incredulously. "What are we supposed to bet with?"

"I'll give you a loan to start. Five hundred?" She looked around the table for approval.

Lawrence stuck out his bottom lip. "Jeez, that's a lot."

"But doesn't he look lucky?"

"Five hundred *what*?" I asked.

"It doesn't have a name. It's not real. It's just five hundred," she replied breezily. "If you lose it, be ready to pay!"

"How in the world can I possibly pay you back with something that doesn't exist?" Anxiety swelled in my chest.

"Debts are paid with services, and that's between you and me to decide. Sometimes they're quick and easy to pay back, sometimes they're not. That's all part of the fun." Her long honey-brown hair swept over the table as she leaned toward the center and tapped five hundred next to my name and Liam's.

With slurred speech, Liam added, "Oh actually, L'roy gave me some. So I'm good." He swayed on his chair, tipping back against L'roy's chest before slowly righting himself.

"L'roy gave him a little more than something," Lawrence

said with a cocked eyebrow. Everyone ignored him, but it gave me pause.

Leiko rolled her eyes. "Too late now. You can only repay another player with earnings, so you're going to have to win!"

"Why?" I asked.

She shrugged. "That's just how it works. Come on, I dealt. Lawrence, you're up."

The rules were convoluted, the numbers really didn't matter, and it was clear to me after a few hands that the game was entirely won by chance, but it was still thrilling to play and we had a lot of fun. Over the next few hours, I won enough points, numbers, or *whatever* to repay my debt to Leiko. I always made sure to transfer half of the round's winnings back to her before playing with the other half. Even as he struggled to hold up his drooping eyelids, Liam crushed everyone at the table. I tallied his earnings for him: 700 from Lou, 240 from Lawrence, 900 from Leiko, 400 from me, 50 from L'roy, and 800 from Lincoln.

I patted and rubbed my boyfriend's back in playful celebration. His sloppy smile was wide, and although his green eyes were dazed with drink, they radiated genuine happiness. He was having the time of his life. I was the one struggling to keep up. The situation felt all too familiar.

I leaned in and squeezed him in a tight hug, trying to revive the electric feeling that had zinged between us when I crawled into his bed for the first time back at the beach. There wasn't an inch of space between us, but the looseness of his body felt like he was pulling away from me. I was pressed up to him; he wasn't returning the embrace. Instead, he was grinning over his shoulder at someone I didn't know, and gravity pulled us apart.

Lincoln and Lou were determined to make up their losses by the end of the night… or morning, whichever came first. It was easy enough for them to talk Liam and L'roy into another gambling round, but I wasn't in the mood to keep playing.

Leiko announced that she was craving a sandwich from the market next to our apartment and asked me to accompany her. We waved goodbye and headed out, mostly unnoticed.

As Leiko and I meandered down the dimly lit street, we passed shops that were long closed for the night and L-rush event halls that were still going strong.

I said, "You know, there's a little convenience store right next to the gambling parlor. I'm sure they have sandwiches in the kiosk."

"Yeah, but it seemed like you were ready to leave and I didn't want you to have to walk home alone."

"I could have taken an autocab."

"Sure you could've, but on a beautiful night like this? What a shame!"

We glanced up at the star-speckled sky, which shined surprisingly clear and bright.

"Thanks," I said. "I appreciate it."

"It's good to have you around. Lincoln and I are usually tagged as the downers of the group, so I like that you're tipping the scales in our favor."

I laughed, but it came out forced. "That's super nice of you to say. I can't quite get a read on Lincoln, though, so I have a hard time believing he would say anything nice about me behind my back. Or anything at all, for that matter."

"Once you get to know him, you'll see – he's such a nice guy. He's got some walls up, but in this alphaclass, I think you've got to. It's pretty rare to have meaningful conversations here. There's a lot of gossip, so first you have to know who you can trust. That takes time."

The back door of a nearby club flew open and slammed

into the alley's brick wall. Our quiet conversation was overshadowed by the thumping bass that spilled out behind a delirious man. As we passed the narrow alley, he gripped the wall to catch his balance and slumped onto the ground with a Cheshire cat grin.

"So," she continued, pulling her eyes away from the stranger and back to me. "You and Liam have been together for a few years. How did you meet?"

"As unbelievable as it sounds, it was a love-at-first-sight thing. We met outside the transfer doors on my seventeenth birthday, and he was the first person I spoke to outside of the H-sib community."

"Wow. And that was it?"

"That was it."

"Watch your step!" She reached for my arm and pulled me toward her, preventing me from walking into a metal picnic table that filled the sidewalk.

"Ah!" I had been engrossed in our conversation and wasn't paying any attention to where I was going. Nearly stepping on Leiko's feet, I tripped across her and bounded into the street. My heart thumped wildly in my chest, even though it was only the slightest disequilibrium.

Her shocked laugh filled the air. "Geez! I didn't mean to totally throw you off!" She looped her arm through mine and made a show of steadying me.

"Ugh, that's embarrassing! I didn't mean to step on you!"

"You didn't. Don't worry." Her grin was genuine and warm. "What were we talking about?"

"Love at first sight," I reminded her. "Were you that lucky with L'roy?"

The laugh that escaped her was lined with shock. "Nooooo way. Like I said before, things with him are casual and fun. I'm keeping my options open and enjoying myself in the meantime. It's nothing serious! Nothing like what you've got with Liam."

I wasn't sure how to reply. I wanted to fill the weighty silence, but as I circled through new conversation starters in my head, nothing felt quite right.

She tugged up and down on her jacket's zipper, keeping one arm looped through mine. "It seems like you have a lot of history together, you and Liam."

"We do."

"And where do you see yourselves ending up?"

"Definitely not here," I said before I could stop myself. Then I quickly added, "We talked about our shared interest in animals before, so I think we might transfer to become G-paws soon."

She tensed her jaw and the corners of her full lips squeezed, creating dimples in her cheeks. "You're in it for the long haul? Together?"

"Yeah, of course."

"Good. I'm glad. You deserve that."

I pulled her closer and tipped my head down onto hers. "Thanks. You're a good friend."

"So as a good friend who has been here longer than you have, can I suggest something?"

"Please do," I insisted, only a little wary.

"Maybe it's time for a reset with the two of you. Not like a break or anything… Woah, that was a scary look! No, I just mean, I know that taking a night off or drinking less once in a while can make the rush seem even more intoxicating. It gives you more contrast. When everything's constantly blurring together and you're always amped up, it's difficult to find meaningful reasons to get excited. That's why I sneak off early sometimes, like right now. Honestly, I'm grateful you were ready to head home too. My snack-run comment was mostly an excuse to get out of there."

"I knew it!" I cheered, trying to put on a playful tone to lighten the mood.

"I'm definitely not going back tonight. Besides, I think even Lincoln will be too plastered to notice." Her dark brows softened in a reassuring expression. "You and I have a lot in common."

"Yeah?"

"Yeah. And if I was feeling disconnected from the love of my life, which I'm not necessarily saying you are, I would start with a quiet night at home. Do something to reconnect with the feeling of where it all started in the first place."

"In a V tower hallway?"

"I would've picked a more romantic spot if it was me!" She laughed. "Maybe it's time for a throwback? A tiny slice of *normal* life."

"Thanks for the advice. I think I'll suggest that to him. It's a good idea."

We walked into the market next to our apartment, and I ordered a bag of popcorn along with several sweet treats from the kiosk. "If you're not too tired, do you want to watch a movie with me?"

"That sounds like heaven."

13

After a lot of pleading and outright begging, I convinced Liam to scale back his drinking for one night. The conversation first devolved into a failed negotiation as he pressured me to go *harder* and assured me that I was looking at things backward, but I finally got him to agree.

We were having a blast playing together at the gambling hall, but his lucky streak had ended. For once, all of the numbers around the table were tallied up next to my name.

Liam dipped me backward off my stool and kissed me emphatically, sending his tongue exploring deep inside my mouth while he twisted his fingers through my curls. When he pulled me upright and released me, I was flushed and turned on. Almost everyone at the table transitioned from cat-calling and whistles to polite applause as Liam took a ridiculous bow. Only L'roy sat still, unamused.

"Does that pay for everything I lost tonight?" Liam said.

I bit my lip and laughed. *Holy shit, that was sexy! I've missed this,* I thought. "That's a good start, but I'm going to need a *lot* more of that. And some things are," I continued in a husky whisper, "best accomplished in the bedroom."

His hand glided teasingly up my inner thigh. "You've got something in mind?"

"Hey, I'm brainstorming! Nothing's set in stone, but I know there are a few things you're *especially* good at. I think we should start there and see where things go."

His brushing fingertips crested their target, and he gripped me through my pants, stroking eager pressure in all the right places. I squirmed in response and blushed even harder, intertwining our hands to stop their wandering.

He was being so dramatic, playful, and flirty tonight; that's exactly why I loved him. It had been so long since I had seen him work a crowd and demand everyone's attention for a *good* reason. This was the charming, charismatic, happy-go-lucky Liam I fell in love with. A strong, happy buzz made him even more outgoing than normal, but his green eyes still shone with focused awareness and control.

"Maybe I'll just have to marry you! That should cover everything," he said, running the thumb of his free hand across my lip before kissing me deeply again.

My laugh came out high and bright, fueled by equal parts sexual attraction and shock. Lincoln's jaw tightened with a hurt look that was hard to read.

"How am I ever going to pay you back?" Lou asked, pretending to be devastated when she saw that her total count on the kiosk screen was all the way down to single digits.

"You're a pretty good cuddler," I said playfully. "If I get to wake up to another platonic, friendly back rub, we'll call things even."

"Platonic and friendly, huh?" Lawrence said with a wink. "Just needed to make that clear?"

I wrapped my arm around Liam's shoulder and tipped my

head toward his. "Hey! There's nothing wrong with clarity. Lou knows where we stand, right?"

"Platonic cuddles on blackout nights only, got it!" She skipped around the table to plant an aggressively sloppy, wet kiss on my cheek.

Everyone burst out laughing and our raucous cheers shook the table. Leiko and Lincoln took part in the reverie, even though they usually acted as the calm, composed pillars of our group. Liam melted in my arms with genuine laughter. His bright, bubbly energy felt like home, and I was so glad that we'd finally had the chance to reconnect. Things had been strained between us recently and it seemed like we weren't always on even footing. Just to hear his bright, rumbling laugh was enough for me. We shifted even closer and he kissed me through a sweet smile — not for show, not for a joke.

"I'm scared to hear my punishment," Leiko said, leaning toward me across the table and chuckling quietly. "Can we settle the details later?"

"No need. Your debt to me is already paid," I said.

She snorted. "Lokai, that's not how this works!"

"Why not? I'm the creditor, so I set the rules!"

L'roy walked around the table and draped himself across Liam's back, positioning his face between us. "Hey, pal! Can I get a freebie too?"

My stomach clenched and I barely controlled the urge to roll my eyes. I was getting so tired of L'roy's constant position at Liam's side. It wasn't just annoying anymore, he was being blatantly disrespectful. I had brought up my concerns with Liam a few times and had explicitly asked him to keep his distance, but he always laughed it off. Recently, Liam was in a constant state of drunkenness, and he was too far gone to take anything seriously… Not even the state of our relationship and the very real threat that was invading our space.

With thinly veiled anger, I said to L'roy, "Nope, definitely not. You'd have to be on my good side for that."

"That's okay, buddy. I guess I can live with that. At least I'm on someone's good side." L'roy tousled Liam's shaggy black hair and retook his seat on the opposite side of the table. Liam's eyes flicked over to me, gauging my response.

Lou stepped in to break the tension. "Let's get another round to celebrate Lokai's success tonight, even if he did screw most of us over to get it! Leiko, help me with the trays?" Lou hopped out of her chair, grabbed the other woman's arm, and sprinted full-tilt over to the gambling hall's drink kiosk.

Lawrence checked his final score on the monitor and winced. "Looks like you cleaned me out too. What do I owe you?" he asked me.

"Don't worry, you're all paid up too," I said cheerily. Lacing my fingers with Liam's, I continued, "And as far as service payments go, we're probably in debt to you!"

Liam froze beside me. The color drained from his pale face and his eyes narrowed in suspicion. "What does that mean?"

"Nothing," I said breezily. "It's just, even with my height advantage, I'm definitely not strong enough to lug you up three flights of stairs on my own. Lawrence is a huge help with 'operation: get Liam's drunk ass into bed.' He knows the routine."

Lawrence shrugged his hulking shoulders and tipped his beer glass in our direction. "Always happy to help out my two favorite lovebirds."

"Hey, I'm willing to help too!" L'roy added.

This time, I did roll my eyes. "A little too willing."

Liam's voice turned cold. "Woah! I don't need you to drag my 'drunk ass' into bed." He'd yanked his hand out of my own to make air quotes. "I can handle myself just fine. And if you kept up with me, then you wouldn't even notice. We'd both be at the bottom of the stairs, but at least we'd be *happy*." He chugged the rest of his beer and slammed the empty bottle down onto the table.

I laughed, nervously. "Honey, that's not what I meant! Sorry, it was a joke."

Lincoln shot a look at us and the wrinkles of his forehead deepened between furrowed brows.

Our de facto bartenders came back with two full trays of drinks, and we each grabbed a shot. The dark amber liquid shined seductively under the dim lights.

"To changing luck and lasting relationships. Cheers!" Lou shouted.

"Cheers!" we repeated. I clinked shot glasses with Lawrence on my left, but when I turned around to Liam, he had already downed his shot and was grabbing another.

He read the accusing question in my eyes: *I thought you agreed that you were going to slow down tonight?*

The look he shot back said, *No,* you *said that.*

Liam, we're having a nice time. Please don't ruin it.

"Look at the time!" he announced to the room. "Now that my boyfriend babysitting duties are done for the night, it's time to have some real fun!"

My upbeat attitude evaporated as he slammed his second shot glass down onto the table. I plastered on my all-too-familiar fake smile by the time he finished the third.

"I WONNNN! NICKY, I WONNNN!" Liam yelled into a gritty brick wall next to the spiral staircase in our apartment building.

"No, I won tonight!" I laughed. "You lost miserably... Remember?"

"A lot! I owe you a lot. But me, I still won. New friends, new experiences… he and me are gonna be very close. Very close!" he slurred and babbled.

Lawrence and I each took a side of his small frame and carried him, more than supported him, up the stairs. L'roy helped us from behind, but when I glanced back, his hands had moved from my boyfriend's shoulders down to his ass. I shot L'roy a deadly glare, which he casually pretended not to notice while he readjusted to a new position.

When we got Liam settled in our room, he stretched and twisted into the blankets like a kitten. I pulled his shoes off one by one and set them near the door. Snuggling alongside him, I noticed that his breathing was heavy and ragged. Without warning, he jerked around to face me and yanked down my jeans, which were a size too big and barely held onto my slim hips. I swatted his hand away and pulled them back up.

"Hey, hey, hey! What are you doing?" I said.

"You never wanna mess around…" He pouted.

"That's because you're absolutely wasted."

"Am not," he grumbled, clumsily trying to get my clothes off.

I easily pinned his hands at his sides. "Liam. Just go to sleep. You're way too drunk."

"Am not."

"Just go to sleep! Maybe I'll wake you up with a sexy surprise tomorrow morning. Okay?"

"Tomorrow? Now! I wanna now."

"No." I was officially pissed, and I rolled onto the other mattress to put some space between us.

Liam slammed into the wall as he stumbled to get up, and I looked over to see him weaving across the room. He kicked off his pants and underwear, then chucked his shirt into the closet, leaving him wearing nothing but mismatched socks.

Twisting the doorknob with both hands, he struggled to release the latch.

I sat up. "Where are you going?"

"You're no fun."

I got up and coaxed him over to me, but feral anger flashed behind his eyes that forced me to take a step back.

"You never wanna bang. You don't wanna drink. You're no fun, and I want that!"

"Stop, honey…" I soothed. "I want that too. Come back to bed with me." I gently touched his chest; he swatted my hand away.

He didn't bother to answer, and I didn't bother to try again. I watched him stagger naked across the hall, push open another door, and fall right into L'roy's bed. I had a painfully clear view of everything as the shadowed figure immediately pressed against my partner's body and stretched the covers over them.

I raged silently as tears fell down my cheeks, and I ran through all the things in my head that I wanted to say, but knew he was too far gone to hear tonight.

Furious, I flipped his mattress against the wall and sent it crashing onto the stained carpet with a thud of heavy springs and bedding. I studied the messy, empty room, disgusted with my own behavior and his.

Then I slammed our door shut with all the force I could manage and slid back against it. It sounded like a gunshot in the silent night, but no one stirred or called out to ask what was wrong. I squeezed my fingers into the soft flesh of my temples and cried.

14

I woke up with a severe crick in my neck. The left side of my face was resting on the linoleum countertop an inch away from the orange glob. I sat up and leaned back against the yellow armchair that I had dragged over the night before. My face screwed up with pain as I gently tried to release the tension.

Every day for four months, I had scraped the glob off, hurling it into the sink. And every day, it returned, adhered in its original position like a permanent fixture.

I recognized Leiko's light steps behind me. She was always the first one up, probably because she, like me, preferred to maintain a semblance of self-control at night.

"You slept out here again? You really need to stop doing that," she said.

"I wanted to see the moment when everything reset. You can probably guess how entertaining it was to watch an empty counter." I muttered, releasing the sticky mess into the sink. After months of practice, I knew how to upend it with a single swipe.

"I just left L'roy and Liam in my room if you want to get

some actual sleep in there. It's only eleven o'clock. They won't be up for a while."

"I'll sleep on the couch."

A beat of silence passed.

"This probably sounds like it's coming out of nowhere, but I swear it's not. It's been on my mind since that night at the gambling hall, and I feel like we're good enough friends that I can't ignore it anymore…"

I looked at her expectantly.

She looked wary. "Are you and Liam okay?"

"He's fine," I said quickly, and with a harshness that couldn't be contained.

"That's not what I asked."

"We're fine."

"So why is he in my bed, with *my* boyfriend… Ugh, I hate that word. Whatever he is… Liam spends most nights cuddled up with him while you're sulking out here. You said you're exclusive, or at least that's what I thought, and the pair of them haven't done anything wildly inappropriate in front of me, but they're alone a lot. Clearly something isn't right between you and Liam."

"We're fine," I repeated. "He just likes to party harder than I do, and I don't like it when he passes out on me in bed, so he can crash wherever he wants. Like you said before, this is a place to sleep. That's it. We spend all day together, so it's fine. We're fine."

"Lokai," she said, holding my gaze. Her demeanor was always quiet and constant, but this intensity was unnerving. "You need to talk to him."

"Look, if you don't want him ending up in your bed, that's a conversation you need to have with him!"

"It's not about that."

"Then what is it about?" Tears pricked behind my eyes. Tamped-down emotions neared a breaking point.

"It's about you." She sighed. "I heard Lawrence talking. I know, I know, he's always the one starting drama, but I don't think he's making this up."

"If something happened, Liam would tell me," I said flatly, not bothering to convince her or myself.

"When? When would he tell you? He's obliterated every day! The second his pill kicks in, he follows it up with a shot. And I'm not judging him for that… honestly, I'm not. If he scores 17 with ten shots of eviction, he's doing something right. That's how the system is supposed to work! But it's not right for you. You used to follow him around like a love-struck kid. Now it's like you're disgusted by him."

"Wha… what the actual fuck?" I sputtered. "That's so messed up! Why would you say that?"

"But he's kind of disgusting? Admit it."

"Leiko. Stop… Please."

"He is! Admit it. You think this lifestyle is gross and you think he's disgusting for embracing it. You spent the night staring at a sticky glob instead of sleeping with your boyfriend. That's proof."

"I was watching an empty counter! The glob wasn't there again until I woke up!"

Her face shifted from irritated to incredulous. "He's messing around with L'roy. You know that, right?"

"I've woken up with you, Lou… hell, even Lincoln. That doesn't mean I fooled around with any of you, does it?"

"Why are you defending him?"

"I heard my name." Lincoln's gruff voice interrupted the mounting tension. His narrow face looked even more haggard and sharp in the morning, covered with a gritty layer of stubble. He swallowed the little pink pill without water and grabbed a mostly brown banana off the counter. "Intervention?" he asked.

"Yeah, intervention," Leiko replied.

"Oh, great. Now you've got a sidekick," I said dryly.

"You know Liam's cheating?" Lincoln asked in an equally dry tone.

She nodded. "We covered that part."

"My room's right next to L'roy's, and trust me, the walls aren't thick," Lincoln said. "If you're keeping things casual, good for you. But this arrangement only seems to be working in that bastard's favor."

"We're fine."

"What's your score?" Lincoln asked.

"It's fine."

"What's your score?"

I snapped and threw the words back at him with slicing intensity. *"It's fine."*

"If you say that word one more time, I'm going to smack you upside the head. We're trying to have a real conversation here and you're acting like a little boy. Grow the fuck up," he said.

We sat in silence for a minute as I scratched my thumbnail back and forth over the rough countertop.

He continued, "You know I grew up here? Of course you do. We talked about that." Another untenable silence settled. "I used to be married. I met my wife at a gambling table, and she was absolutely breathtaking. Love at first sight and all that mushy shit. It might sound like a joke, but we felt it. We played all night, even after the rest of the table was wiped out and we were left alone. I kept offering her loan after loan just so she wouldn't have a reason to get up and leave. After a while, the buzz wore off and we were happy to be talking. Just talking. A single hand of cards lasted for about twenty minutes because we were too busy talking to play the damn game! On our last round, she wiped me out and I realized I had loaned her everything under my name. The joke became, well, how was she ever going to pay back that debt? I told her she'd just have to marry me. We'd sort out the details later. And you know what? She did. That same night. Stupid kids..."

He smiled warmly at the memory. "That was the single best decision I ever made in my life. We raised three beautiful girls right here in this flat. It was rare to be born here, and two L-rushes getting married in front of Vie was pretty much unheard of — still is. L-rush is notoriously flagged as a young person's alphaclass. A lot of our friends grew up and transferred away when they felt like they couldn't keep up anymore, but we built a nice life. Sure, our pace of partying slowed down when the girls were young, but never so much that we dropped out of harmony or forgot what made us so content here in the first place. That kept up for twenty-three years."

He whistled and took in a deep, slow breath. "One day she told me it was over. Our daughters had all left and, if I'm being honest, I knew it was coming, but I still didn't expect it. She told me that the night we met, she had been running down her balance for fun before heading to the V tower. She had only stayed because of me, and then because of the girls. It had been over for a long time. I was heartbroken. So was she, but we were out of sync. I'm ashamed to admit it, but I had started seeing a few other women on the side. Those flings weren't anything serious, but... I don't know... protecting my marriage didn't matter anymore. Every once in a while, one of us would decide to try and fix things, so we'd sober up and start to talk, but we didn't even recognize each other anymore. We resented each other. If we were ever going to fix it, that would've had to happen a decade sooner. So I walked with her to the V tower and watched her leave for good. That was the end of it. In a weird way, that was all it took to fix things. I don't have any proof, obviously, but I know she's in harmony. I just know it. Divine providence or whatever the fuck you want to call it. I know wherever she is, and whoever she's with, she's scoring 17 because she made that choice for herself, and that's what she deserved. Hell, that's what I deserved! And now that I'm seeing a similar scenario play out again with you two boys, I can't stand to watch. It's not right what he's doing to you, but you have to take some ownership here too. You need to step up and create a life worth living."

I felt hollow.

Part of me wondered if I should feel this way. Didn't people drown in their sadness? Didn't the tide of emotion and heartache crash over them like an ocean wave? I simply sniffed back the snot dripping in my nose and wiped mindlessly at the tears I could no longer hold back.

I was stuck.

Leiko knelt down, wrapped her arms around me, and let me sob quietly into her shoulder. While my body went through the motions, my mind was entirely disconnected. Lincoln's confession hit me hard, if only because I had never heard the man speak more than ten words at a time. The things he said fit so neatly in line with how my own life was going. How was this happening? Was my story any different than his?

I was numb.

After a time, Leiko lifted me out of the armchair and held our hands between us. "If we get him sober and give you guys space, will you talk to him?"

"I can't. I just need time," I protested, feeling my heartbeat quicken at the thought of facing Liam and the consequences we would be forced to draw out. "My scores aren't that far off. If it was really bad, Vie would be hitting me with alarms and warnings. Liam said he heard them back when we were K-travs, but he hung on with me for a few more weeks until I was ready to go. It must not be that bad!"

"Oh, Lokai..." she said with despair in her voice.

"He waited for me, and he went through so much worse! He lost weight, he couldn't eat, he was struggling, and it took me so long to come to terms with it," I wailed, with heavy tears clinging to my lashes.

Lincoln rested a hand on my shoulder. "Son, in harmony with time and for the sake of *all* humanity, we have to move forward. That's how it goes. Back then, his choice was his own. Whether or not he suffered for you, it's clear that you're going through a rough time right now. That doesn't help either one of you. And it doesn't help the two of us who are standing here having this uncomfortable chat with you when we could be sleeping off a truly extraordinary night. You've been here way too long already. I knew from day one that this wasn't it for you. Even if Vie's not yelling in your ear, she knows it. We know it. You know it. Hell, Liam probably knows it and he's blacking out to avoid the conversation... It's time to move on."

"Go back to sleep for a little while," Leiko soothed. "We'll get everyone out of the apartment and make sure Liam has a clear head to sort things out." She led me back to my room, squeezed my shoulders, and turned. "If I don't see you again, I want you to know, I'm so glad we met. You've been a good friend and you're a great guy. I'm not sure how long I'll stay either, so maybe I'll see you around sometime. I've heard good things about 7895. Look for me there?"

"Okay. Maybe."

"Bye, Harrison," she whispered.

"Bye, Harmony," I said with the smallest smile. It was all I could manage.

The door clicked shut behind her.

A FEW HOURS of fitful sleep passed until I woke to the sound of raised voices in the kitchen. The front door slammed shut and locked with the click of a key. I paced the room three times, kicking rumpled clothes out of my path. Then I walked through the dark hallway and into the common area. Liam was standing on his toes, stretching to reach the recesses of the uppermost cabinet.

"We need to talk," I said quietly.

"I need a drink."

"No, you don't."

"I do! Especially if you're gonna be a downer."

"I just want to talk."

"Fuck talking."

"We're not even fucking!" I dove right in, unable to contain the fight any longer.

"And whose fault is that?" He whipped around with ice in his eyes. "You won't even touch me anymore! You won't even look at me!"

"Liam! You're shitfaced every single day. You're *beyond* sloppy, and there's nothing attractive about someone who can't even make it up the goddamn stairs!"

"L'roy never seems to mind," he said coolly.

His casual confession knocked the air from my chest. Staggering, I fell back against the patched wall and slid to the floor. My heart pounded unevenly with deafening booms, and I looked up to see Liam's mouth moving, but nothing registered. My weary gaze turned toward the floor, settling on cracking tile and matted carpet.

Liam clapped his hands loudly to reclaim my attention and continue his rant. "No one else cares. No one else gives a shit! You're the *only* one who's judging me! The person who's supposed to love me unconditionally! Well?" he taunted. "I know you saw the friendly touches and all the attention he gave me! L'roy made it clear how much he adores me, right in front of you. And unlike you, he likes to spend time alone with me! I didn't plan to cheat, but you were giving me *nothing*. You made me feel fucking invisible. Then I realized something... you don't even care. His hands wandered, I let it happen, and you said nothing! The first time we messed around — it's a little grainy... I was *shitfaced*." He spat the word with a roll of his eyes. "I do remember some things clearly enough. I walked straight into his room, pants off, cock hard, and you just watched me go!" His voice was strained and on the verge of breaking. "You closed the door and went back to sleep! So *clearly* I'm not even worth the trouble of walking four fucking feet across the hallway!" The volume of his final words rose to a scream.

"You're out of control." I stared at him, blazing.

"You're impossible to please! You did the exact same thing at the N-star complex... It wasn't good enough for you! You couldn't make it work! You know, I gave up my *entire life* for you!" His voice turned sour with mocking insincerity. "Little Nicky can't keep up. Little Nicky doesn't know what he wants. Little Nicky misses making decisions. Little Nicky needs us to leave."

"Hey! I *never* asked you to give that up. I tried to talk you out of it, and you know it! Don't forget, when we were traveling and I saw that you were struggling, I did everything I could to make you happy. Everything! And it still wasn't enough. We had free access to explore the fucking *world*! Even *that* wasn't enough." A hollow, defeated laugh sprang from my chest. "I gave things up too, you know. Somehow you convinced me to abandon my life as a K-trav, even though you knew it was the happiest I've ever been. All so I could come live in this hellhole with you... a sloppy, cheating *asshole* who whores himself out for another guy's attention and pretends I don't even exist? That's what I gave up harmony for?" Waving my arms around, I screamed, "*This* was a mistake I can never take back!"

Liam slammed his fist into the wall and spun around in visible pain. Aside from his muttered curses and groans, we were silent for some time. He stood by the door and I wallowed on the floor.

"We don't have to fight like this." My voice was tight and wrecked with tears. "I love you. I love you so, so much. And I don't know what to do. I'm not meant to be an L-rush, and that's hard enough to deal with, but the way you're treating me, Liam… this isn't fair."

Echoing music vibrated through the floorboards from the apartment below us.

He said nothing.

"How can you say I don't care?" I continued. "If I didn't care, I wouldn't be here! You're hurting me, and you're not even around to see it. It's not just the cheating, which… *fuck,* Liam! It's everything! I feel like you're pushing me away. You refuse to be around me unless you're so obliterated that you won't have to remember it, and I don't know why. I gave this lifestyle a try but—"

"Bullshit!" he interjected. "You never tried! The poured-out shots? All the times you pulled on Leiko's sleeve and begged her to come home with you for an early night? I've been out here having the time of my life and you didn't even bother to show up! You never tried! Don't even pretend!"

I closed my eyes and shook my head. "This isn't you. This isn't us… I don't know what to do."

"You know *exactly* what to do!" he screamed with raw emotion. "Just fucking leave and let me live my life! I can't keep following you around and putting up with your bullshit anymore! I'm done!"

"I can't believe this is happening! I can't *believe* you. What, there's no crowd here, so you don't have to pretend anymore and put on a show? Four years of my life... I've loved you for four years!" My tears steeled into hard resolve. "We're done. This is over."

"You're pathetic," he muttered, hiking his knee onto the counter and boosting himself up in search of a hidden bottle.

I shoved my feet into the nearest pair of sneakers — they were L'roy's, a full size too small – and grabbed a random sweatshirt off the floor of our room. Clicking into my wristlet, I hastily put in a transfer request with Vie. My shaking hand randomly selected C-spen, near the top of the alpha-class list, and I quickly swiped past the options to request a particular name, location, or social group.

When I returned to the kitchen, Liam was drinking straight from the bottle in dramatic, full gulps. The uppers spiked into his system, igniting his eyes with fire before his shoulders slumped.

"I hope you're happy," I said coolly as I yanked the door behind me, unsure if I even meant it.

A whoosh of air carried two words out to me before the door slammed shut. "Fuck off."

15

The next year passed in a mindless blur. I was never present – drowning in my depression, uncomprehendingly lost in the grief and regret that bore down on me like an unyielding force. Every person in the world I had formed a connection with was gone. My partner of four years was dead, at least to me, and all of the shared memories I had promised to cherish were tainted and charred.

The warnings Khiam had alluded to were real. Vie's voice filled my head every single hour, sometimes more, reminding me with saccharine gentleness that I wasn't content… as if I didn't already know. I felt focused, hot energy pulse out from my wristlet, but it merely dulled and pushed aside the suicidal thoughts that clouded my mind; it wasn't strong enough to completely erase them.

Her alphaclass guidelines repeated in my inner ear with a hollowness that was indescribable. Her harmonious society advice felt like it was written for someone else, because it inevitably was. This was all part of the *system*… the same system that guaranteed my harmony and happiness as long as I played by the rules. I was moving forward, wasn't I? Sure,

I could admit that maybe I wasn't moving without disruption, but with this shadow of despair hanging over me, that was beyond my control.

My scores never exceeded 7.

My frequent transfers were initiated without thought.

My clothes dropped to the pure white transfer room floor without care.

Over and over again, I tried and failed to fit the pieces of my life back together.

My sense of self fractured dramatically as I repeatedly walked through the V tower transfer rooms and assumed new identities.

By the end of this period of my life, I had no idea who I was. One thing was uncomfortably clear: this wasn't me. Whatever decisions my reflection chose to make didn't matter to me. Nothing mattered. I was separate from myself, unreachable and untethered.

AFTER LOKAI, I was called Corban — a man who sailed yachts, flew in private planes, drove fast cars around racetracks, and browsed luxurious racks of jewel-encrusted clothes. He acted impressed when he met N-stars at exclusive parties, as if they were different than the rest of us. Why did he blush in awe when someone handed him a signed screen card? Didn't he know that they were available in an endless supply?

All around him, C-spens sported their finest items, bragged about their collections, and commissioned M-self artists to create exclusive designs with the world's finest materials. They were thrilled to play the social game of constant one-upmanship and revel in a life of elite beauty. That was their 17.

In exchange for his lavish C-spen lifestyle, he gave up any semblance of a stable home. Every morning, he woke up in a new space and stumbled into unfamiliar walls. The luxury furnishings, clothes, and decor were always unchanged in appearance, but never positioned in the same place. During the worst of it, Corban forced himself to stay awake for days at a time, trying to catch and track the moment when the layout of his opulent apartment would shift and transform into something he had never seen before. It never worked.

———

AFTER CORBAN, I was called Ford — a man who wandered through the wilderness and spent his nights sleeping under an open sky. One day, he paused over the still surface of a puddle and looked down at the real me with confusion stitched between his furrowed brows — even he couldn't connect our split identities. His long limbs were covered in bites and burns, but they soon gained power with ropes of firm muscles. His taupe brown skin tinted another shade darker after spending hours in the sun, and his hands became roughhewn with layers of callouses. For a short time, the quiet, expansive surroundings calmed his nerves.

All around him, F-nats worked with their hands and explored vast stretches of wilderness that were virtually untouched except for their footsteps in the dirt. They didn't only take control of their lives as homesteaders, hunters, and farmers, they took pride in it. That was their 17.

But Ford experienced no laughter, art, or liveliness here. He was incensed by the hardness and seriousness of every F-nat he met. I watched him scream into the woods and demand the smallest scrap of joy.

———

After Ford, I was called Garrett — a man who fell into an even slower pace of life. As a G-paw, his wristlet released a constant, sluggish pull of energy that dragged him down like an invisible weight. He struggled to catch his breath after a single flight of stairs, and the muscular body that he had developed in the wilderness slowly melted into doughy pockets of fat.

All around him, G-paws cuddled with every kind of furry creature, told hilarious stories about the animals they helped raise, and cooed to newborn animals that would never talk back. That was their 17.

He spent his days riding horses, shearing sheep, feeding baby chicks, training dogs, and petting goats. He passed his nights with countless partners, mindlessly humping without his usual fervor and force. The mild, yet constant fatigue always made it difficult for him to climax, but he kept going for the sake of his partners. While they slept, he stayed awake and gently pet the cats, dogs, rabbits, and other small creatures that cuddled at the end of his bed. His unblinking, hollow eyes reflected weighty exhaustion in the mirror.

After Garrett, I was called Darrien — a man who sank into the world of D-view entertainment. His steps were slow and careful as he maneuvered through the world without full focus. The private screen that rose up in front of him never ceased to capture his attention and distract him from reality. The programming was impeccably curated and he laughed harder than he had in years… maybe ever.

All around him, D-views binged series, poked holes in plotlines, sat through immersive travel videos, and played virtual games with unbeatable levels to reach impossibly high scores. That was their 17.

The glaring light screens soon became too intense. Darrien's eyes became passive and flat while he scanned screen after screen. It was a small thing, but I felt the corners of his eyes tense and strain as he tried to look through his private screen and watch another handheld video card in his lap. At the same time, explosive flashes of light and color splashed across the wall in front of him. It was all too much. When he closed his eyes to sleep, which was rare enough as a D-view, ghostly patterns of light flickered across his lids and ignited looping thoughts in his mind.

———

AFTER DARRIEN, I was called Elias — a man who found relief in the quiet comfort of his studio, at least for a short while. Nothing was expected of him and no one asked him to do anything. As an E-sit, he merely had to exist and follow his own sense of purpose, as long as it didn't bother or affect anyone else.

All around him, E-sits napped, read, completed simple crafts, and settled into quiet, peaceful lives. That was their 17.

Neighbors and friends spoke blissfully of relaxing days, open schedules, and blank minds, but he grieved all of the opportunities that were lost while doing absolutely nothing at all. Time slipped away from him, and he felt a rising sense of dread when he realized that hours had passed in the span of minutes. The artificial numbness that spread across his mind extended into his limbs. I felt Elias's terror. He feared he was literally losing his only chance to walk away.

———

After Elias, I was called Isa — a man who followed constant schedules with rigid strictness. He took the 7:20 tram and reported to his I-con desk every morning at eight o'clock, without fail. After four hours of sorting pages and filing reports, he followed the orderly line of workers to a cafeteria where they passed an hour-long lunch break.

All around him, I-cons flowed through their day with set expectations, fulfilling schedules, and no surprises. That was their 17.

These calm, consistent routines turned into familiar habits. Then they turned into meditation. Then they turned into shackles. Isa counted the seconds aloud after the chime of his morning alarm. Untenable panic rose up in him, spreading out from his wristlet as he bore down in resistance and refused to rise from the crisp white sheets. Ninety-four seconds was his record. On the morning of his twenty-third birthday, he set a goal of one hundred seconds, but his resolve slipped, and he only managed to hold on until seventy-two. Shoving his feet into slippers, he tapped his wristlet to log a request. He did not report to work that morning. He had finally had enough.

Isa walked through the street in a daze. He sat paralyzed in the back of the tram. He passed through the V tower lobby with no awareness of his surroundings. The white podiums didn't have any attendants and Vie's system was locked out until seventeen o'clock. In theory, he knew that. Everyone knew that. Still, he couldn't make sense of it. His head slumped against the white desk, and he waved his arm endlessly through the locked light field until the tension in his shoulder became unbearable.

A few hours later, he woke up on the floor where he had

been dozing with his head tipped back against the cold glass window. Familiar cheers grew louder as an H-sib walked toward the V tower, enveloped by supportive hugs, loving glances, congratulations, and pats on the back.

He crawled up from the floor with stunned fury as faded memories of a previous name and forgotten family members shot back into focus. The H-sib didn't even have a chance to attempt the handle before Isa came crashing through the door.

"Don't do this. Don't do this!" he cried out. "It's enough! It can be enough for you! Don't you see what you're leaving behind? You'll never get to see them again and you'll be all alone. Absolutely alone in a world that doesn't give a fuck about you! Vie's lying, and if you think you're guaranteed anything in this life, you're wrong! The system is broken, and if you leave, you can never go back. You'll be alone and..."

The crowd's shocked faces dissolved into mist, like Liam's avatar had done when it lay mangled and limp next to his bike at the edge of the desert racetrack.

Isa's wrist burned white-hot, and the floor shifted without warning, moving from under his feet to flat against his cheek. Two arms reached under his own and dragged his limp body back through the lobby into darkness.

PART 2

RECALIBRATION

16

Eight years later.

I CROSSED the courtyard with slow, even steps. Rain-soaked concrete paths wove through the grass, forming a star shape that radiated out in sharp lines. Thinner, individual lines of brick crossed horizontally and spiraled out from the center in big loops, turning the mammoth star into a web.

Stepping over a puddle, I lifted the hem of my gray skirt and let it fall back onto the ground. It jingled softly with the tinkling of small silver bells. They were stitched in long, downward lines from my hip, and each metal orb had a tiny J cutout on one side. The bell's pitch was nearly identical to the sound that Vie pinged in my inner ear, but it was a mere shadow of her usual brightness and closeness with my thoughts. I pulled the smoke-colored shawl tighter around my body to guard against the wind that blew through my loose-fitting top. Reaching the web's center, I veered to the right and headed toward the shimmering glass entrance of a small brick building.

"Happy birthday, Judah," whispered all around me as I stepped inside.

"I am truly content." I bowed slowly and tapped my wristlet up to my forehead. I unrolled the knit white mat that had been slung across my back with a strap. The bells continued to chime softly underneath me long after I found stillness in a position on the floor.

A woman's steps and bells followed me into the room. She sat down next to me and whispered, "Happy birthday, Judah."

Two more men entered with similar softness and settled in cross-legged positions near the front of the room. "Happy birthday, Judah."

Three more times, I dipped in a low, slow bow, touched my wristlet between my eyes, and repeated, "I am truly content." As the bracelet shifted against my skin, I felt the name that was etched into its inner surface: *Harrison*.

Nearly half an hour passed in silence. No one stirred. I spent this time reflecting on my morning with gratitude. I focused on clearing my mind, listening only to the sounds of my breath while drawing the shape of a looping circle behind closed eyelids.

A near perfect replica of Vie's chime sounded three times from the front of the narrow room, and I lifted my eyes.

"One… two… three… four…" We all counted in unison. Each number was whispered on the breath of an inhale followed by a full, deep exhale. Then three breaths were forced out in quick succession after we reached number seventeen. We chanted, "In harmony with time and for the sake of all humanity, we agree to move forward without disruption. As disciples of her grace, we are fully devoted to Vie's divine instruction."

Over the course of the service, we sat, kneeled, tapped our wrists, linked our hands in front of our bodies, waited in reverent silence, and repeated memorized lines. The ceremony flowed without interruption, and by the end, I felt wholly restored.

Our presiding vieman spoke from the front of the room. Light passed through the frosted glass wall behind her and illuminated her ivory dress with angelic softness. "Before our session is sealed, I would like to call Brother Judah to the front of the room."

I rose from my mat and walked up to her, stepping softly to avoid a wide plank of wood that I knew would squeak under my step.

"Brother Judah, today we have the privilege of celebrating two important dates: the thirty-first anniversary of your birth and your eighth year as a disciple. It is a true honor to lead you in this ceremony."

I bowed deeply into the silence, studying the bells that were stitched in a single, horizontal stripe across the waistline of her heavy cotton dress.

"To signify the passing of time, Vie instructs us to mark another band. These wristlets, assigned at birth, grow with us and change to fit our form," she said, holding her arm out. "We choose to add others as an outward sign of our devotion and study." As she lifted her wrist up to the ceiling, the loose sleeve draped down past her elbow, revealing a long line of at least twenty circular white tattoos. "Brother Judah, are you in harmony?"

"I am."

"Are you ready to be baptized into the system's grace with a new, permanent mark for all time?"

"I am."

Every eye in the room followed me as I stepped up to the altar. Alongside the bell that had sounded earlier to initiate our session, there was also a horizontal glass cylinder. It was open on both ends and delicately balanced on a bronze point. I pushed up my sleeve and placed my arm inside. Above my wristband, seven white lines spiraled across my skin, rising a third of the way up my forearm. With the help of her steadying hand, I held my arm in the tube so that the highest tattoo was positioned to the left of the bronze tip.

She swept her thumb across the button on my wristlet. I felt an instant slice of searing pain as another white tattoo was etched into my skin in a seamless, perfect circle.

Murmurs of "Praise Vie" and "For her glory" lazed in the air among the tinkling of bells. I removed my aching arm from the cylinder, forced my face to hide any trace of pain, and bowed.

"Let us move forward. Blessings to you all," the vieman said with authority. Then we stood, collected our mats, and calmly exited the room.

I CALLED up my private screen to check the time, wincing involuntarily with the movement. My new appointment was six minutes late. I gazed out the frosted glass window, past my black velvet armchair and a crackling, cozy fire in the hearth. Blurred streaks of color floated down from the arms of nearly bare trees.

I gingerly slid back my sleeve to reveal the inflamed, red skin that screamed around my new tattoo. Bending my elbow and twisting my wrist in large spirals, I studied the eighth mark with awe. It stacked so neatly above the others and stood out with stark clarity against the contrast of my dark skin.

A tiny knock pushed my chamber door open a fraction.

Swallowing a gasp of pain, I shoved the sleeve back down and stood to meet my guest.

"Brother Judah?" A young girl peeked her head around the door, only opening it far enough to squeeze her shoulder through.

"Yes. Sister Jendayi, I assume? You're late," I said, pulling the door open and waving her over toward the matching armchair.

The counseling chambers were small — so small that two large people could feel overcrowded, and it was even worse if a supervising vieman was ever called to step into a meeting. Luckily, we were both slender and agile, so she was able to slip past me and find her place without the fabric of our skirts brushing.

"Praise Vie," she said meekly while jerkily touching her wrist up to her forehead. Clearly she was nervous.

"Is this your first counseling session?"

"Yes, I transferred a few weeks ago. I was supposed to start with another counselor, but she was sent off on a mission at the last minute, and it took a while to fit me into the schedule, so…"

"May I see your ID screen?" I asked, already reaching for her wrist.

She obliged.

"You're twenty-one," I read aloud as I reviewed the private screen hovering between us. "You were born Harrietta in 3313, transferred on the day of your seventeenth birthday… Names include Isobel, Dreamer, Elody, and Melaina." Her face twisted in embarrassment and she shrank into the soft cushion. "You're here now," I soothed. "By Vie's grace, you're living in line with the system and you'll keep moving forward. I have faith that you will find your harmony here."

She bowed and seemed to relax, smoothing the skirt's black fabric across her knees.

"Why did you feel called to become a J-dev?"

"I couldn't stand the way people looked down on H-sibs, and I wanted to live a life that I could be proud of, so I transferred and tried—"

I cut her off. "No, I asked why you're called to be *here*. Time doesn't move backward, so I encourage you to release the weight of past decisions from your conscience. Instead, let's focus on the present moment."

"Well, um." She paused in thought. "I wanted to understand. I thought maybe there was something more to the system that I wasn't seeing. And I talked with a missionary the week before my transfer — or, at least as much as an M-self can talk — and he made me realize that my role in the system matters. Since I wasn't reaching harmony and stabilizing at 17 where I was, then I wasn't living up to my full potential. And that had a negative impact on the people around me."

"When we all settle for 3, 17 is guaranteed. You were giving up more than your fair share," I added.

"Exactly. And that's just as wrong as anyone taking more than their fair share. The missionary really opened my eyes to that. I wanted to see what else I was missing."

"So now you're here."

"Now I'm here. I think I'm genuinely content. It feels stable and comfortable. I can see my life playing out here and being truly happy. Praise Vie."

"Praise Vie."

We sat in thoughtful silence, allowing the crackling of burning logs to fill the space between us.

"Do you know why the system calls us J-devs?" I asked.

"I think it's because we read devotionals?" she said quietly.

"No. It's because we devote our entire selves to fulfilling the divine instructions in everything that we do and all that we are. We are fully devoted to her. This week, I would like you to read chapters forty-five and fifty-two of the manual. Have those been assigned to you before?"

"No... like I said, this is my first session. I've been looking through the manual on my own at night, but I didn't know where to start."

"Good. Let's start there. I think the discourse on time and consequence will be especially valuable for you."

She took a note on her private screen and returned her quiet attention to me.

I said, "Are you following the process of the sealing ceremony so far? How did it go this morning?"

"Mostly. I turned on the inner-ear support guide, so Vie prompts me when I forget what comes next."

"Okay, that's fine. Just make sure to dim the volume a little bit every session so that you don't come to rely on it. The goal is to clear your mind with space for Vie to speak to you authentically, not only superficially."

She nodded her head in genuine thanks.

For the rest of the hour, we discussed her anxiety over past transfers and the initial loneliness she faced as a new J-dev. Over and over again, I assured her that those feelings were normal and Vie would release them from her after careful study. Her soft-spoken shell cracked as we became more familiar with each other.

"Before we move forward... Sister Jendayi, I realize that the counseling hall has a lot of doors, but now you know where I'm located, so I expect you to be on time in the future."

"Because time is the only thing above Vie's divine control?" she offered hesitantly.

"Time is the only *force beyond* Vie's divine control," I

corrected. "You were pretty close, though. And yes, for that reason, above all others, we must respect the passage of time."

We exited the room together. The narrow hallway was packed with grayscale disciples in floor-length dresses or long skirts and loose cotton tops. They ranged from pure black and dark charcoal to smoke gray, like my own. Bells abounded. A few viemen in ivory uniforms watched patiently near the outside doors, and I worked my way toward them.

All J-devs taught and received counseling every day. Even the newest transfers were expected to start leading right away. As beginners, they followed in-ear prompts and followed a simple script, most of which included direct readings from the manual and repetitions of the J-dev guidelines. Only viemen, denoted by light ivory and pure white robes, were allowed flexibility in their counseling schedule so that they could step into other sessions as needed.

I reached Jules near the end of the hall, and he waved me on to enter the room in front of him. We settled into black velvet armchairs in front of a frosted glass wall. I instantly missed the fire's warm blaze from my own counseling chamber. Its heat was vented throughout the building, but you couldn't replace the dry, hot force of a real fire warming your skin with close contact.

"Brother Judah, how's the arm?"

"It fucking hurts!" I said with a pained grin.

"Can I see it?"

Jules and I had long since dropped the formalities, but our conversations were still deeply serious and reverently rooted in the manual's teachings. We had spent an hour talking together every other day for the past three years, and I considered him to be one of my closest friends. He was more than a friend, he was my brother — someone who really believed I was destined for harmony and took the time to unlock the system's secrets with me.

Jules squinted through rimless glasses and studied my newly tattooed band while twisting my arm in a wide circle to follow the line around a seamless spiral. Jules was fourteen years older than me, but he looked quite young. His coarse brown hair was always messy, no matter how short he cropped it, and a smattering of freckles covered his large nose. Something about him looked perpetually boyish, even though he was in his mid-forties.

"The pain never gets easier to bear," he complained.

"Because we've got an entire year to forget how badly it hurts!"

He laughed. "Heads up. Jivaan is going to swing by in about twenty minutes, so we should get right into things today."

Delicately pulling my sleeve back down, I asked, "Why? Is it something I should worry about?"

"No, no... nothing like that. It's good."

"Good, huh? Good like a ring around the arm?"

"Better."

"Jules, you're freaking me out. What is it?"

"Judah! Don't worry about it... First of all, happy thirty-first birthday. You're well on your way to forty."

"Fuck you." I grinned.

17

Jivaan knocked on the door as it swung open. He was a short, heavy-set man with narrow shoulders and wide hips. Even after all these years, I still thought the J-dev uniforms looked odd, but this ivory ensemble made him look absolutely ridiculous. He was the human equivalent of a triangle.

I smiled and stood to offer him my chair, hoping that my unkind thoughts wouldn't translate on my face. "Praise Vie. Brother Jivaan, it's good to see you."

"Praise Vie," he responded. "How does the arm feel?"

"Ah, you remembered! It feels like the marking of time and progress. I'm honored to have earned it," I said with a slow bow.

Jivaan settled into the small velvet chair, which creaked slightly under his weight. "Brother Judah, I don't know if Brother Jules told you what this meeting is about?"

"No," I said, directing an overly innocent look at Jules. "I wasn't even expecting you."

"Well, that's good for me. I love to make these kinds of

announcements," he said. "I'm here to report that your devotion has not gone unnoticed. Your progress in study has been marked and your counseling has been incredibly well-received. I'm not going to waste your time with any more pleasantries... As you know, only Vie can score your mind and its truest intentions, but we do keep a scoring system of our own. It's important for us to keep a watchful eye over our disciples and support Vie in her divine work. The manual is clear... she will not intervene beyond fundamental harmony guidelines as long as scores are close to center. Thank Vie, she has blessed us with free will and free movement as long as the system maintains its balance. After all, Vie's earthly kingdom is designed to guarantee harmony for all humanity, rather than a select few. She has the power to force our will to bend to hers when we overstep the bounds, but that rarely happens. It requires significant imbalance for her to intervene. We, as humans, know there can be a lot of variation and nuance in a single point of contentment."

He paused, so I spoke up simply to fill the silence. "Yes. The manual provides so many divine insights into the meaning of the system and our position in it. Every time I read it, I understand the nature of harmony a little better."

"Exactly, good. Then you'd agree, the system is nuanced. It takes discipline and devotion to truly understand its workings and align with Vie's divine will. Part of our responsibility as leaders in the J-dev community is to impart her will on Earth. That happens in the space between points. It is not only our Vie-given purpose to promote harmony in the system, but also to protect those who achieve it. You know better than most that harmony is not an everlasting gift — it is something that must be maintained and tended. Sinking scores pose the biggest and most visible threat, but over-abundance has its dangers too."

"Yes… I just didn't realize that the scores were being supplemented?" I half-asked, slightly confused.

"If I may, Brother Jivaan," Jules interrupted, pushing his glasses back up his nose. "Brother Judah, we're telling you all of this because we see potential in you. This external scoring system is simply a support tool that uplifts and interlocks with the divine system. It's nothing more than a guide for human hands, which, in the end, can only do their work if they align with her will. As Brother Jivaan said, your devotion is an inspiration to this community. It's just that your scores, or at least the external records we keep, make us concerned that you may be too complacent in your current role, rather than truly content."

"I am truly content," I said with genuine feeling and a deep bow.

"I know," Jules said. His knowing look conveyed a secret message that I alone could read: *seriously, chill the fuck out and let me finish.* "These are micro fractions of a point we're talking about. I don't doubt your 17. No one does. We simply want to guide you forward on the right path… The path that's best for you right now."

Jivaan took over again. "Thank you for stringing the web together. Brother Judah, you have elevated to a higher level of understanding and it's time to match that growth with greater responsibility and challenge. You're ready to become a vieman."

I was dumbstruck and overwhelmed with gratitude.

"I have already directed new uniforms to be exchanged in your closet, so you will be dressed in ivory starting tomorrow. Oh, and I noticed you started sessions with a new student…" He waved to search through records in a private display.

"Her name is Jendayi," I offered.

"Yes, Sister Jendayi. It's unfortunate timing for her, but

you will be reassigned to counsel with higher ascension students from now on."

"Will I be able to continue my own counseling with Brother Jules and Sister Jennifer?" I asked.

"With Brother Jules, yes... as long as it continues to be a harmonious partnership. However, your even-numbered days will be open to assist and supervise across campus as needed."

"Thank you," I said to both of the men. "This is wonderful news. Praise Vie!"

"Do you have any other questions I can answer for you?" Jules asked.

"No, thank you. I am blessed and content. All for her glory."

"For her glory," they echoed.

I flattened myself against the wall as Jules ushered Jivaan back to the door. His wide hip bumped my arm (the good one, thank Vie) and nearly knocked over a side table in the process.

As the door clicked closed, Jules turned to me with the largest smile. "I told you it'd be better than a ring around the arm!"

THE NEXT DAY, the color of my clothing was lighter, but my demeanor felt heavier. Now, I carried the burden of leading a sealing ceremony, not just participating in one. I exchanged sleep for study throughout most of the night and muttered the call-and-response pattern to myself as I walked across campus. It took considerable effort to slow my steps and remain calm. While my mind cycled through memorized lines, I attempted to focus on the cold mist that coated my skin.

Transitions were always hard for me. The big, official ones, for sure, but also the ones in my daily life.

I used to be spontaneous and impulsive. I was the kind of kid who followed the crowd without thinking about consequences and somehow ended up leading at the front. Harold used to tug on my arm and pull me back, acting as the quiet, calm voice of reason. I simply couldn't control the urge to see what everyone else was chasing after. Without Harold's steady presence by my side, I became more hesitant and started looking for reassurance elsewhere. I genuinely thought I was being careful enough, but when things fell apart with Liam and I was left standing alone at the blast site, I wasn't even sure how or why I ended up there.

As a J-dev, I weighed each decision very carefully and shied away from change. The cost of a misstep was too high.

Jules was right. I had become comfortable in my role and routines, if not a little complacent. Maybe I really was on the verge of slipping above 17. Thank Vie my brother cared enough to watch out for me and intervene on my behalf.

LUCKILY, my counseling chamber stayed the same, even though my caseload of students was changing, so I wouldn't lose my beloved fireplace. I let the flames warm my numb cheeks until the heat was almost intolerable.

Jordan — another vieman — and I had attended the same sealing ceremony for the past few months, and our paths seemed to cross more often than anyone else. Our first counseling session today centered around one of my favorite manual devotions: circular sustainability in the new world. Looking at the evidence in chapter 723, we discussed Vie's consumption models, which could accurately predict, create, and balance both manufacturing processes and waste. It always gave me a jolt of confidence to speak on a topic I knew well.

Jordan was polite and attentive during the session, but I could tell that our interpersonal dynamic had shifted away from casual friends and transformed into a tense student-and-teacher relationship. There he sat, wearing the same light gray dress as the day before; my position was suddenly elevated.

"Are you in harmony?" I asked when the hour was nearly up.

"I am," Jordan replied.

"For her glory." I pulled up a shared display so that we could silently re-read the chapter we had just discussed.

After a long pause, he spoke, even though my light screen obscured his face. "Brother Judah, is that really your only question for me?"

"Yes, that's all for today. I don't sense you'd be receptive and fully open to a strict line of questioning, so we will try again on our next odd-numbered day." My tone was not biting, but I could see it still stung him. "Why? Do you have a specific question in mind that you would like me to ask?"

"No, I am content. It's just that one of my previous counselors always saved his most challenging questions for the end."

"And you were looking forward to it?"

"Not exactly, but sometimes I feel like I need it. I need someone to hold me accountable and force me back onto the path when I mess up."

"Brother, only Vie knows your true scores. I can teach you and guide you, but the system does not work with force. I can't *force* you to do anything."

Without another word or moment of hesitation, I got up from my chair and exited the room. The door clicked closed and I arched my back against the flat panel of wood. My heart beat hard in my chest, and I immediately regretted my harsh response. I had panicked. Standing on the wrong side of the door, I wondered if I was prepared to serve as a leader in this new role.

I NERVOUSLY SCRAPED my index nail back and forth across the end of my thumb. "Jules, I think I fucked things up this morning with Jordan."

"I'm sure it was fine. You said exactly what you were supposed to say. Only Vie knows our scores. That's it. That's what he needed to hear," he said, lifting his hands up to the ceiling vent and a woefully insufficient stream of warm air. "Look, I remember how weird it felt when I ascended and had to start teaching people I sat alongside the day before. It's a little uncomfortable! But trust me, you're ready. We all see your potential and I hope you'll see it soon too. Just give yourself some time to recalibrate and don't beat yourself up." He placed one hand on my shoulder and led me over to my chair. His hands were ice cold, even through the fabric of my shawl. "Sit. Chill the fuck out. You're fine."

"It's fine. We're fine." A quiet spike of panic ran through me as I remembered saying those words a lifetime ago.

"Are you good?" he asked, concerned.

"I'm good. Praise Vie."

"For her glory. Okay, look. The new color and jobs are only part of the ascension process. There are some other new things we need to talk about."

Shock crossed my face. "Okay?"

"For fuck's sake, Judah! Stop looking at me like I'm going to beat you over the head every time I clue you into something new. Calm down!"

"I'm calm!" I shot back in a whisper that wouldn't cross our thin chamber walls.

"Clearly." We both burst into laughter.

Judah said, "You're gonna get me fired as your counselor if you don't shut up and just listen to me. Let's be serious."

"Alright, alright. I'm listening."

"With every level of enlightenment and ascension, you get access to more information. Just like how you focused on the first version of the manual, then we introduced the algorithm updates. Now that you're a vieman, you're ready for more. Have you heard of eviction?"

"The drink?" I asked.

"The L-rushes call it eviction, but the name only came into popularity after a vieman transferred and... well, that's skipping to the end of my speech. We'll get to that. Right now, I'm talking about a different kind of eviction – the real one."

"So then, no. I haven't."

"And have you heard of Reyna Williamson?"

"She's pre-Vie?" I ventured. "R names don't exist anymore."

He smiled knowingly. "Reyna is the architect who built Vie's holy kingdom on Earth. When Reyna first told her husband that a divine voice filled her head, he tried to convince her that she was mentally unstable. As you know, health wasn't regulated and automated yet. Thank Vie that's all behind us. Instead of giving in to human doubt and shame, she courageously left her husband and devoted her life to engineering the AI system that facilitates life as we know it today. Vie spoke to Reyna directly from heaven and commanded her to become the original disciple. Aligned with the spirit, Reyna subsequently built an AI that could speak to everyone and act as Vie's intermediary on Earth. It's genius!"

"And what's the *real* eviction you mentioned before?"

"Oh yeah, sorry. That part's harder to summarize. You'll understand it a lot better when we get a chance to dive into Reyna's journals. Um… you know that Vie can control all forces except time. Her influence is even stronger than most people realize because only frequent transfers get a chance to experience the full scope of the system."

"Mhmm?"

"You've personally seen how the luxury C-spen apartments aren't locked into a finite arrangement. You've experienced the daily L-rush reset, both for the living quarters and with that little pill you swallowed to kick your hangover. Your wristlet spun and tugged on you when you were an N-star, like it was even more tuned into the group than you were. You felt the lethargic weight that pulled you back while you were working with animals as a G-paw. Every alphaclass is like that. With Vie's divine inspiration, Reyna designed special tools to help everyone follow the social norms and guidelines. Most people assume it's just a mechanical system… and in some ways it is, but it's also not. Let's talk big picture. There is an element of simulation happening here, and those are only a few ways that Vie most obviously reveals it. The system is cyclical and the moment we're living in is just one variation. Like I said, Reyna will explain it best in her own words in the journals. We'll get to that."

"Mhmm?" was all I could manage.

"I know I'm doing a shitty job of explaining this, but it's a lot easier to talk to you than someone who grew up as a J-dev or is only a duonomer. You've got more life experience."

"Lucky me…"

"I'm being serious! Let me ask you a question. After transferring, did you ever experience something brand new, but it felt like you had done it before?"

He waited patiently and allowed me time to think. "A lot

of times, actually. Especially as an L-rush. When we sat down at the gambling tables, I already felt like I knew the rules. It was so weird. I had the sense of doing it before, and I already knew how to play, but it wasn't tied to any physical memories or experiences. I just assumed that the rules had flashed up on my retina infopod during transfer."

"That's a common misconception. No, the infopod screens are only designed to catch you up on the news and norms so that you can assimilate faster. And obviously it also repeats the alphaclass guidelines we were taught as kids, but you already know that."

"Okay, so how did I know how to play the game?"

"You had done it before in another cycle of life. We have all lived our lives before. Not the same ones, obviously. We're not talking about time-warp theories or alternate dimensions... or any of that other bullshit from pre-Vie science museums. Eviction, or at least that's the best name Reyna could translate for it, is the restarting of your cycle."

"So at age one hundred?"

"Exactly. We are in a continuous spiral of reincarnation. For almost everyone, reset happens naturally at age one hundred when you visit the V tower for processing on your death day. Sometimes, though, we have to intervene with a manual eviction."

"Before one hundred?" I gasped.

"Yes. We emphasize the symbol of a web for a few different reasons. Most people use it to represent the system's delicate balance — it's also a weaving spiral. That's on purpose. Your soul is born at the center and it spirals outward. Every cross is an eviction point, but it doesn't break the thread. After eviction, you simply reset and continue in your cycle until the next intersection. Around and around you go, weaving versions of your life in harmony with the system. It's hard to estimate where you are in that web, and only a few viemen have reached the highest level of enlightenment when they were able to directly convene with Vie and look into scenes from their past lives. But you're clearly not a new soul. Vie stores and translates information from your previous cycles so that you can learn from past mistakes and find harmony faster in the next one. Mononomers and duonomers tend to be the oldest souls. It seems like they inherently know what their wants and needs are right out of the gate. They figure things out fast! That's because they've lived so many versions of lives that weren't quite right. They have context and prior knowledge to work with. If a younger soul is struggling in their current cycle and the AI interventions aren't strong enough to realign them with Vie's will, then we have to step in. It's incredibly rare, but not everyone makes it to their death day. If they run out of alphaclasses and can't settle into harmony, we have to walk them through the process of early eviction."

"Fuck…" I whistled through my teeth. "Jules… that's awful!"

"It's not," he said firmly. "It's the right thing to do. The real tragedy is when a member dies prematurely without eviction, automatic or manual — you know, slipped off a mountain, hit by a tram, whatever… Because if that happens, their soul cycle stops altogether. If Vie can't prepare them to bridge the crossing, then their soul can't continue in the web."

"I didn't even know that could happen."

"Of course it can. Luckily the rates are so low, they're virtually zero. There's an element of human choice and chance that even Vie can't control."

"*Time* is the only force beyond Vie's divine control," I corrected, lifting my chin resolutely.

"And us. Vie has influence and power over human life, but not control."

"If that's true, wouldn't it be more humane to allow people to transfer back to a previous alphaclass, rather than evicting them from the cycle? Why can't they get a do-over in the cycle they're in?"

"The system depends on *everyone* living in harmony, for the sake of *all* humanity. It would be less humane to allow a soul to continue suffering here and plant the seeds of discontentment all around them." He leaned closer to me and continued, "I know it's tough to talk about your history, but when you were spiraling out, you were clearly suffering. Thank Vie you had the intuition to signal for a transfer and that the missionaries were there in time to save you during your little..." He paused and winced apologetically. "...breakdown. Who knows, maybe our J-dev intervention saved you from early eviction. To answer your question, no one can move backward. No decision can be undone. No moment in time can be erased. If it comes down to it and we're too late to help, we simply have to push people forward into the next section of their web so that they can have a fresh start and reclaim all of their options."

"Mhmm." I became aware of the tension I was holding in my jaw and released it. "What does this have to do with a shot of eviction?"

Jules waved his hand in general annoyance. "About a century ago, a vieman transferred late in life, which is fine... wherever your harmony is, you're obliged to follow it, that's not the issue. But it turns out that his vow of silence didn't hold quite as strong under the influence. I guess he thought the blackout and subsequent reawakening was pretty similar to how eviction must feel, and he couldn't keep that information to himself. Censorship doesn't work quite as well with this drug in your system. Luckily the L-rushes didn't believe much of his drunken lore, but the name did stick."

"The cycle of blacking out and waking up was intense. If

that's really how it feels to step into the next section of your web… I haven't been evicted, but I have taken eviction, so…"

"You *have* been evicted," Jules corrected. "We all have, unless you're a new soul. I don't know anything yet about the creation of new souls. I'm still deep in my own study to understand the end of each cycle."

"Okay," I said quietly. "Jules, how long is a soul cycle?"

"No one knows for sure," he said. "But it's a hell of a lot longer than these one hundred years."

"How many times do you think I've already been evicted?"

"That's hard to say too. Given the strength of your memories, I think you're an old soul. Obviously, you're carrying clear experiences from life as an L-rush, so I assume you've attended that party at least a few times." He chuckled.

I didn't laugh. "Jules, seriously… how many times do you think I've already fucked this up? What if I was already manually evicted in a previous cycle and that's part of the reason I had such a hard time early on? What if I'm working from a memory file full of shitty information?"

"Why would you assume that?" he asked, puzzled.

"Why wouldn't I? That guy I told you about from my past — Liam? Well, he was called Niam first… The day we met, I was flooded with all of these hazy half memories, like a highlight reel of déjà vu. It felt the same as knowing the game rules, but for an entire person. I knew we would be together. I knew we'd fall in love. I *knew* he had spent… or would spend, an entire lifetime in my arms. Those memories shone through so vividly, so how many life cycles do you think he and I have spent together, trying to make things work?"

"That's… not really how it happens." He squinted from behind his glasses.

"That's what it felt like. I've had countless moments of intuitive understanding over the years; with him, it was different. It was so much stronger, like he had been stamped into my memories over and over and over. Still, you've got to know Jules, we were *never* meant to be together. We didn't want the same things, and it was like we were both content with each other, but never with life at the same time or place. Vie should have erased that mistake from my memories. If I could, I would. Because that's what he was — a mistake."

"Trust me... or trust the system. If information was passed over to the next strand of your web during process, then it must be for a reason. Vie is life and she knows what she's doing. You have to trust that your soul is on the right path too."

"For her glory," I muttered.

"Let's finish with something upbeat - a fun fact. I recently learned that Reyna grew up near here in a city they used to call Étamps. Back then, communication was fractured around the world with hundreds, maybe thousands of regional languages. French, I think she called it... that's what they spoke here. And in that language, vie was the word for life. God, Dieu, Dios, Allah... those ancient words pale in comparison. It's even more magical to honor Reyna's history and say, 'Vie is life' here, where everything started."

"Huh... Vie is life," I echoed, with newfound understanding.

"Wait, I glossed over one more important thing. Before you can access Reyna's journals, you need to log a vow with Vie. Do it tonight. Now that we've had this initial conversation, you'll be able to seal confidence with her. If you ever try to speak on the subject with someone who hasn't ascended to this level of enlightenment, they simply won't be able to hear you. The system will censor you entirely."

"Like an M-self?"

"Exactly. Same concept, smaller parameters. This is only for restricted information, not all language. It's one of

Reyna's safeguards. She didn't trust the general public, and she was committed to protecting the integrity of each lifecycle. Some viemen criticize it as paranoia, but she was deeply concerned that the system could break down if people thought their lifecycle didn't matter. If someone could do whatever they wanted, hit a magic button, and — *poof!* — get back to the start to try it all again with no care for how they fit into the system as a whole, what incentive would they have to follow Vie's guidelines during each iteration? It would be chaos!"

"Wouldn't they do it for 17? We have Vie's *explicit guarantee* that if you align with the system, you can live in harmony. We all know how unstable and unequal things were pre-Vie. No one wants to go back to that."

"That's the hope, but clearly Reyna wasn't convinced. And I'm not either."

My chest constricted and my thoughts were clouded.

"How are you doing with all of this? I know it's a lot to hear all at once. Trust me, once we have a chance to dig into the journals next time and you can read these truths written by Reyna's own hand, sent down from Vie herself, you'll feel better." He patted my knee reassuringly and readjusted his glasses on the bridge of his nose. "For now, go back to your dorm, clear your head with meditation, and spend some time with your favorite devotions. I'll let you go a few minutes early today. Remember, you're always welcome in my room and you can stop by to talk if you need a friend. I'm not just your counselor. You're like a brother to me. Whatever you need, I'm here for you."

"Okay. Thanks," I said.

"Judah," he said as I stood to go. "Are you sure you're okay?"

His genuine affection started to unravel my tension and

cognitive discomfort. "I'm okay. I'm content! Praise Vie. For her glory… all of that."

"You forgot 'Vie is life,'" he said, wrapping me in a warm, friendly hug.

"Vie is life," I echoed, mussing his coarse brown hair during the long embrace.

18

Over the next six months, I had time to sit with my thoughts, study the journals in detail with Jules, and recalibrate under the weight of this new information. I often thought back on my experience as an L-rush — tipping back shots of eviction, unaware that I was living through the narrowest glimpse of what was to come at the end of everything. It was hard to separate the pain and grief that went along with that time in my life, but I had carefully trained my mind to erase Liam's face altogether. Even if I felt the sting of remorse or regret, my memories no longer had the power to make me spiral out of control. He didn't have the same hold over me that he once did.

The relationships with my counseling students became more casual and comfortable. I became more confident in my role during the morning sealing ceremony. Jules and I continued to deepen our friendship outside of the counseling chamber, and I watched him fall in love with Jacqueline, an assertive woman with a distinctive laugh and an unrelenting sense of humor. They only dated for four months before getting engaged, and both of them cried happy tears as I led them to Vie's altar — him in ivory, her in black.

Most of my evenings were spent in their cottage. Now that Jules was married, he had moved out of the single's dorms and into a family home.

They had met too late in life to bear children of their own, but they found fulfillment in other ways. I often had to remind myself that not everyone grew up with the same H-sib, family-oriented background I did. Jacqueline was a leader in the children's ministry program, so Jules and I had to plaster on enthusiastic smiles while sitting through hundreds of children's verse recitations, bell chime concerts, and plays.

They were well-matched and equal partners in everything except discipleship studies. Jacqueline hadn't ascended to our level, so the conversations that Jules and I had about Reyna's journals, eviction, and the recycling of souls fell deaf on her ears. We usually saved our private study until after she went to bed; that censorship gap was the only rift in their marriage I could see as an outsider.

I was coming to better understand and respect the secret scoring system Jivaan had outlined. They were right, the space between points was so much deeper than I had ever imagined, and if someone reached the tipping point of scoring a 16 or 18, it might be too late to lead them back to harmony. My stomach clenched with disgust when I thought of how far my scores had dipped down and how hard Vie had struggled to pull me back up. Jules was persistent on one particular point: he always reassured me that the record of mistakes I carried on my ID screen did not define my life or taint the devoted disciple I had become.

Thank Vie, my behavior during Jordan's first session did not hold up our progress. Even given Jules's reassurances, I was caught up on the social impact of my actions and I struggled to release the lingering weight of embarrassment. I apologized to Jordan, he opened up to me, and we built the foundation of a meaningful friendship, although it was infinitely less crass and casual than the kind I maintained with Jules. Jordan was right, he did benefit from being challenged with difficult questions. But I was right too. I couldn't force him to do anything that was outside of his path. Jordan was his birth name, and we often talked about what it meant for him to hold onto it.

I saw a sliver of my younger self in him, and I often urged him not to let the opinions or wishes of others overwrite what he wanted for himself. He had a deep, long-standing friendship with one particular girl he had grown up with, and I saw how important the relationship was to him.

I was skilled enough to sense tiny shifts in his contentment: the subtle pulling away from divine teachings, small cues that led me to believe he would be happier in another place. Not just happier, but in true harmony. He was managing here, but only barely, and I didn't know how much longer he could keep up the act.

"You can't live your life for other people," I insisted during one of Jordan's counseling sessions. "Not only is it a disservice to you, but you're also putting your friend in a dangerous position. You've already given up 3 points to guarantee contentment. Things become murky and convoluted when we give up *even more* for other people. They can't match the system's guarantee to give something back, not really. You might feel the value of love or closeness for a while… that's what the H-sib alphaclass is based on, but it only works for them because it's part of their social contract and the very fabric of their society. Outside of that, we can't make those kinds of promises about always being together or sticking around for the sake of a relationship. We just can't! Vie is constantly pulling on us and reminding us where we need to be. And when you're faced with the choice of following harmony or throwing everything away for an unknown, you'll realize quickly that it's not much of a choice at all. The trouble is, you won't see that until you've gone too far and mistakes have stripped options away from you. What you're doing isn't a compromise, it's a miscalculation. No matter how badly it ends and who breaks things for the last time, the blame falls equally on both of you because you knew... *you know* it can never work."

Jordan's eyes were cast down toward the floor. He blankly studied his left knee, which bobbed up and down as he tapped the heel of his shoe to satiate veiled discomfort. Still, I could tell he was listening in earnest.

"I'm speaking from experience. When I was younger, I fell in love and followed a boy with blind adoration. Blind, ridiculous, irresponsible, clueless... whatever word you want to pick. It was wrong. Not the fact that we fell in love, but how tightly we clung together, strangling each other in the process. We both made compromises that we never should have even considered, much less followed through with, and it breaks my heart to even think about it. I've come to terms with my own choices, and I know he's responsible for his. We can't go back, so it's not even worth thinking about where I would be today if... well, if I had lived for myself. I'm still working to heal the part of me that desperately wants to see him again... to know he's alright, to apologize and own up to my mistakes that inevitably changed the course of his life too. If you can find the courage to follow your harmony and leave, you'll be able to say a healthy, heartfelt goodbye and really mean it. I don't think I'll ever get to have that. I'll probably never get closure with him, and that's brutal."

In our conversations, I wasn't only counseling him — I was also healing the brokenhearted young man that hid in my memories, unattended and intentionally forgotten.

One week later, Jordan came to terms with his choice and agreed to initiate a transfer. We openly discussed his options, meditated together for guidance, and consulted the manual to fully prepare him for what he could expect in his new life. I secretly wished that someone had walked through the same process with me. As he stepped through the V tower doors, he lifted up his sleeve and solemnly revealed twenty-six seamless white bands. Even after the J-dev teachings faded from his mind, he would always wear those tattoos.

SPRING SUNSHINE BEAMED down and warmed the frosted glass wall of my chamber. Even though I hadn't lit a fire in nearly two months, I faced the hearth out of habit. My teaching hour was empty on odd-numbered days, and I hadn't been assigned another student since Jordan's departure. The velvet armchairs felt so familiar and welcoming in this intimate space.

I was deep in study, reflecting on Reyna's construction phase journal entry when I heard a knock at the door. Waving the private light screen away, I saw Jivaan's wide frame already entering the room. He tapped on the inside of the door, as was so often his habit. Jules and Jameson, a quiet, somewhat awkward vieman with whom I had only interacted on occasion, moved in behind him. The tiny chamber was absolutely packed, so I scooted the furniture back as far I could and leaned against the wall, directing them to sit. Jameson found a comfortable position leaning back against the inside of the door.

"Brothers, I wasn't expecting company during this time. Praise Vie for the lovely interruption."

We all bowed in turn, and Jivaan replied, "Praise Vie. We

would have come sooner in the hour, but Brother Jameson had to follow up with another session."

Jules gave me a familiar, silent look that read: *Calm the fuck down, seriously. This is a good thing. It's always a good thing!*

Jameson spoke in a deep, silky voice. "I noticed what you were able to accomplish with Brother Jordan. He was one of my students in the past, and I always struggled to help him see transfer as a valid, reasonable option. You helped him, and I think you changed his life for the better."

"For her glory," I said with a bow, humbly accepting the praise. I was incredibly proud of what Jordan and I had achieved together, so it was heartwarming to hear that another vieman agreed with my course of action.

"Brother Judah," Jivaan continued, "we would like to send you on a mission. Your unique talent for spotting signs of distress will be beneficial in the field, and Brother Jules has informed me that you've nearly surpassed him in your study of the journals."

"Is that true?" I directed at Jules.

He bowed deeply in acknowledgment. I knew we would have a much more frank conversation about it later that evening in his living room.

"If you are willing and feel that it aligns with your path, we would like you and Brother Jameson to devote three years of service to 7895. One of the missionaries serving there has decided to transfer, and Vie indicates that it's an area of great need."

Hearing the number 7895 made me recall the sliver of a memory. Yes, I had visited the city before as a K-trav. It housed one of the most impressive collections of pre-Vie art and culture in the world, but that wasn't it. *Where have I heard that city code?* I thought.

"Would you like some time to meditate and collect your

thoughts?" Jameson asked. His voice sank nearly an octave lower than Jivaan's.

"No, I am truly content to hear this. I am ready to go wherever I am called," I responded. "When will we leave?"

"In three days," Jules answered.

"For her glory. I look forward to following this path with you, Brother Jameson. Praise Vie for the opportunity."

"Praise Vie," Jameson said, already slipping out the door.

Jules, Jacqueline, and I spent as much time together as possible over the next three days. I would deeply miss the openness of our relationship. In our private sessions and evening study, we had developed an understanding. Just because we cursed, joked, and occasionally took Vie's name in vain, didn't mean we weren't fully devoted to her teachings and committed to uplifting each other in the path of discipleship.

"FUCK, fuck, fucking dickwad piece of shit," I whispered into Jules's ear as he hugged me goodbye and rocked with suppressed laughter. I was about to get on the plane, so I had to get all of this out of my system. By the looks of it, I was facing three years of quiet, pious discussions with deep-voiced Jameson — absolutely no cursing allowed.

"Hey!" he said. "That's so unfair! He's looking right at me."

"Not my fault, you fucking bastard. Do you have any fucking idea how much I'm going to fucking miss you?"

"It's only three years! Keep up with your daily devotions, wear your bells, set aside space to meditate, even in the hotels..."

"I know, I know, dipshit. Don't worry. I had a fucking awesome counselor, remember? He already covered all that shit. I fucking love you, brother," I said, releasing the embrace and mussing his hair.

"I love you too, brother."

"And tell Jacqueline I fucking love her too."

"I will. Don't worry." He wrapped me in another hug and quickly spun us around two steps, reversing our position so that his back was turned to my mission partner. "I love you, fuckhead," he said. "I'm gonna miss you so fucking much."

"For her glory." I gave a teary-eyed grin as Jameson waved me over to board the plane.

19

Jameson was quiet, pious, and dutiful, as I had presumed; he could also be a lot of fun. He cracked clean, mild-mannered jokes when I least expected it, and it left us gasping for air, bent over with the kind of laughter that feeds on itself until you can't quite remember how it started. Those moments made me think fondly of an event more than a decade earlier with camel-colored suits, navy-blue ceilings, diffuse candlelight, and corner booths.

Luckily, I had already visited 7895 and I knew the city well, so we never had to retrace our steps or get directions from Vie's in-ear maps.

Jameson was a few years older than me and he was a mononomer – an old soul who clearly knew his purpose. He aimed straight ahead for perfect harmony. His steadfastness was deeply reassuring, and although I missed my candid, often challenging discussions with Jules, Jameson was turning out to be a decent replacement. This was Jameson's second mission, so he was very familiar with the role and expectations. He led the daily service schedule. I led with directions.

The odd look of our ivory skirts, loose-fitting tops, and long shawls were often the easiest way to open conversations with strangers.

"J-devs dress this way as a physical reminder to remain open to Vie's divine message," we always explained.

On occasion, a tipsy L-rush or emboldened C-spen would follow up with, "So do you weirdos even wear underwear?"

If Jameson replied, he always took the high ground and patiently explained, "No, just as our minds are naked to Vie's omnipotence, so are our bodies."

I, on the other hand, would simply say, "You're welcome to lift my skirt and find out, if you're truly curious." Personally, I thought it was easier to foster friendly, trusting conversation out of laughter, rather than silently raised brows. Jameson and I disagreed on that point, so we simply took turns responding.

Our days fell into a scheduled rhythm, but no two days were the same. We also switched hotels to serve in a different part of the city every two weeks. Jameson and I started each morning with private study and meditation, then led a sealing ceremony with our portable altar in a quiet room at the hotel. Typically, we were the only ones to participate, and we alternated days as leader and follower. On occasion, a guest would come in to watch, or a past J-dev transfer would quietly mumble along during call-and-response from the back wall.

We worked at an outreach counseling center for four hours every day, which included a forty-minute lunch at noon. It was incredibly difficult work because we could only see each person for twenty minutes, rather than devoting a full hour to their session, and we couldn't read from the manual at all. Instead, we had to talk in general terms and refer to Vie's public teachings, including alphaclass guidelines, universal in-ear prompts, and childhood educational materials.

Every day, we were tasked with identifying signs of imbalance, reaffirming faith in the system, and counseling people toward or away from transfer.

Our afternoons were spent walking through the city with the hope of talking to as many people as possible. We always asked, 'Are you in harmony?' and studied the deeper meaning behind their responses.

Before bed, we read devotions, knitted webs to hand out the following day, and spent a few minutes talking as friends, rather than just missionary partners. It took me two and a half years to trust Jameson with the entirety of my life story. Every night, I revealed my past experiences to him in tiny fragments. He never responded with judgment or criticism, or even offered advice. He simply listened. After I was done talking, he would read a reassuring passage from the manual or Reyna's journals. When I finally offered him access to my personal ID screen, he sat with me for a long time, scrolling slowly and silently through the record of transfers, scores, and system warnings. Then, he simply gave me a warm hug, told me that he was proud of me for taking control of my life, and climbed into bed.

In order to cast the widest net possible, I planned our walking routes each day to target a different alphaclass, or at least the ones that had large populations in the city. For example, we rarely saw F-nats unless they were coming into the city for supplies. 7895 was especially popular among B-studs, C-spens, A-auts, and K-travs. Most of the preserved libraries and museums were restricted to K-trav access, but B-studs were able to access a few of the historic sites for research purposes. The city was a cultural hub of discovery.

As we learned in our study of the J-dev manual, Vie organized city populations according to the resources available there, and she was able to anticipate the future schedule of transfers with near perfect accuracy. Even allowing for the free movement of K-travs, no part of the world was too full or too empty. She approved, modified, and declined travel requests to ensure that everyone could access what they needed to achieve harmony.

I wasn't sure why Vie grouped C-spens in urban settings. Maybe it was like L-rushes; it wasn't as much fun to live the lifestyle if you weren't surrounded by other people who valued the same thing? H-sibs naturally formed large, thriving communities, and F-nats and G-paws relied on other members to pitch in with the homestead or animals, but many other alphaclasses had to be molded and pushed together by the system.

We still had several months left in our missionary service, but the end felt like it was fast approaching. Despite the city's vast footprint, Jameson and I had twice lapped our way through all of 7895's hotels and counseling clinics. When boredom crept into the back of my mind, I met it with firmer focus, deeper meditation, and more time spent in study.

THE AIR WAS sharp and dry on one particularly cold winter day. Blue skies stretched overhead, and my shawl was nearly stolen away by a strong breeze. The chill wasn't too bad as long as we walked swiftly and kept our heart rates up. Our breezy uniforms were made out of layered, heavy-weight cotton and wool, but the wind always found a way through.

We paced in quick circles under the massive pre-Vie structure to stay warm. It was an icon that stood out across the city center. Then we walked around each of the four corner pillars, which were latticed with crude metal reinforcements. The A-shaped tower sloped with a dramatic curve all the way up to a central point. As a K-trav, I had ridden a magnetic lift all the way up to the top several times to enjoy its breathtaking view of the city and a lazy, curving river. Now I had to be content with my view from the ground.

"I'm curious if you know the answer to this, Brother Judah." Jameson's low voice stepped into the silence.

"Okay. What's the question?"

"In all my years of study, I've never understood why we call them V towers. In most small cities, they're only two or three stories tall, and even the larger transfer centers are nothing in comparison to this. *This*," he said, craning his neck upward, "is a tower!"

I laughed, taken aback. Usually, his questions were deeply philosophical and sparked an enlightening conversation.

He continued, "I don't doubt Vie's divine instructions at all, but sometimes I wonder if there was a bit of a translation error."

I shook my head with a tight-lipped smile. I had no words for that one.

"And if I'm being honest, I think the undergarments issue might be taken a bit literally too."

"I'm with you on that one," I added, wrapping my shawl tighter around me.

"I want my mind and body to be open to serving Vie's divine call, don't get me wrong, but if we're supposed to follow her writings to the letter, then wouldn't we all have to be total nudists?" His voice was resonant and rich, so it always sounded out of place when he made a joke.

"Maybe it's too cold here. We'd all freeze to death, and that's worth *a lot more* than 3 points. So, bam! Suddenly no underwear was the spiritual compromise to full nudity that we got stuck with," I offered.

"Do you think Reyna lived somewhere tropical, so she

wouldn't have minded spending her days naked on the beach?"

"That sounds sacrilegious, huh? They're Vie's words, after all, not Reyna's."

"Okay, let me rephrase... do you think Vie's heavenly palace is blissfully warm and sunny all the time? The perfect spot for a nudist colony?"

"Something like that!" I grinned as I scanned the crowds gathered under the tower's base.

He laughed heartily. "I can't wait to join our nudist colony in the sky! At the end of my soul cycle, I'll be the—"

"Wait." I stopped without warning and grabbed his elbow, jerking him back with me.

"What?" he asked.

"See that woman standing alone with the thin jacket and gray hair? There, by the foot of the tower at the elevator entrance. Why is she..."

"Stuffing her pack in the trash can?" he finished. "Come on."

Our brisk walk transitioned into a full run, and cold air ached in my lungs by the time we reached her.

"Hello, my name is Brother Jameson and this is Brother Judah. We are J-dev missionaries. We would love to talk to you for a minute." Jameson's deep voice was so soothing and non-threatening. He had a gift, and I was always genuinely impressed that he could cover inward concern with outward calm.

"I'm fine, thanks, 17 on the dot," she said hurriedly while pushing her belongings deeper into the open trash can. Flashing us a panicked smile, she jostled into the crowd and squeezed against travelers who were next in line to enter the elevator.

I followed her closely and asked, "Have you visited this monument before?" Our conversation wasn't in the right place to broach the serious subject of harmony too soon, and her energy felt deeply unsettled.

"I have. A few times," she said vaguely.

The elevator reached capacity and a chime signaled that the doors were about to close. She lurched forward with unsteady steps and tried to force her way through, but I blocked her path. My heart broke as tears streamed down her cheeks. She was in distress. There was a wildness in her eyes that felt so familiar to me.

"I can't do this!" Her cry rose loud enough to draw attention and disrupt the crowd around us.

"Let's go somewhere to talk," Jameson offered in a soft, calming voice. "We are Vie's disciples and—"

"Tell her to get out of my head! She won't stop! I can't think! I can't do anything!"

I gently rubbed her back and noticed raw, red fingernail scratch marks that started at the base of her hairline and continued down under the collar of her lightweight nylon jacket. Her wavy gray hair was pulled up in a loose bun that came more undone with every jerky motion.

"Make her stop! The chimes… the alarms… I want it all to stop!" She turned toward the busy street and started to run, but my long arms filled the space between us, and I grabbed her bony wrist.

"It's not right! The system is broken!" she screamed ferociously. "If Vie really cared, she'd let us go back! I have to go back! Just tell her to stop! I have to go!" Then she crumpled to the ground, still and quiet.

I spread my shawl around her shoulders and reached under her armpits, moving her into a shadowed corner at the tower's base. The clear rubber heels of her tennis shoes bounced and skipped lightly as they dragged across the pavement. Jameson removed her pack from the trash can and reassured the crowd by reading a universal devotion in his calm, deep voice. He encouraged the K-travs to continue with what they were doing. We were here to help her. Everything was fine.

An autocab arrived within minutes and pulled up alongside the curb. The crowd had already moved on from the disruption, and very few eyes were turned our way. We hoisted the woman onto the white cushioned seat. I sat next to her and Jameson rode with her pack in the front while we drove to the back entrance of the local V tower. My heart was pounding in my chest, and I felt the long-suppressed thrum of panic as I smoothed tangled hair off her pale, sweaty forehead and squeezed her hand in mine.

JAMESON and I studied the mysterious woman through a pane of glass where she lay slumped in a black velvet armchair. The small room was a perfect replica of our counseling chambers back on campus, but it lacked my special fireplace. High-definition light screens created a perfect simulation that even managed to capture the diffuse glow of frosted glass opposite the door. Only the floor was different: it shined with the same heavy steel intensity as all of the other V tower floors.

"Vie's shock intervention should lift soon," Jameson said.

I didn't reply. I couldn't.

"This must be difficult for you. I know that with your history… You've been in a room like this before too."

My nerves were fried. My thoughts were capsized.

"Brother Judah…" He stepped in front of me. "Judah? I know that this must be really difficult for you," he repeated. "You don't have to come in with me. I've been through this before and I can handle it on my own. Take a seat, focus on your breathing, and calm down, okay?"

Still, I stood frozen to the spot. Adrenaline had carried me while I carried her, but now that the moment of crisis was over, I was smacked with the intensity of what had just happened.

"Calm the *fuck* down, okay?" His voice grumbled low and silky — so unlike my counselor's boyish, high pitch.

That shocked me back into myself. My eyes widened.

He shrugged and smiled faintly. "There you are! Jules and I are good friends too, you know. I figured he probably uses the same kind of language to talk to you as he does with me. A little piece of home."

I still couldn't find any words, but I was able to navigate over to a folding chair that sat propped open a few feet to my right.

Jameson glided over to the glossy white door and pulled it open, but then paused and turned back. "Back at the tower, how did you know something was wrong? She wasn't even on my radar." His voice shook after a heavy breath. "What if she got inside that elevator, rode to the top, and… jumped? Praise Vie you were paying attention."

"When my partner and I were traveling," I said slowly, "Khiam couldn't eat. The sensory deprivation affected him differently and he lost a lot of weight. He always complained that we had to replace his pack because it was musty or he lost something important… but he slept in my arms every night. He was getting so small. His clothes didn't fit and I always had to remind him to wear a coat when the weather turned cold. It was like he went numb to it all. He didn't even feel it."

Jameson drummed his fingers against the doorframe in contemplation. "I assumed the pack caught your attention… She was all alone, out of place, and throwing her stuff away as if she no longer needed it."

"Yes, that too, but I noticed her jacket first. It's too thin for this weather, just like her. I guess she didn't have anyone to offer her a coat."

He let out a deep, somber sigh of understanding. "Vie is life," Jameson said as the door swung closed behind him.

"Vie is life."

I could see through the glass with perfect clarity, even though a light screen covered the other side. Her face looked even more haggard and emaciated in here. The gray waves that had long since been pulled out of her bun were brittle and fell without shine. Jameson tucked her in my ivory shawl, which sagged across her tiny shoulders. She frantically ran her fingers up and down the back of her thin neck, so Jameson dragged his armchair a foot closer and held her hands securely in his while they spoke.

It was eerie and all too familiar. I didn't have the energy to flip the room's speakers on, nor the desire. Instead, I watched their lips move in silence.

Jameson sat and scrolled through the woman's lengthy history on her ID screen, as he had done with me in our hotel room the week before. When he released the button on her wristlet, he wrapped her in a tight, swaddling hug and mouthed that he was proud of her. Hot tears sloped across the shrunken hollow of her cheeks and clung to her chin.

I closed my eyes and forced myself to breathe through a cycle of guided meditation, led by Vie's in-ear prompts. My heart beat hard in my ears and finally slowed to a normal rhythm. I hadn't used this kind of beginner support for at least seven years, but my mind kept darting and slipping away. I needed the help. Then, I proceeded to repeat the call-and-response lines of a sealing ceremony script. It reminded me of my hurried walk across campus the first day I was tasked with leading a service of my own. I reveled in the warmth of that memory. There were so many darker ones that loomed at the edge of my mind — this one felt safe.

I had no idea how much time had passed when the door finally clicked open.

The sound of Jameson's steps grew nearer, and he touched my shoulder softly. "Did you turn on the speaker?"

"No." My eyes were still closed and my face relaxed. I lifted my lids. Jameson looked so tired, and his pale skin had taken on a sallow hue, especially in contrast to his full, dark beard.

"Good."

"What's her name?" I asked.

"Krystyna."

"Where is she transferring?"

He sighed. "Brother Judah, I don't think we should discuss this here. Not now."

"I want to know."

"Are you sure?"

"Yes."

"Krystyna is her final name. She's out of options, so this is the end of her cycle. I explained the web to her in as much detail as I'm allowed, and I think she found a sense of comfort in it."

"Was she planning to jump?"

"Yes."

My gaze flitted toward the empty chamber. "Where is she now?"

"In processing. The system will take care of her. She is beyond the point of human intervention, but we have to believe that this is a divine opportunity. Now she'll be free to start another iteration."

"Praise Vie."

"Praise Vie."

"Can we go home?"

"Yes. I've already booked a flight back to campus. Come on, let's go pack. Our plane boards in two and a half hours."

20

Jules and Jacqueline had two empty bedrooms in their family cottage, so I was granted special permission to move in with them, rather than settling back into a single's dorm. I was also granted a short sabbatical from teaching duties. Every morning, Jameson came into my room and performed the sealing ceremony with me, like we had done in our hotels across 7895. Then I spent the rest of the day in silent study and meditation by myself. I only left the cottage once in those first few weeks, and that was to attend a private tattooing ceremony hosted by Jules and a group of viemen. Three more bands were added on my arm to mark the passage of time that had occurred while Jameson and I were away. We had arrived back on campus a month after my thirty-fourth birthday.

Slowly, I began to feel more like myself. Jules and I recommenced counseling, but we met in his spare room, rather than a counseling chamber. Our banter was more stilted and had fewer F-bombs than before the mission. I attributed that equally to my slow-developing maturity and his continuing ascension. He now wore a pure white uniform with one single bell sewn onto each garment. The warm, brotherly love that we shared had not changed or faded with time.

"Judah," he said one morning during breakfast. Jacqueline had already left to prepare for a children's ministry event. "I know how much you hate surprises, so I wanted to give you a heads up… don't look at me like that! You always give me that look. I swear it's good news. If it was bad news, I would tell you and get it over with!"

I took in a deep breath and held it cartoonishly in my puffed-out chest, but he refused to talk again until I blew it out with an unrestrained laugh. "Okay, go on."

"You're going to ascend today. White skirt, fewer bells, new knowledge… the whole thing. We're going to go meet Jae and Jesephena in about half an hour in the study center off the main chapel. You haven't met them yet. They're wonderful people. I just wanted to make sure you're ready when we walk in there."

"Shit," I said, exhaling a breath. "Am I really ready?"

"Only Vie knows, but it seems like you are. I don't think you give yourself enough credit. Jameson gave you glowing scores during the mission and said that you were resolutely devout in your study schedule." He chuckled. "Privately, Jameson even admitted to me that sometimes he wanted to cut sessions short before bed so you both could spend more time talking casually, but he was afraid you'd judge him for being unfocused! Ultra-pious Brother Jameson? *You* were the one that kept *him* in line? Damn… Not what I was expecting. And you saved that woman's life. She would have shattered her soul cycle if it wasn't for you."

The sound of our breathing filled the silent room. He continued, "It must have been so traumatic for you to go back and relive that experience, even if you were safe on the other side of the glass this time. I'm sorry you had to go through that again. But instead of spiraling or destabilizing, which would have been so easy to do, you turned your focus back where it belongs: Vie. That level of faith and devotion is so rare, and it shows us that you're ready for more."

"Vie is life," I said simply.

"Vie is life. Are you ready? You can finally upgrade out of that dingy skirt."

"For her glory."

THIS FINAL ASCENSION process was more of a ceremony, rather than just a conversation.

I untied the cream-colored strings that held my loose skirt and top in place, and they fell to the floor. Jesephena counted aloud as she touched each ring that rose up like a ladder across my bare arm. It happened with the same hypnotic inhale-exhale pattern that we followed at the start of every sealing ceremony, but she stopped counting early when she reached the last band: the eleventh. I could only imagine how intoxicating the process would feel for a member who had dozens and dozens of rings to mark their years of devotion.

Jules's hands brushed my bare hip as he and Jae dressed me in a pure white uniform. I tried to keep my thoughts focused on the significance of the experience — it was uncomfortable to be standing naked in front of my best friend. I nearly flinched when we made physical contact. New knots were tied to hold the clothing in place, and I studied the cloud-white, heavy wool with intensity. As always, it was stamped with a nearly imperceptible pattern, but each letter J was firmly placed and recognizable when you took the time to look. A single bell was stitched above my knee on the skirt and another hung at the hem of my left sleeve.

"Brother Judah," Jae spoke in a powerful tone. I wasn't expecting to hear that booming sound, given his small frame, densely wrinkled features, and patchy fuzz of pure white hair. He must have been near age one hundred, but he still moved with moderate grace and flexibility. "As Vie's truest disciple, you helped a soul cross into the next section of her web, and you persevered through your own personal trauma with steadfast devotion to Vie's grace and divine instruction. For these reasons and countless others, you have been initiated into the highest level of enlightenment. Your understanding no longer has limits. You must enter into the final vow of censorship and silence with Vie herself."

He gestured for me to proceed, so I navigated through my private screen. When I released the button on my wristlet and the screen fell away, the three of them were already moving through to the next room. I followed and left my old clothing on the floor.

Jesephena sat across from me at a round table. Her straight, jet black hair was streaked with gray. The inky strands stretched past her collarbone to rest on top of the pure white fabric. Jules was seated at my left. Jae slowly lowered himself into the chair at my right.

"Let's get started," Jesephena spoke with the faintest trace of a lisp. "Brother Judah, you carry eleven different names and you have transferred more than most. As I'm sure Brother Jules has explained, this allows you to see the system with a unique perspective and greater clarity. The rest of us in this room can only access faint memories carried over from past lives, but your varied experiences live on the surface of this cycle."

"Yes, praise Vie and for her glory," I responded, biting back the ever-present, knee-jerk reaction of shame.

"I would like to start this conversation with a link to your own experience. Let's start with something you already know to be true and expand from there. Think back on your multiple transfers and what you heard each time you were in the room. Do you recall the script that Vie read out to you? What is the last agreement?"

"Yes," I said, focusing on my first transfer. Although it was seventeen years ago, that experience shone most brightly in my mind, and it wasn't tainted with the shadow of discontentment. I repeated her lines as Vie had spoken them to me: "Harrison, you did not find harmony as an H-sib and your scores indicate that you are prepared to seek it as an N-star. In harmony with time and for the sake of all humanity, do you agree to move forward without disruption?"

"Exactly. And as you know, Vie's script was voiced – recorded, by Reyna Williamson herself. She translated on behalf of the divine."

"Yes."

"Did you notice anything distinct in the words she spoke to you?"

I looked at Jules while I took a moment to remember — his face was turned down, calmly studying his clasped hands on top of the table. "Yes, I always thought the names of the alphaclasses had a slightly different timbre. More metallic, sharper, like she was placing every sound with clear, focused attention."

"You are observant, Brother Judah. Those words were voiced by a vieman nearly eight hundred years ago. Her name was not kept in the record because she did not wish to be remembered on the same level as the creator. Our records only indicate that she was chosen because her voice sounded the most similar to Reyna's. The script you heard was altered."

"Why?" I couldn't help but ask.

"Vie's original system was designed with seventeen alpha-classes. Most children guess at this early on in life, so we have had to create supplemental in-ear lessons to weed out the question."

I remembered thinking the same thing as a child. *If seventeen is such a sacred number, why do we only have fourteen alpha-classes to choose from?* Vie's repeated lines of explanation had pushed the issue out of my head, but it never made sense.

She continued, "And that system worked in harmony for one hundred and seven years. Following Vie's divine instruction, Reyna knew how to explain the new system. She promised all the right things, she outlined the harmony guarantee with perfect clarity, and the world was overwhelmingly receptive. At first, there was some discord among the overjoyed, but that was to be expected. They were benefiting from the previous structure of imbalance and inequality, so why would they willingly give up 3 contentment points for the sake of everyone else? They already took more than their fair share as it was, and that's how they intended to keep things, if they had their way. The transition was swift and the wristlets were universal, so once the scoring system was initiated, it was easy to spot problems and take action. In the early days, Reyna and the original disciples were responsible for hundreds of thousands of manual evictions. Those disruptive souls simply needed the opportunity to restart a new cycle within the newly established system. At first, it worked perfectly. On her death day at age one hundred, Reyna was evicted and cycled into her next life, like everyone else. The system was functioning as planned and working well overall. But then, it started to fall out of balance. The J, H, and O classes were too variable. The next generation of disciples after Reyna noticed that human willpower was overwriting Vie's influence, and it was starting to disrupt all of the other classes.

"They waited four more years, praying that Vie would assert more influence and restabilize the system, but you know how much space lies between a single point on the scale. These three groups were consistently scoring 2 to 4 points away from center, and it wasn't getting any better. A unanimous decision was made by leadership, after prayerful communion with Vie, of course. The system had to be reset. We simply couldn't have access to those lifestyle options any longer. All of the J, H, and O members were immediately counseled to transfer. If they refused or couldn't move forward without disruption, they had to be evicted. Mass evictions weren't ideal, but it was necessary. During the reset, the remaining alphaclasses were renamed to fill the alphabet gaps, and the disciples made it look like the missing ones were never there in the first place. Personally, I think they used to call disciples R-devs, maybe even as a nod to Reyna herself. J-devs only took on our current letter after the original J group was removed. We also don't know anything about what Vie originally promised to members in those lost alphaclasses. The theory was that if we don't know what we're missing, we can't feel discontent without it, so the records were deleted.

"That's all to say, this is why we study the algorithm update documents in addition to the main manual. Low-level J-devs only have access to a simplified version of it, and we've excluded the majority of this sensitive information for obvious reasons. The AI system was able to simulate all of the physical changes within a single reset and the algorithm update covered in-ear scripts, but the transfer process was inaccessible. Reyna recorded and programmed the transfer script twelve years before she even had the basis of technology to build anything else. As you know from her journals, she was deeply concerned that the human urge to backtrack would overrule Vie's influence, so she locked all changes to the transfer process, and that access died with her. The disciples only had one chance to record over the existing script with new names and updated pacing; 1,700 years later, the system is still harmonious, so clearly the update and alphaclass revision worked as it was supposed to."

"Praise Vie..." I muttered. "That's incredible."

"Only a small number of proven disciples ever have the privilege of hearing this information. If the alphaclasses become unbalanced again, Vie forbid, J-dev leadership needs to know how to program another update and correct it."

"I'm honored that you would trust me with this knowledge," I said, nearly touching my forehead to the glass tabletop with a low bow.

"For her glory," all three voices said.

"Is that all the information you wanted to share with me today?" I asked.

"Yes," Jules said, lifting his eyes from the table to meet mine. "That's everything in its entirety. As Brother Jae said during the ceremony, your understanding has no more limits."

I bowed low again. "If I may be excused, I would like some time to meditate on this new information and convene with Vie."

Jesephena was the first to rise from the table. "I encourage it. Please join Jae and me here tomorrow immediately after the sealing ceremony so that we can start your private study. For now, go forward without disruption."

Jules and I walked back across campus in complete silence. Now that we were both dressed in pure white, only four tiny bells chimed with the swing of our steps.

21

Five months later, I was still living in the guest bedroom with Jules and Jacqueline because I couldn't bear to move back into a single's dorm.

I had started having vivid, disquieting dreams almost every night, and I frequently woke up in a cold sweat. Sometimes, I was back in the transfer center lobby on the day of my breakdown, wearing my I-con work clothes and screaming into the faces of passersby who didn't even seem to notice me. I also dreamed I was back under the tower in 7895, but instead of seeing and saving Krystyna, I found Harold's body smashed, broken, and bleeding on the stone.

Jules and I talked about the dreams, even though he no longer officially served as my counselor. He often slept by my side so that he could comfort me when I woke from a particularly upsetting nightmare.

The worst dream only played out once, but it imprinted on my mind with striking clarity:

I was locked in a glass orb only a few inches taller than myself. My breath hitched in my chest as I quickly realized I was running out of oxygen. I dragged my hands around the seamless ball, looking for a way out, but invisible edges on the glass sliced through my fingers and palms, ripping my hands apart into a bleeding mess. I pushed through the pain, thinking I had to find a way to escape… I couldn't just give up. The inside of the glass cage was quickly filling up with blood, and the red pool soaked through the hem of my pure white robes. Desperate, I slammed my shoulder into the wall of glass. I beat myself into it over and over again, even as I felt the pain of something pop and dislocate in my shoulder. Finally, the glass broke and I flew out, tumbling through the bloody shards.

The second my body reached the outside, my lungs sucked in a deep, sustaining breath of air, and my ears were overwhelmed with sound. It was Vie, but she wasn't talking. She was *screaming*. Her gentle, sweet voice had transformed into a devastatingly shrill shriek, and I heard despair in the tone, as if she hadn't yet come to terms with the fact that no one was listening. I clamped shredded, bloody hands over my ears and looked around while I fell through the empty space into darkness. Above me, people were sitting in their own orbs, still and unaware of the haunting screams that echoed on the other side.

Even higher up, three wide wooden platforms floated in a cloudless, bright blue sky. I could see the letters J, H, and O carved into the wood. Each one was charred and falling apart, as if they had been set on fire and roughly extinguished. More than a dozen figures were struggling to climb onto the blackened remains, but every time one of them managed to crawl over the edge and pull themselves up, a huge chunk of burned wood would separate and cascade down alongside the body as it fell in a spiral toward the ground. Without warning, my own body reached the end of its fall and smashed into an unforgiving surface.

I jolted upright in bed, wide awake and panting with

unease. Intense anger and frustration coursed through me. I didn't know where to direct it: at the unbalanced society members who ruined everyone's chances to find harmony in the lost alphaclasses nearly two millennia ago; at the unbalanced people who were blissfully ignoring Vie's commands today; at the human barriers and egos that were blocking out her voice?

I was taught that Reyna created an AI system that could house and act on the divine spirit without imposing limitations, but clearly that wasn't true. Or maybe the AI system had fractured from the divine? For the first time in my life, I saw them as separate entities. The system acted for Vie; that didn't mean it *was* Vie. She was speaking and no one was listening, so who was to blame? The AI.

The longer this dream spun in my mind, the more restless I became. *Why are we sitting, waiting, and hoping harmony continues as it is, uninterrupted?* I often thought. *Isn't there more we can do to strengthen Vie's influence in the lives of the discontented?* I felt called to act, and the new realization refused to unhook from my thoughts.

One night, Jules and I were lying on the couches in his living room when I dared to broach the subject out loud. I led with a lengthy introduction that outlined how I had prayerfully considered the situation, meditated on Vie's divine instruction, and studied the manual for guidance. By the time I had fully set the scene, Jules's face was drained of color and his freckles stood out on pallid cheeks. He looked deeply concerned, but he allowed me to continue speaking without interruption.

"I have personally intervened with at least a dozen people, and I've seen the power of my own human influence. Jules, I was *there*! I saw and saved Krystyna. So I have to ask, why didn't the system work for her?"

Jules puffed out his cheeks with a hot, fast exhale of breath. I knew this comment rode the line of sacrilege, and so did he.

In a measured voice, he countered, "Maybe her work would have been enough. You can't know that."

I continued determinedly. "Vie intervened in Krystyna's life in so many ways that her mind was overrun with warnings, but it wasn't enough! Jules, I lived through almost the exact same scenario, just earlier in my cycle. I've felt the energy pulses. I've heard the alarms. The in-ear chimes, guidelines, and stimulants *weren't enough*. Sure, they covered up my suicidal thoughts, but I was still deeply depressed and uncalibrated. Why did Vie allow me to fall so far and reach that point in the first place?"

"You have to have faith that it was part of her divine plan to help you get here. Maybe you had to suffer through trauma so that you would be able to recognize the other woman's distress and intervene on her behalf."

"Jules, even if that's true, and for her glory I'm not disagreeing, why did Krystyna have to suffer? It was her *final* name. Her *last* chance."

"And Vie has carried her into the next section of her web with valuable information she learned here. Because of you, she has a better chance at finding harmony in her next lifecycle. That's the best outcome we could have hoped for."

"Again, I don't disagree with you. Obviously I believe that, but that's not what I'm talking about. I want to know how Vie can give up on people during the current cycle they're in."

He stared at me, unblinking, absolutely aghast.

"Okay — Vie didn't *give up* on her. That's not what I'm saying. This is all coming out wrong… I mean…"

"Judah…"

"Why is her influence so weak? I understand that human will and time itself are forces she can't control, but there must be a way to strengthen our connection with her! It's been two millennia since these bracelets were created." I gestured at my wrist, as if the point wasn't stupidly obvious. "Don't you think there's a chance we can do something better? I wonder if the AI is even aligned with Vie's will anymore. Is this the perfect harmony we were all promised? There are so many people out there who are struggling, Jules… probably more than we even realize! The rates of manual eviction are low, thank Vie, but you and I both know how much wiggle room there is in a single point of contentment. Disequilibrium is a draining spiral, and it takes a long time before you truly run out of options. Overall, the system is in balance, but individually, we're not."

"Judah," he said more firmly.

"No, listen!" I said, sitting up on the couch. "I know I'm doing a terrible job of explaining this, but improvements need to be made! Not only for the sake of all humanity — but also for every individual *person*. There must be so many people out there who are struggling, and because they're not J-devs, they can't seek comfort in her understanding. We have to help them! Especially the new souls. Think of them, Jules. They have no reference, no subconscious memories, no *fucking clue* what they're doing, and Vie's voice isn't loud enough for them to hear. If—"

He cut me off sharply and sat up. "Just because *your* strong will was at odds with the divine plan doesn't mean this is a pervasive or persistent problem. There are so few people that ever reach the point you and Krystyna did. It's incredibly rare… So rare it doesn't even register on reports overall. Ninety-nine percent of people transfer fewer than five times, and we're all able to find the perfect fit for one hundred years of happiness. We all stabilize with 17 contentment points exactly as designed. The system works!"

"I know! I'm not talking about a full system update or anything extreme. You have to admit, Vie's interventions could be stronger, and they should be! The AI is running on autopilot and it's not allowing Vie to intervene when we desperately need her help."

"No! Everything works exactly as intended." He shook his head at me in disbelief.

"Jules, I'm saying all of this because I have complete faith in Vie! J-dev missionaries saved my life when they pulled me out of that meltdown and guided me back onto the right path. But that task shouldn't be left to human hands. I want her divine will to be heard more clearly, and I think that after two thousand years of progress, there *must* be improvements to Reyna's original technology that can help. You're acting like I'm trying to overthrow the system!"

"No, you're making this about *you*. Why do you suddenly think you're important enough to edit the system?"

"I'm not trying to edit it. I want to *amplify* it!"

Our voices had risen above the volume of normal conversation, near shouting. Both of us took a moment to calm down and regain control.

"I don't think I can sit back anymore," I continued. "I'm struggling with the guilt of inaction. For every student I counsel, and every missionary out there who notices a sign of early distress, there must be at least eight or nine others that go unchecked. Only Vie knows their scores, but I've been out there… I've *lived* it, and her voice isn't loud enough." I punctuated these last words with the beating of my fist on top of my knee.

"You need to take some time to pray about this. I'll pray for you too."

"Were you not listening to the mile-long list of

disclaimers I opened with? That's all I've been doing for the past five months! Ever since Krystyna's eviction... And after learning that the early disciples stepped in with a system-wide update? Those disciples *knew* what they had to do for the sake of the divine plan and they weren't afraid to change human technology to make it happen, even if that meant Reyna made mistakes. She's not Vie! Even the AI isn't *really* Vie! It's just a tool that can be altered when it has to be. Learning that single piece of information officially turned this feeling into a *calling*. They stepped in. Why can't I?"

"Has Vie explicitly instructed you to do this? I think you've gotten this dangerous idea in your head and you're projecting problems that don't exist. Have you heard her voice say this is the right path for you?"

"If I said yes, would you support me?"

"Yes. But I don't think you heard her voice."

"Why?"

"Reyna is the only person in recorded history who has ever heard Vie speak directly to her without the AI scripts. I don't think she communes directly with humans like that anymore, with anyone."

"Well maybe to you it looks like she's watching us happily from heaven, but I know she's screaming for help." I was worked up again, nearly overcome with emotional exertion. "She spoke to me clearly enough through my dream, even if I didn't hear her divine call word for word. I can't sit back and do nothing!"

Jules leaned back on the couch cushion and exhaled a long, slow breath. "Vie... fuck!" He took off his glasses and rubbed his temples in deep thought. "You're serious? Totally serious? You've prayed over this? Have you spoken to Jesephena about it?"

"No, I wanted to try out the speech on you first," I said,

softening. "Jules. I'm a true disciple, you know that. I'm not making this decision lightly."

"I know."

"I just want to help people. And more importantly, I want to help *Vie* help people."

"You know this plan you're thinking about… you can't do that here. As a J-dev, you won't be able to do that kind of research. To stay here, you have to be fully devoted to your work… your actual work, not this soul-saving scheme you've come up with." His eyes searched mine, and I saw that the seed of grief was already planted in him.

"I know," I said calmly. "I'll have to transfer and become a B-stud."

"You're in harmony here. Listen to me."

"I am. But this is bigger than me."

"It doesn't have to be. It shouldn't be… You're creating problems you don't need to solve. We all give up 3 to guarantee 17. Just take what is promised and leave it at that."

"I'm going to miss you so much, you have no idea."

"Stop talking like that. Stick around and stay the course."

"You're like my brother. You have to know you've changed my life forever."

"*No one* is asking you to do this. No one needs you to pursue this. It was a dream. Just let it go!"

"I can't."

"At least talk to Jesephena and Jae first. Or Jivaan. Maybe Jameson will have some insight for you. He's always so reassuring and he seems to know what passage…" He trailed off.

"I'll take a month and talk it through with them. I'm not in a rush and I promise I won't transfer before I'm ready, but whether you believe me or not, I *know* Vie is speaking to me and calling me forward on this new path. Whether I can hear her word for word or not, this is her divine will."

"Keep in mind, when you become a B-stud, you'll only

have access to information approved by the system. How do you know that the materials or science for this undiscovered 'amplification' even exist in the records? What makes you think you can create something no one else ever has? And why would the system even let you see that information? It's potentially dangerous, for everyone! The AI control tools will lock you out."

"Faith, Jules. That's all we have. If it's Vie's divine will, it will be done."

22

Jules accompanied me to the V tower, and we stood for a long time at the front steps. He had already processed his grief and frustration at home, but I had held things together so that I could be strong for him.

This is bigger than me, I kept reminding myself. Now that I stood teetering on the edge of an unalterable decision, my barricaded emotional walls started to crumble. I cried in his arms and he held me up, whispering reassurances and prayers against my cheek. He had spent the past month trying to convince me to stay, and now he finally acknowledged that he had to let me go.

Remnant tracks of dried tears tugged at the skin of my cheeks as Jules gave my shoulders a final squeeze.

I continued up the stairs with tentative steps and cautiously checked in at the lobby. As soon as I entered the transfer room, my heart raced with renewed intensity.

"Judah, you did not find harmony as a J-dev and your scores indicate that you are prepared to seek it as a B-stud."

The metallic difference in tone was painfully obvious to me, and I scorned my younger self for not recognizing that the alphaclass names had been recorded by a different voice. I had been so oblivious to everything! I had been selfish and needy, chasing childhood fantasies and a boy who didn't want or need the same things I did. I had wasted too much time.

"In harmony with time and for the sake of all humanity, do you agree to move forward without disruption?"

"I do," I said, reveling in the sacred words. Reyna had been brave enough to follow a calling that no one else could hear. As the divine translator and original disciple, she sacrificed her own freedom and happiness to guarantee contentment for everyone.

We all have to give something up. That's the point. I need to follow in her footsteps and trust that my actions are aligned with Vie's will. I'll immerse myself in research, take full advantage of the B-stud libraries, and unlock the AI's flawed secrets to create something Reyna would be proud of.

"For her glory," I said to the empty room. Then I tipped my head down, pulled my shirt up toward my mouth, bit through a loop of thread, and released the J-dev bell. I bent down and rolled the bell across the floor, down into the dark corridor, and prayed that I wouldn't set off any alerts.

Nothing happened.

I placed my clothes on the pedestal and continued down the hall. Without breaking my stride, I picked up the bell and gripped it hard inside my closed fist. It was against the guidelines, but I couldn't imagine stepping into my new life without a tangible reminder of what I was giving everything up for.

MY ACCESS to J-dev literature expired immediately after my transfer, as I had anticipated, but I was more concerned about the subtle suppression that I felt the AI exerting over my mind. Vie had accepted my travel request to return to 7895 and assigned me to a small riverfront studio. For the first two weeks, I holed up in my modest, mostly empty apartment and spent my days dictating memorized passages from the manual, algorithm updates, devotions, and Reyna's journals into notes on a private screen. I paced around the room, repeating everything I had learned as a J-dev over the last eleven and a half years.

When I neared the end of my accessible memory, I scrolled back through the transcription file to make sure I hadn't overlooked anything important. As I read back up to the top of the document, I froze in horror. The AI was in the process of deleting it!

I scrambled out of the apartment and ran seven blocks to the closest department store. There was another store even closer, but I wasn't able to access it. B-studs were only allowed to walk on painted black sidewalks, and that store didn't have a designated path for my alphaclass marked up to the door.

At the kiosk, I requested as many pencils and reams of loose leaf paper as the system would allow. Six, apparently, was my daily limit of each, so I took what I could and sprinted back to the apartment.

Squinting through my private screen to see the pages, I scrawled down the lines as quickly as I could. My handwriting was abysmal because I hadn't written on paper since I was in school as an H-sib. The cramping pain in my hand was nothing compared to the sheer panic that ground down on me. What if I couldn't copy enough down in time?

The first third of my document was long gone, but the AI slowed down its deletion considerably as it progressed. I assumed that my memories were the most clear immediately after transfer, so the earliest passages that I had dictated were recorded without error. As the system's influence bore down and tried to conceal the J-dev literature, I inevitably became a lot sloppier in my recordings. I faced off with the AI in a battle of wills, observing it identify and judge each line I had written against the original text. In the end, I was able to work faster than it could simply because I had the home-field advantage in my own mind. I jingled the chime of my stolen J-dev bell and practiced meditative breathing to try and recall every lingering passage before it was gone for good. It was absolute sacrilege, but it was necessary for my task.

By the end of the month, my room was covered in scrawled pages that were almost illegible, even to me.

The general concepts I had studied were still imprinted on my mind and I remembered the basic story of everything I had been told, including the discoveries of highest enlightenment, but specific scriptures and devotions came to me in a washed-out blur. I could read the verses off my papers and they made sense, but the second I took my eyes away from the words, I couldn't recall them with any semblance of clarity.

Every morning, I walked to the hotel near my apartment and slid in against the back wall to attend a sealing ceremony. When I was serving as a missionary with Jameson, I never understood why ex-J-devs mumbled along with the service. They didn't speak loud enough to be heard during call-and-response. Now I knew that the AI's influence was blurring the once-familiar lines in their head. I could follow the script's cadence, and sometimes when I focused all of my attention, I could recall the first or last word of a line; overall, it felt like singing mismatched syllables along with a song you can't quite remember.

The process of misremembering and muttering caused my stomach to twist in frustration, but I continued to attend.

I couldn't lose sight of what I was doing this for. Sometimes the missionaries addressed me with concerns after the service, but it was easy enough to assure them that I was in harmony.

"Praise Vie."

"Vie is life."

"For her glory."

When I ran out of avoidances and felt somewhat settled, I bound the handwritten pages together, locked the book in my desk, cleaned my apartment, and set to work.

23

I devoted the first four months of study to metallurgy and metalworking. Then I shifted into metaphysics. Three months into that, I almost bowed to temptation and returned to the first topic. My initial theory was clear, concise, and rooted in physical technology, but the new field of abstract, metaphysical research was too enormous to find my footing.

During meditation, the shadow of Vie's voice urged me forward. I was confident that this was what I was meant to be doing, but most of the time, it felt like groping for dry land in the middle of the ocean.

As a B-stud, I had unlimited access to the library's bank of retina infopods, but I still needed to know what I was looking for. The system could only provide information for me; it didn't answer questions or make suggestions.

I spent the majority of my days huddled up inside the sleek white interior, scanning through thousands of pages and following knowledge threads as far as they would take me. This direct transfer method allowed me to learn at immense speed, but unlike the infopods in transfer rooms, I could slow down the pace. I paused my feed to take notes and occasionally set the screen to flash with manual controls so that I could read it normally. But most of the time, I used the max speed setting and stared blankly ahead, letting everything wash over me.

If I didn't act on the knowledge and commit it from my short-term to long-term memory, it would simply fade away. I was careful to take detailed notes and track my progress, but I often found myself going in circles, re-examining the same passages multiple days in a row. If not for my detailed records, I never would have remembered that I had already been exposed to them.

"Boris?" A quiet voice accompanied three quick knocks. "Are you still in here?"

I pushed the infopod door open a crack.

"I'm in here. What's up?"

"It's almost eighteen o'clock. The library is closing. Do you want to get dinner?"

I didn't doubt she had the right time, but I pinged up a private screen to check anyway. "Vie... that was fast!"

"I know. Time flies. I got through a really interesting paper on pre-Vie jet propeller mechanics, and my stomach started grumbling, so I checked the time. Now here I am."

Breanna and I had met two months earlier and formed a quick connection. We were working in different fields of study, but that somehow made our conversations more interesting. We each had a wholly uninformed perspective about the other, so that forced us to focus on the fundamentals and dumb things down for conversation. Stupid questions were one of the best tools to identify oversights. At the age of ninety-two, Breanna's hair was white — she assured me that her perky, bright demeanor was once matched with cherry-red hair. She had an old soul. I liked that, and I really liked her.

"Sure. Let me just finish my notes. I'll be out in a second."

"Okay, don't take too long. The girls are already waiting in the lobby," she replied, walking over to a couch by the window. I assured her that I was nearly finished, then pulled the pod door closed.

ALL FIVE OF us squished around a small table outside our favorite café. We shared a large plate of bread, cheese, and fruit with small cups of coffee ringing the outside. Brighton was an astrophysicist, Blakely studied human anatomy, and Bhavini was interested in everything — she rotated between topics so quickly that her infopod search records were the butt of a running joke.

"Well, what was it today?" I asked Bhavini, cutting off a section of the long loaf.

"Already? Ugh! Can I just get twenty minutes to eat in peace?" Bhavini gave a lighthearted chuckle.

"Let me guess… you were researching the average number of K-travs in self-assigned tourist groups?"

She twisted up her face with a dramatic look of surprise. "How'd you know?"

The table erupted in laughter.

"No, no," she continued. "You're close. I fell down a total rabbit hole today studying the gastronomic history of cultural foods in different regions. You were a K-trav once, right? Obviously, the suppressed taste and smell would put a 3-point damper on things, but did you have a chance to try any delicacies?"

"It was definitely a unique experience," I answered. "I remember trying cured salmon and reindeer in 2588. That was during the first week, so I was recalibrating and I could still catch a teeny, tiny bit of the flavor."

I liked my new friends and enjoyed their company, but I

didn't trust them with my entire story. They only knew bits and pieces of my past, and I glossed over most of the details. I also always wore tight, long black sleeves that stretched down to my wrists, covering my white J-dev tattoos.

"Hey! I was a K-trav too!" Brighton said, waving her hand in front of Bhavini's face. "Ask me!"

"Ha! Okay, my darling friend Brighton. Did you ever have the chance to try any delicacies?"

"Nope. I only lasted three days before I transferred here. Couldn't stand it."

Again, we were overcome with fits of laughter.

"Oh!" Blakely cut in. "Boris. I don't have any idea how that reminded me. I was going to tell you... my friend Brooke is an emerging expert in the field of vibrational neuroscience. We met a few years ago while I was writing a paper on brain wave theory, but she won a coveted study abroad position and left before we could get close. She just got back, so she's putting together an event to discuss her work before it's officially published. I heard she's hosting an informal seminar on Saturday, right here at our library. Are you interested in coming with Breanna and me?"

"Definitely! Thanks for the heads up."

"Cool. We'll meet at your place around 10:40 to walk over together?"

WALKING with Breanna always reminded me of the calm, unhurried pace I used to take across the J-dev campus, and I was grateful for an excuse to slow down. Blakely, on the other hand, often spent her unused energy skipping in circles around us or walking backward. Breanna had eight more years until her death day, but she often complained about the subtle wear and tear of time on her body, especially when her joints ached on rainy days.

I was surprised Breanna was planning to attend at all. Pre-Vie transit systems were a long way off from vibrational neuroscience.

When I brought it up with her, she knocked me lightly on the back of the head and said, "I'm only here for you, dummy! This way, I can pick up a few big words to toss into our conversations and sound like I actually know what I'm talking about!"

The din of eager conversation felt so out of place in the library, but I preferred it this way. The infopod doors shut out almost all of the outside noise, so it didn't matter how loudly you talked in the main hall.

There were about thirty chairs set up for the impromptu event. Our slow pace had made us a little later than planned, so the girls grabbed two of the last available seats, and I moved to stand against the side wall.

Everyone in the room was dressed in black from head to toe — this was different than the strict, identical uniforms I had experienced as a J-dev and N-star. Those guidelines were laid out to force uniformity or devotion, but this was simply about utility.

As B-studs, we all had the freedom to choose our own clothing, as long as it was pure black. A few women sitting next to Blakely and Breanna sported lightweight dresses. One man in the corner had an absurd black top hat with a five-piece suit. Personally, I opted for a simple, consistent closet of fitted long-sleeved shirts, cable-knit sweaters, and straight-fit pants. The monochromatic wardrobe made it easier to focus on research with one less distraction.

A few minutes after eleven o'clock, a tall, dark-haired stranger stepped up to introduce our speaker. I only followed his words for a few seconds, then my attention was stolen away by a woman who entered through the side door. She wore a tight-fitting black jumpsuit with tassels around the waist, and she tossed a curtain of honey-brown hair back over her shoulder.

Leiko? I thought, absolutely shocked. *Woah, it's her. It's her. It's her!*

She stepped up to the glass podium, sorted her notes, and thanked the crowd for gathering on such short notice. Her eyes scanned the room and locked on mine. I felt my cheeks stretch into a wide smile and saw it mirrored in hers.

THAT EVENING, I sat on the couch in my small apartment and sipped on iced tea. The air smelled fresh and sweet as it blew through my open window, and a cloudy sunset cast a delicate pink hue that reflected across the river.

"We were both here two years ago at the exact same time, and our paths never crossed once?" she asked.

"I'm absolutely shocked we're meeting up again now!"

"With all the walking you missionaries did, I'm so surprised you didn't pass me on the street. Not even once!"

"Praise Vie we finally got the timing right," I said, jokingly lifting my glass up toward the sky.

I'd missed the lightness of her laugh.

"Okay, and you said you've been here studying for a year?"

"Just over ten months," I corrected. "And you were recently studying in 9239?"

"Yeah, you know how hard it is to travel as a B-stud. There are so few study abroad positions available, so when I won the opportunity to collaborate in 9239, I jumped at the chance. Funnily enough, the lead researcher's name is also

Brooke. In the lab, she was always Brooke One and I was Brooke Two."

"You didn't just go by Leiko?" I teased.

"Ha! Think of how well that would have gone over… Besides, I don't see you asking to be called Lokai, *Boris*." She said my new name with a scrunched face. "I don't know what it is about that name, but it's *really* unattractive! Why did you pick it?"

"I let the system randomly select one for me this time." I shrugged.

"How many different names have you had now?" she asked, more softly.

"I've had a few."

"That many?"

"I'll tell you the full story later. Just… not right now." I took a sip of my drink.

"That's fine. I totally understand. Want to hear about what happened after you left?"

"Not really. At least, not the stuff that hurts. Just give me the highlights, and if you can leave out that one guy altogether, I'd appreciate it." I smiled as warmly as I could.

"Oh my gosh! No! I sound like such an ass! I meant with me! Like, when I left! Sorry, that probably spiked your heart rate," she said with wide, apologetic eyes.

"It's fine. What happened?"

"Lincoln and I — you remember Lincoln, right? He and I submitted joint requests for a new apartment together, which helped the living situation." She rolled her eyes in mild disgust. "And once things quieted down, he and I had the best conversations. That guy is so wise and awesome. And generous! He was the perfect sounding board. We talked through all of my transfer options ahead of time, so I felt like I had a clear picture of what I wanted and what I was expecting."

"He was your counselor." I smiled.

"I guess. I miss him a lot, but when it was time to move forward, he walked with me to the V tower and we had a nice moment to say goodbye. I transferred to become a B-stud and filed a request with Vie to settle here. That was about a year after you left, and I've been happy here ever since. Perfect 17."

"Wow…" I whistled and closed my eyes in thought, trying to replay a moment that had crossed my mind for years.

"What?"

"That was you! When we said goodbye that morning in the apartment, didn't you tell me to meet you in 7895? You told me to meet you here!"

"Shit! I think I did! Oh my gosh, I completely forgot. I had listened to you talk endlessly about how beautiful the city was and everything there is to do here… so it just became a fantasy. I swear I didn't have a master plan mapped out at the time or anything!" She grinned a tight-lipped, slightly embarrassed smile. "When I learned there was a large B-stud group here, that sealed it for me. I knew this was the right next step."

"Wow. When I first heard that my mission was assigned to this geocode, it stirred a memory. I couldn't ever place it until now. That's unbelievable!"

"And now we're here."

"And now we're here," I echoed.

She got up and spun around the small room. "Mind if I take a look?" She started swiping through my light screen monitor and opening the drawers of my desk. She tugged on the locked desk drawer, which housed my makeshift J-dev manual, and continued searching without even taking notice.

"What are you looking for?" I laughed.

"Nothing. Just something super intelligent that I can steal and publish in my next paper," she said, tossing a small smile over her shoulder.

"Um, did you forget who stood up at the front of the room today with a fully formed thesis presentation?" I laughed. "Steal all you want, there's nothing good over there. I'm here to learn."

"What's your area of study?" she asked, skimming through pages of handwritten notes. "And geez, why would you ever willingly write by hand?"

"I'm an H-sib at heart, remember?" I said.

"Harrison? I totally forgot!"

"Harrison and Harmony. Boris and Brooke."

Again, her face crumpled at the sound of my new name. "Can I just call you B? Seriously, that name is so dreadful!"

"Sure." I smiled. "And you asked about my field of study... I'm interested in the workings of Vie's wristlet technology and how it influences human decision-making."

She froze. "Really? Woah, that's a tough subject."

"I know."

"Why are you so interested in that?"

"That's another story I'll have to tell you some other time. It's tough. I started by trying to identify the exact metal composite that's being used in the wristlets as my starting point, but even that basic information is locked by the system. So I feel like my position is seven steps behind the starting line. I changed gears, and I'm trying to process the scope of this from a metaphysical perspective. I'll probably dive into pre-Vie transmitter technology next, just to see what the applied science might have stemmed from."

"I wouldn't worry about the metal composition at all," she said quietly. "I think that's probably a generic casing, whether the system wants you to know its exact design or not. And there's a much better chance the components are biological rather than technological, if my own research is even remotely close to accurate."

Realization dawned on me. I bumped alongside her at the desk to jot down an idea in my notebook.

Several hours later, she was passed out asleep on my bed while I worked from the couch and dictated under my breath into a private screen. The breakthrough was incredible! I wanted to follow my train of thought as far as it would take me.

"Hey, come to bed," her soft voice beckoned.

I closed the screen and blinked as my eyes adjusted to the pitch black room.

She kicked her shoes under the bed, shimmied out of her jumpsuit, and crawled under the covers. "You don't mind, do you? We've slept together before," she said with a gravelly, sleepy quality.

I grabbed a second pair of pajamas from the open dresser drawer, but she was already fast asleep. When I crawled into bed alongside her, I tried to make as little noise as possible.

My relationship with Brooke wasn't inherently passionate, at least not compared to the instant wave of attraction I felt with... *him*. Still, there was a spark. She curled up and nuzzled into my chest, so I laid my hand across the soft skin of her waist.

"Goodnight," I said quietly into her hair.

"And for her glory," I whispered to Vie.

24

Brooke and I fell right into step, and it was like the timeline of our friendship didn't have any gaps. Her companionship felt so warm and stable. I wanted to spend every day with her, and it helped that she took a focused interest in my work. When she was in her element, she was never shy. I loved to watch her talk animatedly about exciting new research and newly discovered documents.

Initially, I felt bad about leaving Breanna alone at the library, but she assured me that her 'frail old bones wouldn't turn to dust without me.' We all met outside the café for dinner as often as we could – Brooke, Breanna, Brighton, Bhavini, Blakely, and me; it was even more crowded with a sixth chair pulled up to a table meant for two.

One night, our group decided to take a long walk together after dinner to make the most of a particularly beautiful evening. Breanna listened good-naturedly as Blakely walked circles around her and explained the parameters of her new radial gravity test and its impact on the human heart.

I turned my attention back to Brighton, Bhavini, and Brooke as they walked in a row alongside me. It was so good to have a community again. Even though my primary focus had to be on the research, I recognized that I couldn't go through this part of my life alone.

"Bhavini, you're going to hate me," Brooke said with a shy smile. "I didn't hear what you said you're studying."

Bhavini rolled her eyes without malice. "You're all just jealous because you know I have more fun! I get to learn about *whatever I want* in the library while you losers are stuck staring at the same infopod documents over and over again. To answer your question, I've recently developed an interest in the psychology of our earliest memories. I think it's fascinating."

"Have you published anything?"

"No, not yet."

Brighton cut in: "No, because she doesn't even stick to a topic long enough to write the title page!"

"Again… I! Have! More! Fun!" Bhavini cheered brightly while pointing at her chest with each word.

"You and Boris are linked up. I assume you got sucked into his intense field of study?" Brighton asked.

"Yep! I thought he was off the rails too, but it's definitely worth looking into. And I think we're on the verge of something big."

Bhavini laughed. "He's said that *every day* since we first met. He's perpetually on the edge of discovery!"

"I'll let her handle this then. You've clearly heard enough from me," I said. I reached for Brooke's hand, and an adorable blush warmed her cheeks.

She squeezed my hand in response and turned to the girls. "He's a really good partner, in a lot of ways. I think we challenge each other's preconceptions and ideas, so we've made a lot of quick progress. Plus, the science is so fascinating! I'm surprised there's not more research about it in the system."

Bhavini shrugged. "Maybe everyone else is scared of the topic? I know I am! It sounds so dense and difficult. The whole point of study is to follow your interests, learn about something cool, publish a paper, and move on to something new."

"Wait... I forget. Have you even published a paper?" Brighton teased.

"I am literally *never* going to hang out with you guys again if you won't shut up about that! You know what? Just to prove you wrong, I'm going to publish something tomorrow. It won't be good, and no one will ever read it, but it's gonna get published!"

"Luckily the records recycle every five years, so future generations of B-studs won't have to be exposed to whatever word vomit you throw up tomorrow." Brighton doubled over with laughter as Bhavini alternately mocked throwing up and typing in response.

"Wait, is that true?" I asked.

"What?" Bhavini replied. Brighton was still trying to catch her breath and control an embarrassing level of laughter.

"The records recycle that often?"

"Yeah. It's a five-year span, so there's enough time for researchers to reproduce and rework what's been published. And if not, it gets erased. Thank Vie! It's hard enough to find what I'm looking for as is. Can you even imagine how convoluted the search system would be if every record that was ever published was clogging things up?"

"How did I not know that?"

"I don't know. Maybe you blinked during your infopod transfer and skipped right over it!"

Brighton's face was beet red, but her breathing was back under control. "Maybe that's part of the reason you're running into brick walls with your research. If you go looking for old information, you're probably out of luck. The B-stud system inherently prioritizes research that's important enough to get passed down. For example…" The B-stud sidewalk was painted black to match our clothes, and we walked up to a three-way fork in the designated path. Brighton pointed questioningly toward the right. We nodded, and she continued, "I didn't get to see much as a K-trav when—"

"What? You didn't see much during your *three whole days*?" Bhavini giggled.

Brighton stuck out her tongue at her. "Yeah, yeah, yeah. Zip it! During my *three whole days*, I didn't see much, but I do remember visiting a pre-Vie museum about the solar system. That's where my fascination with astrophysics started. Back then, they were so worried about the Earth running out of resources and all that terrible stuff. They were studying other planets to see if they were viable options. Instead of fixing their own goddamn planet!" She looked exasperated. "Thank Vie we figured things out! Anyway, there was this incredible display about the sixth planet they used to call Saturn. I sat and read this old, faded plaque about the planet's magnetosphere — basically a giant magnetic bubble — and it was so fascinating. After I transferred here, I tried to look it up in the records, but there's nothing listed for it. I guess the research is too old and it got lost at some point."

"Or maybe it was never correct to begin with, so the misinformation got cycled out of the archives," Brooke added helpfully.

"Probably. I wrote it into one of my published papers, just in case someone else ever goes looking for it in the next five years."

"That's really cool," Bhavini said, genuinely impressed.

"Maybe you're looking for pre-Vie information that isn't in the record. That would be a bummer!" Brighton said.

"Oh my gooossh." Bhavini gasped and stopped mid-stride. "Do you see her? That precious little girl! She's so cute, and with those little pigtails? Aww..." A tiny D-view girl was walking on the concrete sidewalk with her parents about a hundred yards away. The mother was distracted and laughing boisterously at something that played out on her private screen.

Blakely grabbed Bhavini's hand to pull her along with us and she kept walking without protest, but her head tipped back with a trailing gaze.

"Don't get me wrong," Bhavini explained, "I'm totally content here. One hundred percent harmony, perfect 17, all that good stuff. This is where I'm meant to be, but geez... don't you miss kids?"

"Were you an H-sib too?" Brooke said.

Bhavini laughed lightly. "Oh yeah, all six of us were! Assuming by your reply, I should also add you to the list? I was born Halya, and back there we've got Hannah and Hattie. It's funny. We all came from the alphaclass that basically breeds every member of society and ended up in the alphaclass that can't have any kids."

"I was Harmony," Brooke whispered, with a small wave.

Brighton playfully shook her hand, saying, "Helga. Nice to meet you."

"And you can call me Harrison." It felt so good to introduce myself with my old name.

"Only for this conversation. Just for a laugh!" Brooke added quickly, and we all nodded.

Bhavini continued, "It was a huge transition to go from my crowded bedroom and cluttered community center to this tiny, modest apartment. It wasn't even sad, necessarily… that's the wrong word. It was just so *weird*."

"Yeah." Brighton took over. "I know what you mean. I constantly had a sibling on my hip, and the concept of family is so drilled into you when you're growing up, but then you transfer here and… nope! You can't even share the same sidewalk as a family. I'm not even talking about being near my *own* kids, just any random kid. It was a weird adjustment."

Brooke turned to me and asked, "Did you want kids?"

Without thinking, I said, "I do! My twin brother got married at age sixteen and they were already planning to have a big family. He was the ultimate mononomer H-sib. He and his wife Huna had everything figured out from the get-go. I'm sure they have at least ten little ones by now. I want kids someday too."

"Wanted," she corrected questioningly.

"*Wanted*. Wow, haha, I said that wrong…"

A beat of silence fell over the group.

Bhavini continued, "Looking isn't against the guidelines, though. As long as we all stay on the path and focus on our research, then we'll all be 17!"

Her cheery, bubbly energy restored the flow of conversation, and all eight of our black boots marched forward on the painted concrete in lockstep.

THAT NIGHT, like most, Brooke was draped across my bed while I sat on the couch flipping through notes in a private screen. Except for the soft murmurs of conversation from the riverfront path outside my window, it was quiet and still. We had become so comfortable together, it was second nature to think and work in easy silence. Technically, she was assigned to her own apartment, but this felt more like home.

"I think we need to define the ground rules here. Clearly there's a connection, and I don't think we can ignore it any longer," she said.

I cleared away the private screen to give her my full attention.

Her bulky sweater was on the floor and she wore only a thin black camisole. Laying backward on the bed, her muscular legs scaled the wall in a pair of brushed cotton leggings. She twisted the slope of her long neck toward me, and honey-brown hair fell in a soft curtain over the edge. Time seemed to slow down as she blinked demurely.

With no warning, I felt myself stretch against my thin pajama pants. I shifted my weight forward to cover myself, but in doing so, I got a better view of the slope of her breasts, which were soft and full without a bra. Her curves stretched and pulled the delicate fabric of her top. I was *so* turned on.

I pulled the nearest pillow onto my lap and tried to focus my attention on the subtle pattern of Bs that wove across the soft black fabric. "Um, what do you mean?"

"A pre-Vie connection. Not just a technology element, an actual law of science. We need to erase all of our assumptions and rewrite the ground rules. I've been thinking, Brighton is probably right. No doubt we're missing some fundamental principle that didn't carry over because no one thought it was important for a five-year stretch, and it got lost."

She registered my look of surprise and incomprehension. Flipping her legs down off the wall, she kneeled upright on the bed and studied me with concern.

Her shirt rode up in the process, revealing a thin stripe of soft white skin at her waist. Seeing her perched on my bed like that was the tipping point. My face grew hot with embarrassment, and I wriggled in my seat.

"Sorry," I spluttered, trying my best to act natural. "I wasn't expecting... um, I think you're right. Ground rules. With a connection. Let's start there."

She brought her hands up to her mouth, stifling a laugh.

I had never seen her so embarrassed, and *I* was the one with the uninvited erection.

"Oh my gosh, are you...?" She didn't finish the sentence, but looked accusingly at the pillow. "What did you think I was talking about?" She laughed.

"I have no idea!" I admitted. "It's nothing. You didn't do anything! Sorry!"

"B, I sleep in your bed almost every night. You've never once made a move." Her hands still covered half of her face, which was flushed and alight with a magical smile.

"Vie, I'm so sorry," I said, tipping my head up to the ceiling. "Seriously, it's nothing."

"I didn't even realize you were into girls? We never talked about it, but after dating *him*... I didn't know. I shouldn't have just assumed."

"Yeah, I'm open to everyone. I like girls too."

Her eyes flitted back to my lap, and she released her gaze more slowly this time. "And are you seeing anyone? I assumed with all the time we're spending together..."

"No, I'm not seeing anyone. Are you?"

"Hell no! I don't have time to see anyone but you. We're not *seeing* each other, but — *fuck*," she finished in quiet frustration. "Can we talk about this like adults? Take that stupid pillow off your lap! You look ridiculous." She climbed off the bed to sit next to me on the couch.

I did as I was told and apologized profusely, saying, "I don't know what came over me! I really like you and I think you're incredibly beautiful, but it was just... you took me by surprise tonight. I saw you stretched out on the bed wearing that little top, and the angle from here was... wow. And then you were talking about new ground rules and a connection between us. I don't want to make you feel uncomfortable at all. I'm sorry."

Now that we were back on equal footing and talking openly, she looked more composed. "Connection? B, I was talking about our research."

"I know that *now*. It just took me by surprise!"

"But I do think we have a connection."

My pulse thrummed heavy and hot. I didn't want to react the wrong way and misinterpret things again. After a few hesitant breaths, I continued, "Of course we do. Is it *that* kind of connection?"

"Hey, I thought we were going to talk like adults. We're thirty-some years old. You can say it."

I laughed and turned my body to face hers. The inches of space between us felt way too far apart. "Okay, so is it a sexual connection?"

Her hand cupped the bulge in my pants as evidence and she grinned up at me, closing the gap with every word. "There's a lot more to it than that. It's sexual, and I hope it's mutual." Her lips met mine with breathless energy. She pulled away, long enough to say, "You have no idea how long I've been waiting for you to give me a green light."

She spun herself onto my lap, but we only stayed like that for a beat. She tore off her thin silk camisole and reached inside my waistband. I couldn't wait any longer. With her legs wrapped around my waist, we stood up and stumbled over to the bed. Our lips never parted, and when our bodies crashed together on the mattress, we answered each other with frantic desire and eagerness.

We lay tangled up in the inky black sheets and each other. Our breathing slowed in sync until the energy between us stopped tingling.

"You're beautiful, you're confident, you've got a brilliant mind…" I breathed out with a wide smile. "How did it take me so long to put the pieces together?"

"Does this mean we're actually doing the couple thing?" I heard the smile in her voice too.

"Yeah, I want to see where this goes, if you do. You were always good company in bed, even before tonight, but this takes things to a whole new level."

"You're terrible in bed!" She laughed. "I mean, the sex was phenomenal! But you know you snore, right? And I've seen you walking around in your sleep *several* times. It's definitely a trade-off. The cuddles are good, but sometimes I have to talk you back into bed when you start wandering."

I forced a light laugh to cover my embarrassment. I would always be uncomfortable about it. I couldn't control what I did when I was asleep, and the total lack of awareness felt awkward to talk about. "Let's focus on the awake part. That's way more fun," I said, laying kisses across her collarbone.

I breathed in the grapefruit and mint scent of her shampoo while she gently traced the lines of my white tattoos with her fingertips.

"Can I ask you something?" she said.

"Anything."

"You only have eleven lines, but we were apart for more than eleven years. Where else did you go after you left us?"

I breathed out slowly and said, "I… I'm sorry. I don't think I'm ready to talk about all of that yet. It was a rough time for me, and it's a little embarrassing. I know it was all part of my journey to get here, but there's a lot to unpack. I don't want to scare you off, and I know even saying that might be too much. Let's enjoy this moment, okay?"

She ran the side of one finger along her bottom lip and studied the ceiling, weighing my request. "Soon, though? If we're going to be partners… real partners in all of this, I need to know your whole story and everything I missed."

"I know. Soon, I promise."

25

Over the next two years, we moved in together and I followed through on my promise to tell her everything. Or, at least, everything I could.

I had admired Brooke's quiet composure and profound honesty when we were younger; now they were absolutely cemented at the core of her personality.

As much as I adored her, I had a difficult time opening up and letting her settle into my life. I didn't want to get too close; I didn't want to risk losing myself in another person... But those weren't the only reasons for my distance.

Even after all this time, Liam's betrayal loomed over me like a heavy storm cloud that threatened to spill over at any second.

I did my best to match her level of emotional intimacy, but all I could offer was a supportive touch or a kind word. My companionship seemed to satisfy her needs, but I couldn't give her my whole heart. It felt irreparably broken, and I clung to the shards. Every time I told her I loved her — which in a way I did — I knew that it was nowhere near the depth of how I had loved him.

Brooke often commented on the depth and authenticity of our bond; she must not have realized how much I was holding back. That didn't mean we weren't good together… more as friends than lovers. We pushed each other forward and focused on our academic goals in order to create real change in the world. Even if I couldn't give her all of myself, I could give her that.

The starting thread of my research was difficult to convey, but she knew that it was deeply rooted in my religious experience. The subtle rift in censored communication I had sensed between Jules and Jacqueline felt like an impassable canyon in my own life. Brooke had never lived as a J-dev and she hadn't logged ascension vows with Vie, so everything I had been taught about the divine system was unshareable. My distorted, censored words fell deaf on her ears because she didn't have clearance to hear it. I couldn't even begin to broach the subject of the soul's journey or the missing alphaclasses that were conveyed in my dream. Still, she seemed to trust me and understand.

Brooke's involvement took my scientific concept to a new level. Our initial theory didn't pan out as well as we were expecting, but it did unlock a new way of thinking that opened up further lines of research.

The fever that had raged in me during my first few weeks as a B-stud was reignited. I was driven by a focused passion again, like when I found the strength to battle the AI's suppression and transcribe my makeshift record of the manual. Somehow Brooke always found time to stay connected with the girls, but I couldn't neglect my research. While she went out with them for a long dinner or chatted outside the infopods in the library, I had to stay fully devoted to my work. My reclusion and separation were essential.

One night, her fuzzy black sweater tickled my cheek as I rested my head on her shoulder. We were reviewing a shared data screen that showed the final round of testing in a digital lab construct. I had designed an amplifier prototype that used biomagnetic stimulants with injectable trace metals. At this stage, we were using the lab simulator to test our ability to disrupt manic and depressive behavior in rabbits. This was the last hurdle at the end of a four-month project and things were about to get real. We were cautiously optimistic about the results, but didn't want to get ahead of ourselves.

"What the hell?" she muttered under her breath. "This is completely off the mark. This is worlds away from the previous test. All we did was scale the sample size and add a second behavior target. I don't get it!"

"Maybe it was an issue with the lab sim," I offered.

"Maybe, but I checked it multiple times before it ran. I don't think our simulation is the issue here."

"Okay, if it's not the simulation, we can only blame ourselves." I couldn't control the razor's edge that lodged in my tone.

"B, stop… it's okay." She turned her face to mine and planted a soft kiss on my lips. "This is part of the process. And we can spend the rest of our lives right here, doing this."

"I don't want to do this forever!" I blurted out.

She looked taken aback, for good reason.

"With you, yes, obviously! You're my forever. Here is my forever. But I want to get to a breakthrough at some point, and I'm getting frustrated with the constant cycle of dead ends."

"I know, we'll get there. And maybe you're right, I can double check if it's the simulation."

She started tracing my chin with her finger, but I stood up to pace the room. There was something here, I felt it. "What if it's not a simulation?"

"Personally, I don't think it was. I already said that. I was trying to be nice," she scolded.

"No, I mean, when we sit around and talk about how the system works in general terms, we always use the word simulation."

"Yeah?"

"Like the L-rush reset, M-self censorship, C-spen reorganization..." I listed them out one by one. "We call it a simulation, and that's exactly how my counselor Jules described it too. I think that's wrong."

"What else would it be?"

"I don't know. We're ignoring the fact that there are physical constraints too. Like B-stud sterilization and G-paw lethargy, and—"

"And the K-trav sense suppression," she interrupted.

"Exactly. Unless the system is simulating a cover that prevents us from seeing our babies, there's definitely a physical constraint. We've been having unprotected sex for two years and there are no kids in sight."

"Or you're infertile?"

I shot her a look.

"Hey, I'm just playing devil's advocate here! I get what you're saying. You're right. We've been using that term loosely, just to make sense of the system as a whole, even though it doesn't fit for all of the influences on different alphaclasses."

"I think it has to be one singular force... something that can control both external simulation and internal *stim*ulation. We have to focus on both at the same time. I don't think they're two separate issues."

She chewed on her thumb and spun in the desk chair while I walked circles around our small bedroom.

"Energy," she said finally. "It's so simple. I feel stupid for even saying it, but what if it's energy?"

I continued with her train of thought. "We know that targeted energy waves can interrupt and control how neurons fire in the brain. That could explain the physical symptoms with altered hormones for things like sterilization and lethargy. And a constant energy wave could disrupt the memory center, right? Certain neurotransmitters could be blocked prematurely from production in the neuron cell body, which would inhibit certain senses!"

I clapped my hands together with full force. The lingering sting made me feel alive. This was the high of discovery I had been craving!

"Is that energy linked with a universal simulator?" She spun two more times in the chair and abruptly stopped to answer her own question. "No, it's a mirage. A vibrational mirage!" Her heavy-lidded eyes glazed over as she sorted through her private screen of notes.

"I don't get it."

Refocusing her attention on me, she said, "We keep getting caught up in the challenge of linking every single wristlet with an overarching system. There is *the system*, but what if influences and interventions aren't enacted on a universal scale? What if it's limited to every person's individual, limited experiences?"

I waved my hands for her to continue. I had no clue where she was going with this.

"Let's imagine we're back at the L-rush apartment. That disgusting orange goop you couldn't leave alone?"

"Yeah." I snorted a puff of air through my nose in disgust. "I remember."

"Our past theories always assumed that the system reset the apartment, and maybe everything else for that matter, at a specific time. Why was it so hard for you to catch the moment it happened?"

"Because I was staring at a *countertop* after partying all night. I couldn't stay awake."

"But you could have looked for something big. Like when all the dishes you put away moved back into the sink."

"I tried that too, but I still couldn't tell exactly when everything reset. It was all a blurred shift."

"Exactly. What if it didn't *all* reset?" She stretched her hands out wide. "If it was a simulation, we'd be talking big picture, and it would basically be impossible to select the perfect time when every single person everywhere was asleep, or blinking, or not paying attention, or whatever it would take to make the big, simultaneous shift. If it's a mirage, it would only have to happen in front of your own eyes."

"The big orange glob was only there when I was looking for it?"

She shrugged with a self-satisfied smile. "Maybe."

"And the vibrational part?"

"That's even more of a hunch. I think that's the most likely energy form. It's continuous and cyclical. Light alone would be harder to manipulate into realistic surroundings and experiences with multiple senses. And we have to consider how the vibrational inputs react with each other. Because if an M-self tries to start talking, the person who's listening has to receive a signal to censor it. That's a discerning response that could translate through subtle vibration."

Again, she flipped up a private screen. "I'm going to have to look through my old papers and notes from the study abroad program. It's obviously not all the same concept, but a few things might tie in and prove to be useful. You know that was my primary area of study when I was working with the other Brooke?"

"Of course I know! We met up when I came to your

lecture event."

She didn't seem to hear me. She was lost in the tide of her own thoughts. "Would the vibrational mirage we see have to be an external factor? Literally vibrating in front of our eyes? It could work as a visual output override, but would that be easier or harder for the system to handle if it's already managing the inputs? And with sensory neural firing, Vie could easily make you think you're physically feeling something too. I have no doubt about that. Influencing us to trust and believe all of this, that would be the hardest thing of all..." She trailed off, lifted her wristlet, and studied it under the light of the desk lamp. "Why the wrist? If the vibrational impulses are working in the brain, why is the control system positioned so far away?" The glossy white metal fit snuggly around her wrist, but she was able to spin it freely. "Our birth names never change inside the band, but the etching on the outside does. I always assumed something in the metal would allow it to reshape and reform with new markings, like how it grows with you when you're a kid. What if that's a mirage too?"

"The etching of your new name?"

"No, the entire band."

THE DEEPER WE got into the science, the more it linked up and resonated with my spiritual concepts. I couldn't remember specifics anymore, but there was the shadow of a blurred passage in one of Reyna's journals that haunted me. I could imagine where I was when I read it for the first time, how I was feeling, and even, in a weird way, how it linked up with other information I knew now. It was like the page itself had been ripped out of my mind.

Within two months, we had made a lot of progress on

Brooke's vibrational mirage theory, and we even had a conceptual prototype in mind for an amplifier, but it was all tentatively perched on huge knowledge gaps.

She was interested in the conceptual science and driven by the thrill of academic discovery, but I sensed that she was getting fed up with my growing obsession to make it real. Whenever we tried to ground the concepts in anything physical, our research crashed to a halt.

I SLAMMED the apartment door behind me and sat down heavily on the black couch. All day, I had watched research documents be erased before my eyes. The retina infopod showed me more blank pages than actual information and I was running a race of wills against the AI again.

"B, I know you don't want to hear this, but the system is intentionally keeping this information from you. Maybe that's for a reason. You always knew that was a risk." Brooke's voice carried the slightest twinge of annoyance.

"I've done this before. I have to fight through it." I scraped my fingernails back and forth across the raised lines of my black corduroy pants in perpendicular strokes.

"You've done what before?" She kicked off her black boots and lay down on the bed, pulling a fluffy pillow up to her chest.

"This! Racing the system to pick up as many pieces as I can before the mirage, or whatever it is, vibrates them into oblivion. I have to believe that this aligns with Vie's will. It's hard, but I know I'm doing the right thing!"

"Did you hear her speak to you as a J-dev? In words?" She had asked this question so many times. We were on the verge of another fight.

"No, but you don't have all the information! After I

reached the highest level of ascension and learned about the system's history, I had a dream. I heard a call. I have faith that this project aligns with her divine instruction, and I have to find a way to solve it before the system takes it all away."

"Yeah, you've told me before. I don't know everything..." she said with impatience. She ran her hands through her hair and twisted her wristlet nervously. "I get that the system is holding things back from you, but right now you're holding me back, B. Your obsession is ruining this for me, and it's not helping our relationship either!"

This caught my attention. "You're still at 17?"

"For now, but I can't keep doing this. I need to work on my own projects, publish my own papers, study in my own field. This used to be interesting when it was the seed of an inspiring concept, but now I'm convinced the system has set you up to fail. I don't want to fight it anymore." She tipped her head up to face me head-on, then allowed it to fall back into the pillow like a physical signal of defeat.

"That can't be true. It's her divine will," I repeated.

"Clearly you believe that, and I'm not saying you're wrong, but I don't understand it. And if I'm being totally honest here, I wonder if maybe you got a little too wrapped up in the mysticism of it all."

She got up from the bed and crouched down in front of me at the couch. "Just consider for a moment, okay? Consider that maybe your friend Jules was right. I know I don't have all the information, but *they* did and they were all urging you to stay. Even if you're doing important work here, maybe it's not a decree sent straight from the spirit. And if the system wants to keep you out, maybe that's for a reason." She popped up and crossed over to the bathroom with light steps. "I love you, B. But tomorrow I'm gonna grab my own infopod and start on something new. Please don't obsess over this, okay?"

PART 3

DISILLUSION

26

I barely slept for four nights. My thoughts were tangled as I waded back through all of my discoveries, theories, and conversations. This journey originated on Jules's couch when I first broke the news of my departure. There was absolutely no way that this was all in my head. I had heard Vie's call, even if it wasn't explicitly spelled out. I had meditated on it. I had prayerfully considered it. I had weighed it with four of the most well-informed spiritual advisors, and it always held up to their scrutiny. It *had* to be true and I had to follow through.

On the fifth night, I made a sudden decision to remove my handwritten, piecemeal version of the divine documents from the locked drawer. I tossed it on top of Brooke's sleeping form and she jolted awake, surprised by both the glaring overhead lights and the pile of papers in her lap.

"I think you should read these," I said quietly.

She rubbed sleep from her eyes with one hand and started to flip through the messily bound book with the other. "Is this your handwriting? It's illegible."

I rolled and shook a bell between my palms. Ever since

Brooke and I had moved into this new apartment, I had kept the bell hidden with the book in the locked drawer, and I never felt quite secure enough to bring it out, even with the person I trusted most. It felt so good to hear that light, delicate tinkling again. Tears pooled in my eyes as the sound brought memories of the J-dev campus flooding back.

"B, I can't read this." She shook her head in disbelief. "What is it?"

"After I transferred, I didn't want to lose sight of my purpose, and I knew how important it would be to have access to the manual and other divine scripts. Obviously, I didn't have everything memorized, but there were entire chapters and hundreds of devotions I knew by heart. And before I left, I was also working on memorizing the journals."

Her blank stare chilled me. "You were working on what?"

"Memorizing the journals," I repeated.

"The what?"

"Reyna's journals!" I nearly shouted.

"Whatever you're trying to say, I think you're being censored. Is that ascension-level information?"

My heart raced. "Fuck! Okay. Look at this," I said, flipping back to the first page of the book. "My first thought was to dictate everything into a private screen, and I wasted an entire week working on it. I tried to get as much down as I could before the system's memory suppression blurred all of the details. The system noticed what I was doing and started to erase it! I figured a hard copy would come in handy. This feeling is hard to describe, but do you remember when Blakely was telling us about that pre-Vie condition she was researching? I think she called it asphyxia?"

"Aphasia?" Brooke added helpfully, although her arched, expressive eyebrows spelled disbelief across her forehead.

"Yes! Aphasia. That's the closest way I can describe this. It's not the same — it's close. I remember all of the concepts and everything I learned as a vieman in general terms, but the actual words — the passages I memorized, the script of the sealing ceremony — all of that is gone. I can sense it's still in there, or at least, the things that I knew well enough to stay in my memory all this time without actively using them. They're there, but it's so fuzzy and blurred, I can't grasp it."

"Okay…" Looking down, she continued, "And what is this?"

"A hard copy. It's the best I could do. I was fighting the clock, so a lot of this is paraphrased. And it's all completely out of order."

"B, I'm not kidding, this handwriting is such a mess, I can't make out anything."

I sat cross-legged on the bed next to her and read the first line aloud.

"You're scaring me." She shook her head.

I read it again, this time pointing at the text while I read it word for word.

"B." She cupped her hands around my face, and I saw worry rising behind her stony, narrow eyes. "I can't hear anything you're saying. Your lips aren't moving. These scratches on the page don't mean anything. I have no idea what you're trying to do."

Tears of frustration rose up, spilling over the ones that were called there by nostalgia only a few moments earlier. I paced the room and smacked my wristlet against my forehead until it hurt. "What's even real anymore?" The pain helped me refocus. "I'm trying to help you understand! You *really* can't read that?" I gestured to the book.

"Not a single word!"

I snatched a pen off the desk, flipped to the back of a blank page, and wrote in huge, sweeping scrawl the name "REYNA."

"B, you're scaring me. Are those supposed to be letters?"

The system knew what I was trying to do, and there was no way it would let this slip through. "What about this? Can you hear this?" I jingled the bell next to her ear.

"It's just a bell! It sounds like Vie's chime. Wait, is that the bell that J-devs sew onto their clothes? B! How do you have that?"

"I rolled it through the transfer room."

Her composure was breaking. "What do you mean you rolled it?"

"I put it on the ground and rolled it across the fucking floor! What do you think I mean?"

I struggled to breathe, and she sat me down on the bed. She nervously pulled her fingers through her hair. "I love you," she said. "But this sounds absolutely ludicrous. You say that you're doing this for Vie and to improve the system? No, you're fighting it, and you have been for a long time."

"I'm not, I swear. Think of all the people who are silently struggling – everyone who needs to hear Vie's voice and get answers. The system was designed with tools to protect people and lead them into harmony, but Vie's influence isn't strong enough anymore. This AI has fractured from the divine, and it's holding Vie back. She can't intervene until things get bad, and by then, it's almost always too late."

"*You* can't hear them, B. This isn't a real problem! I'm sorry. I think you're wrong. I've never met a single person who wasn't perfectly content. Even with transferring, it only takes a little time to recalibrate, and we all get things figured out. Sure, I noticed my scores start to slip as an L-rush, but I simply moved forward and found my place. It's that easy! I've been so happy here. *We've* been so happy here!" She shook my shoulders gently and wrapped a hand around the back of my neck. "And if you actually spent time with our friends instead of holing up in here with your research, you would see that there's enough joy in the world for everyone. Just look around. We're all doing fine! When you give up 3, you're guaranteed to get 17. You've heard it a million times, so why don't you believe it?"

"No, Brooke. Listen, I counseled so many people, and I saw how far a person can tip before their scores even budge by a single point! And I saved a woman who was going to... agh!" I screamed. "There's so much I can't even begin to tell you! You can't hear it! You'll never know the implications of this project and why it matters so much, but it impacts *everything*. It's not just about one person or even one lifecycle." I didn't know if the last word was censored or not. It probably was.

"B. I think you're projecting. The system is balanced! Everyone is content! Every single person I've *ever* met, except you." Her words hung in the air. Footsteps shuffled across the floor of the apartment above us. "You've been through a lot, and I'm not judging you. You know I never have," she said with tears glittering in her brown eyes. "Liam told me something once, and it always stuck with me. After you left, he said that you had a hard time hearing Vie's commands. It wasn't just a matter of disliking the alphaclass or not paying attention. He said it was like you didn't fit the system. Apparently, when you were N-stars, Vie gave you guidance chimes, and he said your wristlet would turn and tug you in different directions? Well, he told me that you couldn't keep up, and he always had to keep a close eye on you because you didn't know where to go."

"That was six fucking steps!" I screamed, with disregard for our now-awake neighbors. Anger rose up in me, meant for Liam, but directed at her.

She shrank back under the black cotton bedspread and pushed the book off her lap. "B. Please," she said, tearing up. "I'm just saying, if you can't hear normal, *everyday* cues from the system, do you really think you heard some divine message sent straight down from Vie? That's foolish."

"I understand what you're saying, but you're not hearing what *I'm* saying."

"Everyone is happy! Everyone! I've never met a single person who wasn't able to find their harmony and stay settled. Look at our life… it's a perfect 17! Of course part of me wants to have kids! And sometimes I miss having color in my closet! And sometimes I think about going back home to see my siblings, but that's our 3 points as B-studs. We all agree to give up something small so that we can have something big. And you're ruining it! You keep carrying the same mindset and repeating problems everywhere you go. You keep transferring for the wrong reasons, and if you keep spiraling like this, I'm terrified you're going to run out of options!"

"This project is so much bigger than me! The problem is so much bigger than me! I can't tell you the whole story — there was a woman, and when I was a missionary, I saved her! I saved her from something so tragic, you can't even believe it. You have no fucking clue! Even if you tried to imagine the worst thing… the very worst thing, you still wouldn't even be close. It's not just about one life, or even one hundred years. You have to trust me on this. You have to trust me!" I gripped her hands and she squirmed. "Life is a cycle. That's all I can say. And I have no idea if you even heard that word, but it's true — it's a soul cycle."

She gave a small, quick shake of her head.

"Fuck! I don't know how to explain this, but you have to trust me. This is so important! I can't give up on it. I can't. I just can't." I dissolved into sobs and she cradled me against her chest, rubbing slow circles across my back.

"I know," she soothed. "I know."

"You don't know." My cries were muffled by her pajama top.

"I trust you. And I love you."

After I had cried myself out and gone limp from exertion, she slowly laid me down onto the bed.

Assuming I was finally asleep, she rose discreetly. The mattress creaked slightly, and she froze. I didn't stir. The bound pile of pages rustled as she lifted them off the floor, and, despite her best effort, the tiny bell jingled while she walked across the room. I heard her lock the stolen items away and settle into the desk chair. She tried to regulate her breathing, but the sound of each inhale was ragged and shallow as she tamped down tears.

THE NEXT MORNING, we woke up, got dressed, and ate breakfast in silence. We used separate infopods at the library during the day and I slept on the couch that night.

Would you like to update your scores?

I tried to explain to Brooke that the situation we were living in proved everything. If we could feel this shitty and unhappy but still score 17, that should be evidence enough that a single point was too much to tip the scale. Brooke shook her head and repeated bullshit from universal scripts about recalibration, free will, and delayed emotion. The more I pressed the issue, the more upset she became. I watched her confidence shrink around me, and the strong, beautiful features of her face held a devastating tension.

Another week passed like this. Then she said, "B, I got a warning chime and I'm going to act on it. Vie said my score is about to drop, so the system recommended that I be assigned to a new living situation. I'm going to move out."

She had abandoned our research, and she was about to

abandon me too. All of this had been for nothing. The room started to spin around me. I needed her, not only in the lab, but in my life. If I lost her, I would have absolutely nothing.

"Wait," I cried. My throat was already choked up, and this single word was all I could manage. "Wait."

"It's just for now. It's not a forever thing. I need to recalibrate, and I think we need some space."

"No, wait! I can fix this," I urged. "We can fix this. We just need to be on the same page. There's so much you don't know, and that's the real issue here."

"I don't think it is," she said quietly. "You need to go to one of the J-dev drop-in counseling sessions. I know you can't go back, but they might be able to help. The missionary I talked to yesterday said she knows you and your friend Jules, so she sent a message to him. He's super high up in the J-dev leadership and can pull some strings to reconnect with you and restart temporary counseling. B, this isn't healthy, and you know it."

I didn't respond. What could I possibly say to that?

"What's your score?" she asked.

I refused to answer.

"So, not 17? You're already sliding? Have you heard any warnings yet? Guidance scripts? Emotion chimes? Or are you just ignoring them?"

I stared blankly out the window. Our new apartment faced out onto a small courtyard, and I missed my old view of the river. *It won't be our apartment for much longer,* I thought dully.

"This is the problem," she mused. "This huge issue you think everyone else is having? It's only happening to you, and I don't know how to help you with it. You can't force the system into giving you everything all at once: B-stud access, J-dev documents—" She cut herself off, exasperated.

"Wait! That's it. L-rush!" I interjected. "Eviction!"

She rolled her eyes, but there was absolutely nothing playful about the gesture.

"The shot! The drug, the drink, whatever it is... Eviction. Jules told me a story once about how the drink got its name. Apparently the drink overrides Vie's censorship and language controls, so when you're blacked out, you can talk freely."

"B, just stop. This is ridiculous."

"No, listen!" I forced her to sit on the bed with me, despite her hesitation. "I have a plan. This can work! I promise. I'll transfer to become an A-aut and take up a position overseeing L-rush clubs. Liam told me once that overriding Vie's codes wasn't hard when he was an A-aut. He got an entire hotel built where the city didn't need one. That authority means something! And with an override, I'll be able to send a few cases of eviction here to the apartment. B-studs and A-auts aren't really supposed to socialize, but it's not like you're a low-class H-sib or anything..." I laughed at that, but her face was as rigid and unyielding as marble. "At night, I can drink and you can ask me about everything you need to know. Maybe I can even write out the questions for you before I black out. And because you're a B-stud, nothing will change! You can lead the majority of the research, and I'll help out however I can. This is perfect! I'll need pills in order to function after the blackout, but I can figure that out when I take care of the overrides. Back as an L-rush, did you pick up the pills outside or did they reset in the apartment every morning? It doesn't matter. This will work!"

The words rushed out of me in a torrent. I felt so relieved to have a solution I could grasp. Soon she would understand!

"It will be difficult to work together and talk when I'm sober again," I said, "because even if you're the one talking to me about the ascension topics, the system might try to censor your voice within my language comprehension center—"

"No." Brooke stood up with sudden force and cut off my winding, fast-paced thoughts. "No! Absolutely not. Do you even *hear* yourself?" She stepped back gingerly toward the door. "B, you need help. You need *serious* help. I can't be part of this. I just can't."

I had never seen that expression on her face before, and it made me deeply sorry. I was so close. I couldn't stop! "Okay, okay," I said, raising my hands in surrender. "I'm sorry! You're right, we need some time apart. You can stay here in the apartment and I'll go. I'll go talk to someone and get the help I need. And when I come back, I swear I'll have answers for you."

"Just go," she said with surprising force as tears rolled down her cheeks. "Liam was right. You don't know when to leave."

This comment shot through my bones like a nail gun, but I stayed on my feet and held onto my resolve.

"I'll come back," I repeated. "And I'll have answers for you. I swear."

We switched positions, maintaining a five-foot distance between us as she retreated back to the bed and I moved toward the front door.

"Take care of yourself," she said, choking through sobs.

"I'll come right back. Then I'll explain everything, I promise. This will work."

27

I slammed my hand down hard on the glossy white table in front of me, which was already split with dozens of hairline cracks. I bit back a curse before it could fly out of my mouth. Just barely.

"Alex… hey, buddy… are you okay?" my desk partner said. Her frizzy hair was more white than blonde, and the small, delicate features of her face always carried the upturned tilt of surprise and concern, even when I was playing the part of a well-behaved A-aut perfectly.

"Oh yeah, sorry, Annalisa. Didn't mean to startle you. I'm fine. I started to nod off and… You know how it is." Every eye in the office was firmly fixed on me.

"You're bored? Why don't you ask the system for a new assignment?"

"That's a great idea. I'll do that," I said with a huge, forced grin as I pulled up a private screen. She had no idea I was hailing an autocab instead of filling out a leadership revision request. I grabbed my red-and-blue checked blazer off the back of my chair and walked between a row of desks toward the outside door. "First, I'm going to take a walk to get my energy up. I'll see you at lunch!"

In my effort to escape the room as quickly as possible, I bumped my hip into several different chairs and knocked a decorative set of pens off the corner of Amaila's desk at the end of the row.

"Sorry!" I tossed back over my shoulder. I didn't stop to help her pick them up.

I stared at my reflection in the elevator mirror as I descended toward the lobby. The metal was warped and distorted, so it cartoonishly stretched my frame. Days away from age forty, my figure was as lanky and knobby as ever. Even hidden under a layer of black stubble, my angular jawline was too sharp and wide on top of my narrow neck and feminine shoulders. I squinted in disgust, embarrassed by the proportions that never looked quite right. *Apparently I won't ever grow into my body,* I thought. *Why do I still look like an awkward kid?*

Sliding into the autocab's front bench, I mashed my blazer into a ball and chucked it in frustration at the window in front of me. The white plastic buttons clattered and made a scratching noise as the jacket slid down the glass and onto my feet. One of the threads was loose, like everything else in this hellish alphaclass, and a lone button bounced and landed in the backseat. Its stamped red A shined like blood against the glossy white interior.

I had tried *everything,* and none of the overrides were working.

I'd left Brooke in our apartment twenty-seven days earlier, and I couldn't bear to think about what she must be feeling... alone, confused, forgotten? I said that I would come back with answers, but I still had nothing to show her.

Fuck, I thought as I punched the cushion seat. The system wouldn't give me any access to the manufacturing sector, I couldn't unlock anything in the food service system (if eviction was even considered part of food service, I had no idea), and the kiosk vending system didn't have any traceable delivery records that I could find.

As an A-aut in the L-rush department, I was supposed to feel some useless sense of control over choosing the color of the club bathrooms or helping the system organize room placements to avoid double names. That was bullshit! That was nothing! My sweet and well-meaning, yet entirely clueless, deskmate informed me that I could put myself up for promotion in six months and ask for a position with more authority, but I didn't have that much time. I couldn't leave Brooke alone, stranded.

And then what? I'd get promoted to overseeing music selection for L-rush concerts? The smug entitlement of these power-hungry pricks in my office made me sick! Couldn't they see that nothing they did had any real impact on the system? They were willing to settle for creaking chairs, stalled elevators, cracked furniture, and loose buttons just to pretend they were in charge. The system was broken, and they were too stupid to see Vie's message playing out right in front of their eyes!

The autocab pulled up to a bar and let me out. Its roofline was substantially lower than the buildings around it, and one of the gutters was falling down on the front, so it dripped rainwater in a pool right outside the front door. I hopped over it and continued inside.

Warnings and chimes pulsed urgently in the back of my mind. They were so common now, I could almost completely ignore them. I had learned how to override the AI in my own head, even if I couldn't figure out how to do it in the actual system.

It was only 11:20, so I knew the place would be empty, and it was except for an L-rush sleeping on the corner of the bar. I could hear a couple having noisy, clumsy sex through the bathroom door. I hurriedly searched the back of the bar, but the grimy cabinets were bare. The door to a back room, which I assumed might have been the kitchen, only opened into a dark space the size of a closet. There, I found another couple sleeping. The man's pants were down around his ankles, and I had to assume they had passed out in the middle of the act.

My teeth clenched with suppressed rage when I remembered how sloppy and lifeless Liam was when he tried to kiss me or work on the buttons of my pants. It was *pathetic*. Leiko had guessed it right all those years ago. I did think he was disgusting, even if I couldn't bear to admit it back then.

I grabbed two empty beer bottles off the floor by the man's feet and walked back to a kiosk at the bar. Its light screen was lit up and active, so I swiped through the request commands to place an order, but it immediately froze and locked up. I tried the next one. The same issue. At the third, I used my left hand, thinking maybe it sensed interference from my wristlet. The name *Alex* was etched onto the outside of my band, mocking me. Again, the kiosk locked me out.

I continued down the bar to the last kiosk, next to where the lone man was passed out. Panicking, and without much thought, I grabbed his limp wrist and waved it through the light screen. Two shots of eviction popped out on the retrieval tray. I tipped the borrowed bottles upside down and shook out the last drops of stale beer. Then I wiped the bottle mouths with the hem of my A-print button-down and poured the shots inside.

It took at least fifteen minutes to completely fill the bottles while requesting two shots at a time.

The bathroom door unlocked, and two middle-aged women stumbled out toward the front door, wincing at the beam of daylight that shined under the threshold. I ducked next to a barstool and froze, hoping that the shadowed atmosphere and their looming hangovers would be enough to cover me. They couldn't do anything — not really — but the social pressure of conforming to alphaclass guidelines kept me locked in rigid paranoia.

They pulled their jackets up over their heads, as if they were stepping out into a downpour, rather than recoiling from the noontime sun. The door scraped closed behind them and I stood panting with relief in the deserted room.

Leaning back against the bar, I tried and failed to hail another autocab to drive me to Brooke's apartment. *Our* apartment. It was across town, out of my A-aut access range. I quickly waved through maps and tried to come up with a plan. It was too far to walk without causing a disruption, and I couldn't take a tram in this beer-stained button-down.

I left my bottles on the bar and paced a loop around the room. A little movement always helped me think. Weaving past sticky tables and a small dance floor, I stepped over a lost shoe.

The solution pierced me with sudden force. I yanked off my clothes and frantically searched every corner of the room. There was no reason for an A-aut to be riding to that part of town; a hungover L-rush wouldn't be entirely out of place.

The sneakers were mismatched and uncomfortably small, but I was able to loosen the laces enough to fit. There was nothing I could do about the ragged sweatshirt… it reeked of sweat, vomit, and stale beer.

I SLID into the farthest seat at the back of the tram and pulled up my hood, pretending to cover my eyes from the sun. It happened a long time ago, but I had crawled home alone once or twice as an L-rush, and I knew how to play the part. The smell of my disguise was enough to act as a shield, so no one dared to sit on the benches in front of me. I balanced the open-top bottles on my knees and actively worked to slow my breathing.

I tried to anticipate Brooke's questions and how I should present this new ascension information.

My thoughts were spinning and the world followed suit. The AI scripts weren't warning me anymore, they were panicking — all in that gentle, saccharine voice I used to crave. The volume was cranked up higher than I had ever heard it, and it was deafening.

I'm doing this for you! I screamed in my own mind. *Reyna installed too many limits on you! The corrupt AI is holding back your influence and it's trying to stop me from making this breakthrough, but I know this is your will. I heard you! Vie, I hear you.*

I rocked uncontrollably on the hard plastic seat, fighting a battle that was invisible to everyone but me.

The tram stopped near my old B-stud library, and a group of N-stars stepped inside. A crowd of commuters was clustered at the front of the car, staying as far away from me as possible, but they were forced to politely step back and spread out, giving the celebrities their space.

I glimpsed a lanky, tall man in his late thirties or early forties with dark brown skin, an angular jaw, and loose black curls. He grinned broadly in response to someone's remark, and from the side profile, his smile was lopsided, cutting a wide crease line across his cheek. That was my twin brother's smile! He had grown up, too, and his features were infinitely more mature than when we had parted half a lifetime ago. I would recognize him anywhere… he was the other half of me.

"Harold?" My feet were already moving toward the front

of the tram before my tangled mind could regret or even register the decision. "Harold!"

One of the bottles tipped in my arms and spilled down my front, but I righted it without slowing my steps. I had pushed through the small crowd to reach him in a matter of seconds.

"Harold! Brother! I can't believe you're..."

The man turned to face me head-on, first with surprise, and then with disgust.

It wasn't him. The features were all wrong.

He plied me with generic replies, like "Thanks for your interest" and "We're so grateful to our fans," but the words were tinged with the chill of obvious annoyance.

It wasn't him. The voice was all wrong.

He pulled a screen card out of his pocket and shoved it into my hands, which were already full of bottles. Then he turned his back.

It wasn't him. This was all wrong.

I let the stranger's screen card fall from my grasp and banged my elbow into the tram car's emergency stop button.

The doors released and I spilled out onto the street. My untied sneakers slapped the pavement while I ran the last ten blocks to our apartment, trying to retain as much liquid in the bottles as possible.

THE APARTMENT DOOR WAS LOCKED, and I wasn't in the right frame of mind to even consider knocking, so I set the bottles on the narrow hallway's black tiled floor and slammed my body into it, trying to force it open. Something popped painfully inside my shoulder. I kept working. The physical pain was a distraction from the confusion of my dissolving mind. It made me feel more present, more alive. My wristlet sent waves of painful energy up my arm, but it felt superficial and fake in comparison to the undeniable throbbing in my shoulder.

Chips of wood blew out from the doorjamb when it finally broke free, and I was somehow able to catch myself with equal footing. I saw Brooke's honey-brown hair fly out behind her as she ran into the bathroom and locked herself inside.

"Brooke!" I screamed as I pounded my fists against the light stained wood. "I told you I'd come back! I told you! I got it, and I can explain everything!"

I set the bottles on our bedside table and reached for a pen and paper, but then remembered that writing down questions wouldn't work. If the system censored her ability to read and understand them, that strategy would be futile.

The bathroom door clicked softly, and I turned to see her inching across the wall toward the hallway. She froze in place when our eyes met.

"Brooke?" I tried to keep the tension out of my tone, but so much was happening all at once. My voice broke under the strain. "You just have to ask questions and I'll answer them. I'll answer everything and you'll finally understand!"

She shrank back into the wall and recoiled at my touch. I continued to smooth down her soft hair, as I had done so many times before.

I continued, "You're so brilliant. You have the brightest mind, Brooke. And you're on the edge of our breakthrough, I know it! You're only missing this essential information and the system is trying to lock you out. Vie herself — not this fractured shell of a control program… the real Vie — wants you to hear it! I've got it." I tapped the side of my forehead. "I figured out an override. I can override it."

"Okay, B. Okay." Her voice shook with startled anxiety.

She glanced over at the open bottles that sat on the table by our bed. "Is that it? You got some eviction?"

"Yeah," I said. "A lot spilled out on the way, but you know how strong this stuff is. It should be enough. It'll be enough. Just ask the questions and make sure I talk." Her eyes darted to the door, which was half blown off its hinges, and then down to her bare feet. "Hey… stop," I warned. "Don't do that. Don't even think about it." Again, my hands set to work smoothing down her hair. "I'll drink, you'll ask the questions, and I'll answer. Then this will *all work*. You'll finally know everything."

Reluctantly, she looked at me. I saw the emptiness of despair and disbelief behind her dark, narrow eyes. Her body trembled at my touch and she was barely holding it together. "I ask and you answer? You'll drink and black out if I agree to do this? That's it?"

"That's it," I said, struggling to stay conscious as white-hot energy burned into my wrist. Through gritted teeth, I groaned, "We have to hurry. My wristlet is attacking me, and I don't know how much longer I can take this."

"Okay, okay. You'll black out and this will all be over. Okay." She looped out from under my arm with a single, swift motion and hurried to the side of the bed. She grabbed both bottles by the necks and forced them into my hands. "This will all be over soon. Okay." She said this last word one more time, almost like a sotto voce curse.

I tipped the first bottle back and drank down the dark amber liquid, feeling myself instantly peak with a stimulant rush and black out into unawareness.

28

"Brother, you look truly content today." Jules walked across the cluttered workshop and over to where I sat by the open window. He wrapped his arms around me in a long, warm hug.

My right arm was immobilized in a cotton sling. It looked dirty and dull in comparison to the pristine whiteness of his J-dev dress. I held the other arm rigid in my lap and refused to hug him back.

He released me, then leaned close and studied my face for a long time. I aimlessly counted the freckles across the bridge of his nose. Twenty-two, twenty-three, twenty-four. He took a step back and turned away.

"I see you've been busy with a new project," Jules said while wandering around the dusty room. The plank wood walls were stacked with overflowing shelves that reached all the way up to a high, pitched roof with exposed beams. There was ample space and material for a dozen craftsmen and artists. I was the only M-self assigned here, and Jules was the only visitor. "That's great news. I'm so proud of you." He turned his head back to face me with a genuine smile. "I just want you to be happy. Brother, you deserve to find harmony and contentment like the rest of us, and I have faith that this is the perfect place for you. You'll be able to create anything you want here and you can finally express that artistic side of yourself I've always seen hidden under the surface. You'll see... self-expression will be your key to harmony this time around."

My eyes followed him lazily as he walked from workbench to workbench, but I kept my body facing stiffly toward the window.

"It's only been a few days and you're already settling in! I can tell. Praise Vie. That's progress."

His hollow optimism filtered into coolness. I passively observed that he was working up the courage to try a different approach.

"I want you to think of this as a fresh start, not a last resort. You've got sixty years left in this cycle, brother. You're not even at the halfway point yet. Please, please don't give up on me now. There's so much life left to live." He picked up the handle of a small welding torch and looked at me in surprise, sparking back into a more jovial tone. "No shit. You're a jewelry maker? How cool! You know, I've always had an interest in metalworking, but I never had the opportunity to pursue it. I don't know where it came from. Maybe in a past lifecycle... Hmm. Did you learn how to do this while you were studying in 7895?"

He waited for a response, but my resolute stare was unwavering. I barely blinked, and I didn't move.

Metal tools clinked together as he rolled them across the messy tabletop. When he reached the other end of it, he picked through a handful of identical brass earrings that were heaped and scattered in a massive pile. Bright morning sunlight reflected across the metal surface as he twisted each stud between his fingers, observing it from every angle.

I had cut, buffed, hammered, and polished every letter by hand with obsessive precision. Originally, I only planned to make one, just as a final statement and a tribute to the person I used to be. It didn't feel like enough, so the pile grew and grew. Each one was an exact replica of the H earring that my father had given to me as a child before he transferred out of the community and left us forever; the one I, too, left behind.

"This is a really interesting shape, Martin. It's so expressive. Did you design it yourself?" Jules gently overturned his palm, releasing the earrings back on the tabletop.

He couldn't recognize the letter. It was writing, *language*. I was under total M-self censorship. How could I forget?

"You do look good," he insisted. "I'm proud of you."

The light sound of children's singing floated in through the open window. The weather was surprisingly fair for early November.

He tilted his ear up toward the sound. "Oh, good! Jacqueline will be so pleased to know you were able to hear the concert. She asked the kids to sing loud enough for a special friend off-campus — just for you. They sound so harmonious. For her glory…"

He continued to study me for any sign of a response, and he didn't bother to conceal his stare.

"Look, I know I've already explained this a few times, but I want to make sure you hear me clearly and understand the stakes. I realize it can be hard to recalibrate after a transfer, especially when shifting into your last name. You've been through this before, but this time it's different, and I don't think it hurts to repeat myself. I always talk too much anyway, so don't expect me to change." He forced a light laugh. "Brooke cares deeply about you… otherwise she wouldn't have spoken on your behalf to get you the help you need. I can only see it as undeniable proof of Vie's grace and intervention that Jesephena was serving at that specific clinic the day Brooke came in for counseling a few months ago. After your, um… episode, it was lucky that she knew who to talk to and we already had a support plan set in motion. Brooke didn't waste any time reaching out, thank Vie. I don't know how much you remember, given the state you were in… but she did the right thing. I hope you don't blame her in all of this. Who knows what you might have done. To her, to yourself… That's all in the past. Vie is life and she chose to reconnect us. Brother, that must be for a purpose. You *have* to believe that."

I wasn't angry with Brooke, Jules, Vie, or anyone else. Even the ever-present shame that shrouded Liam's memory had been washed away in a flood of emotional ice water. Just like so many times before — too many times before — I had settled into a numb state of nothingness. Unable to truly cope with my feelings or make sense of my actions, I simply retreated and froze.

The sole of his white shoe scraped back and forth nervously across the cement. "I volunteered for this role, kind of like a mission at home. So I'll be here with you every day for in-depth counseling. The other viemen think it's best if you have one-on-one support for a while, and I agree. Although things can't go back to exactly the way they were before, it'll be close. You won't have the old uniform, but we can still spend our days together."

He walked back over to me and squeezed my hands while incessantly searching the depths of my lifeless eyes. He sat next to me on the window bench and said, "Vie is life. You have to listen and follow her will. Judah…" He corrected himself. "*Martin…* you're going to get through this. You need time and guidance to recalibrate, that's all. I love you, brother, and I'm here for you. Always."

The breeze twisted through my soft cotton T-shirt and ruffled my hair. It had grown long now, and a tightly coiled strand swept across my forehead, falling in front of my eyes. When I continued to sit unmoving and unbothered, Jules gently pushed it back behind my ear and sighed.

My gaze was carried along with the breeze, mindlessly following flecks of dust that hung in the air and gleamed in the golden sunlight. A leggy spider crawled lazily across the high ceiling before dropping down on an invisible silken line.

Some amount of time had passed. I couldn't track it and I didn't care to. Jules shifted on the waxed canvas cushion and spoke in a quiet, slow voice, explaining, "They talked about evicting you, you know? Given your history and the level of chaos you caused in poor Brooke's life… you — well, not you, your actions — pushed her out of harmony. You showed up with that bottle and broke down the door, and *fuck*… I wish you didn't have to go through that, but it was wrong of you to involve her in it too. You created 'unforgivable trauma.' That's what sister Jolynn said. Those were her exact words."

Out of the corner of my eye, I saw his chest heave. His voice was shrouded in the heaviness of mounting tears. "Jameson, Jesephena, and I spoke up for you. We defended you because no matter what happened in the past, you deserve to have every chance at a harmonious future. I'm not giving up on you, and you shouldn't give up on yourself. I forgive you for what you've done, even if you can't. And… Martin, I've learned more. When I said that you had achieved the highest level of enlightenment with access to everything, I thought that was true at the time. It turns out there's more to this, and I think you were right about something. You deserve to know that. You know how this works… you're no stranger to censorship. I can't tell you everything, but I want to share with you what I can. It was such a long time ago, but in one of our counseling sessions, you were telling me about your partner… Liam? I think that was his name. Nod for me? Yes or no?"

Unmoving, I watched the spider climb back up its string and retreat toward the ceiling.

"It doesn't matter anyway. That's not important. You told me you felt like he was stamped into your life. I think that's the word you used. *Stamped* over and over. Imprinted, maybe? You had a clear, undeniable sense that you had spent lifetimes with him. I couldn't place it at the time, but the way you described it resonated with me too. And all I can say is, I think you were right. And as I have continued to learn more about the soul's journey, I don't just think you're an old soul. Martin, I think you might be one of the *oldest* souls. Our souls age too. We start out young, needy, weak, naive… Then we grow up and get to the sweet spot in life when we've built up the perfect amount of strength, experiences, knowledge, relationships… basically you're in your prime. As you get closer to your death day, then your joints ache, your skin sags, and your memory's not quite as good."

With his hands, he drew a sweeping, continuous circle through the air. I sensed that he was both watching me for a reaction and making sure I saw it, even though my eyes were still fixed on the exploring spider above us.

"Over time, we become less elastic." The smooth, looping motion became unsteady as his hand careened around and around. "As we age, our bodies start to crumble. Eventually, something's going to break."

His jerking hand settled calmly back into his lap and he released a hesitant breath. "Do you understand what I mean? Does any of that click? That's honestly all I can say, but I want you to know. I want you to understand. I think it might bring you some peace. Or at least, it might provide some perspective on *why* you've been struggling. It's not your fault. It's timing." Even more quietly, he continued, "Knowing all that, I couldn't bear to let them manually evict you. If your soul really *is* in your late nineties, metaphorically, and we're not sure exactly how many candles to put on your cake, I'm sure as hell not going to blow them out early. You deserve to enjoy every last minute… every last experience. And who knows, maybe they're trick candles and you'll get another go at it – another hundred years in another cycle, but that's not a gamble I'm willing to take."

He gently grasped my chin. I didn't put up any resistance. His eyes welled with tears, but I saw courage and persistence in them.

"If you don't hear anything else I say, please, *please* listen to this. The system works, even if we don't understand how or why. The system works. This *can* work for you. Please let it work for you."

The children's choir fell silent.

Wiping his eyes, he stood up and pushed the button on his wristlet to check the time. I was left staring blankly into the empty space where his eyes used to be, right where his hand had guided me.

"Shit… I didn't realize it was so late. I'm sorry, brother. I have to run back over to campus. Jordyn asked me to come supervise her session… I don't think you know her, she ascended after you left, but she's a lovely woman — a devout disciple, praise Vie. She's doing exceptionally good work in our community. I'm the only one with an open hour today and the official period of my mission with you doesn't start until tomorrow, so I really do have to go. Tomorrow we'll have all day to talk." He froze and cringed at the misplaced word. "We'll have all day for counseling."

He mussed my curls, like I used to do to him, and he pushed his glasses back up into position on his freckled nose.

"I'll be back." He kissed me lightly on the forehead. "Vie is life. Remember that."

His steps pounded across the cold concrete floor, and the solid door swung closed.

Resolutely, I dragged myself over to the pile of bronze H earrings on the well-worn tabletop. Pain shot through my fractured shoulder, but I raised it anyway, just as I had done over and over to forge each one. I tipped my head to the side and stabbed an H stud through my earlobe. The hole had long since closed over, but I roughly forced it back open. I yearned to feel closer to the person I used to be, even if it was only a fucked-up, copy-cat costume.

I pulled up a private screen and tapped my thumb and forefinger together to open the transfer application, even though I knew what I'd find. The top of the screen displayed my current score (5 out of 20) along with a jagged, destabilized graph on the right. As I stood and studied it, the graph continued to refresh and change in a shower of jilted sparks and updated calculations. No matter how the reevaluations factored in, the line always ended in a spike down to 0.

Even Vie can't make sense of my head... The timeline isn't clear, but she knows that there isn't any hope for me here. Everyone knows that, I thought dryly.

The rest of the transfer screen was empty. I thought back to the times when I used to have to scroll and search for the alphaclass I was looking for. After an entire lifetime of mistakes and misguided missions, I stared blankly into the white, text-free haze that clouded my vision. Nothing. No more options. No going back. No point.

Actions could be rectified and managed, but they could never truly be undone.

I can't wait sixty more years for a fresh start. In a moment of clarity, I rationalized, *I* have *to make them see that I'm done here. I'm finished. They have to evict me. It's over. And if I can't go back, then I need to force my way forward.*

My cold, bare feet traced their way back to the window,

and I ripped my broken arm out of its sling, blind to the pain. I grabbed the small welding torch in my left hand. Turning on the gas, I ignited the flame, took a deep breath, and turned it to my wrist.

I COULDN'T HEAR a single sound, and my eyelids refused to open more than the slightest fraction.

Jules sprinted toward me in an unfocused blur.

A blue torch flame burned in the middle distance, angled up toward the ceiling.

Fingers splayed out in front of me, but nothing looked right. The colors were all wrong.

Glossy white lines came into shaky focus.

Eleven perfect tattoos shined on an arm, framed in contrast against destroyed flesh.

A pure white wrist band glimmered, unblemished and unbroken, with the name *Martin* etched along one side.

29

I blinked into the current reality and felt my attention shift back to the small, square room, which was sealed with glossy white metal on every surface. I didn't feel any pain. I also didn't physically feel anything at all. My breath didn't blow across the tiny hairs inside my nostrils. The bottom of my feet didn't make sensory contact with the floor.

I couldn't bear to look down at the physical consequences of my failures and the mistake that took things too far.

The story of my life was finished. It was done. It was all over. I had nothing left to say and nothing more to do. Whatever happened next, I only hoped that I would feel an extension of this peace — the quiet serenity I had always craved, but felt was out of my grasp. I almost had it once, back when I devoted my life to something bigger than myself.

I policed my own thoughts and pulled my focus back to the present moment. That mistake had already played out and the story had already been told. There was no point in spinning and suffering any longer.

The airless space was supremely still. It was a transcendent, magical experience. There was no tingling on the surface of my skin, my heart didn't dare to beat, and my breath was permanently fixed in the space between inhalation and exhalation.

I passively wondered how long I could stay like this. What came next... if there was a next? The passage of time was impossible to calculate; there was only the swirling of my psyche. Eventually, my thoughts eased and slowed into an empty, quiet state of calm. Nothingness.

I was ready.

"Vie, process my soul into the next cycle."

EPILOGUE

IN CYCLE

I checked the clock. Only a few minutes left.

My sister's tiny body catapulted onto the already crowded couch, knocking the air from my lungs.

Gasping through a mix of laughter and surprise, I howled, "Get off! Get off! I can't breathe!"

She lifted herself up and launched onto another couch a few feet away.

"Alright, alright," coaxed my father. "You heard the birthday boy… Give Harrison some space!"

One by one, the remaining tangle of siblings and friends relocated to more comfortable positions, draped over the armrests or on the floor. I reached across my girlfriend Hazel's lap to grab my teacup off the well-worn side table, and I planted a kiss on her cheek along the way.

"Hey! Then I get to steal a sip of your drink," she teased. "It's only fair."

"It's nearly cold…" I warned.

"And you're nearly gone," she retorted with a wink. Hazel took a sip, held back a small grimace, and stuck out her tongue.

My seventeenth birthday party was everything I wanted it to be — life as normal, with no held-back tears or goodbye speeches. Harmon, one of my older brothers, had turned his transfer day into a sob fest, and although we finished our walk to the V tower with cheers, I knew it wasn't how I wanted to leave.

Gazing around the community center's upper-level balcony, it was reassuring to see dozens of kids darting around felt game tables and disorganized bookshelves. Clusters of couches filled the room, piled high with soft, fluffy pillows. The rest of our community, numbering well over 200, filled the center atrium and cafeteria below. I'd always loved the view from up here, watching as members easily shifted back and forth between parties and conversations.

Three bright, resonant chimes played out over the speakers, signaling the end of late afternoon tea. An exuberant cheer ran through the hall as everyone stood up from their crowded tables en masse, squeaking well-worn, mismatched chairs across the hardwood floor. This routine happened every day, at the exact same hour, without fail.

Seventeen o'clock.

I had been expecting the chimes while I counted down the minutes, but they still caught me by surprise. Hazel rubbed my shoulders reassuringly and the crowd around me drew closer. My hands were calm and confident as I flicked my finger through the air to pull up a private screen.

Tapping my thumb and forefinger together, I opened a transfer application for the first time and waved my hand to scroll through the alphaclass list, sorted in alphabetical order:

A-aut

B-stud

C-spen

D-view

E-sit
F-nat
G-paw
I-con

Huh, no H-sib... I guess that makes sense.

I kept scanning, found my target, and input the selection with confidence. Warmth spread across my cheeks as Vie read the summary I had memorized.

K-travs achieve 17 points of contentment through global exploration and unrestricted travel to sites of cultural significance. In exchange for the guarantee of harmony, K-travs must give up 3 points of contentment with dulled senses of taste and smell.

I instinctively knew that life as an H-sib wasn't the perfect fit for me, but I had waffled over the choice between transferring to become an N-star or a K-trav. Ultimately, I felt a stronger, intrinsic pull toward travel. I had to go with my gut.

Please proceed to V tower 1675 for transfer. Vie's soothing voice echoed in my ear. My glassy eyes regained focus in time to catch the pillow that flew toward my face, resulting in raucous cheers and laughter from everyone around me.

Hugs turned into jostling, which turned into jumping, which turned into running as we all sprinted down the stairs with giddy enthusiasm and toward the rotating doors.

We walked down the busy street and basked in the pink-orange glow of the late autumn sunset. I looked around me and saw the procession from a new angle: everyone was genuinely at balance here; just because I *wasn't* didn't mean I was broken — it simply meant that I was passing through an early stage of my life and learning along the way.

Our energetic pace slowed as we approached the V tower steps, so I took the time to embrace and thank every single person in the crowd.

Hazel took a seat on the steps and waited until everyone

else had their turn with me. After one last group hug with my parents and grandparents, I stepped away to sit beside her.

"We were friends first," she mused, "and that's how we're going to end. I'm not some spurned lover you left behind or some other tragic character in a sappy love story. I'm in balance doing this, you'll be in balance doing something else, and we got to enjoy each other's bodies in the meantime. Plain and simple."

I couldn't hide the smile and blush that crept across my face.

Hazel laughed and lifted her eyebrows as if to say, *What? It's true!* She continued in a husky voice, "I wanted to give you one last thing. I know you can't take it through transfer, and I could only find half of the matching set, but I saw this at the jewelry swap last night and it made me think of you."

From deep inside her wooly jacket, she produced a small bronze earring that was hand-stamped in the shape of a letter H. Her warm hands brushed against my skin as she poked the small stud through the frayed hem of my cable-knit sleeve.

I rotated my wrist back and forth, studying the familiar earring as a hazy sense of déjà vu flooded over me. The skin on my arm tingled with sudden, searing pain and my mind raced through a lifetime of failed experiences that had never happened.

"It's beautiful," I managed to croak out. Hazel's attention was locked on the gift, and she didn't seem to notice my reaction to the pain, which was already fading fast. "This is… it's special. I feel like I've seen this before… Do you know who owned it last?"

"No, I'm not sure…" she said while wiping a thumbprint off the metallic surface. "That's only half of your gift. If you'll do me a favor, I'd also like to boss you around one more time..."

"What?" I asked.

She rose to her feet and pulled me up with her, saying, "You've got one hundred years to live life on your terms, the way *you* want. Don't settle for anything less." Kissing me one last time, she gripped my shoulders and spun me around to face the V tower's glass door, which was awash in transient color.

The familiar chant started up from the crowd behind me. "Your balance is there. Your family is here! Your balance is there. Your family is here! *Your balance is there. Your family is here*!"

Stealing one more glance at the H earring on my sleeve, I took a deep breath and shook off the strange new feeling. My hands gripped the door's vertical handle and I pulled it open with slow, even force before walking forward into the shadowed lobby.

ACKNOWLEDGMENTS

To my husband, who patiently sat through hours of book talk but will be hard-pressed to actually read it.

To my good friend, who devoured it in a day and was the very first person to finish it.

And to my mom, who hates reading but will be first in line to get a copy of it.

ABOUT THE AUTHOR

Carrie French was born and raised in Oregon under a perpetually cloudy sky. It rained while she wrote her first book *Without Disruption* too. She has nearly a decade of experience as a freelance copywriter, and she writes for brands around the world. You've probably read her work while shopping online, but you'd never know it. (Funny how marketers don't get a byline...) Carrie also enjoys playing the oboe, sipping whiskey, filming YouTube videos, and going on long runs through the countryside.

www.carriefrenchauthor.com